1903. A darkness has descended over London after a series of grisly murders. Trophies were taken from the victims, their bodies arranged and soon there are whispers across the city of Jack the Ripper's return.

A new client arrives at Baker Street seeking Sherlock Holmes's help: Dr Jekyll claims his friend has been wrongfully accused of the hideous crimes, a friend called Mr Edward Hyde, whose very existence relies on a potion administered by the doctor himself.

But the case becomes more complicated, more unsettling than simply proving Mr Hyde's innocence – for Holmes and Watson unearth beastly transformations, a killer who moves unseen, a secret organisation and then they find a traitor in their midst…

SHERLOCK
HOLMES
&
MR HYDE

Also by Christian Klaver and available from Titan Books:

The Classified Dossier: Sherlock Holmes and Count Dracula

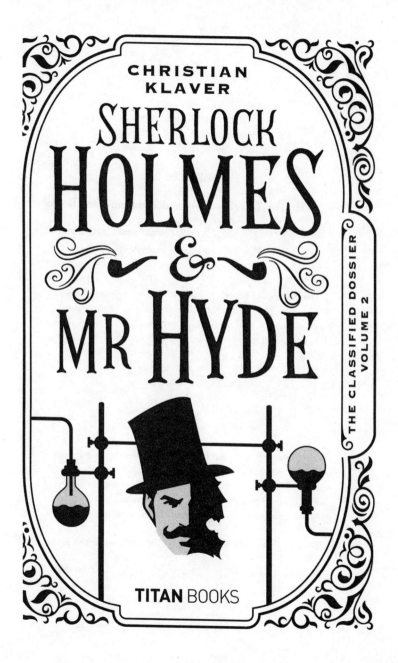

CHRISTIAN KLAVER

SHERLOCK HOLMES & MR HYDE

THE CLASSIFIED DOSSIER
VOLUME 2

TITAN BOOKS

Sherlock Holmes and Mr Hyde
Print edition ISBN: 9781789098693
E-book edition ISBN: 9781789098709

Published by Titan Books
A division of Titan Publishing Group Ltd
144 Southwark Street, London SE1 0UP
www.titanbooks.com

First Titan edition: September 2022
10 9 8 7 6 5 4 3 2 1

A CIP catalogue record for this title is available from the British Library.

Printed and bound by CPI Group (UK) Ltd, Croydon CR0 4YY

To Dad, for instilling a love of all things Sherlock

Part One

DR JEKYLL AND MR HYDE

Chapter 01

THE RETURN OF JACK THE RIPPER

During my long acquaintance with Mr Sherlock Holmes, there have been many cases where Sherlock Holmes has been thrust into the limelight, such as during 'The Case of the Raven and the Shroud', and also 'The Disappearance of Mrs Graham's Wedding'. There have also been a few cases where it has been necessary, at the request of a client who wished to keep their lofty names from being attached to a public scandal, to keep my records unpublished. But in this instance, the case itself is so famous and prominent in the public's eye that this task is an impossible one. In addition, Holmes's involvement was so slight and no progress was made for years, so that there was scarcely any point in constructing a narrative. Now, however, matters have finally offered a resolution of sorts after so many years. Thus, it is with some relief and some trepidation that I take up my pen to write of the grisly affair surrounding the activity known as the Whitechapel Murders, and the deeds of the persona the newspapers have called alternately the Leather Apron, the Knife and, most enduringly, Jack the Ripper.

Even though London's most famous detective, along with Scotland Yard and a great many other law enforcement agencies, spent a great deal of time on the case, it is a matter of public record that there were few promising suspects and in the end, no arrests.

Though the facts are still fresh in the minds of many of my readers, I will lay out a short summary here.

While there was a great deal of disagreement regarding the case, Holmes posited that the murders of Mary Ann Nichols, Annie Chapman and Catherine Eddowes could be linked to the same perpetrator, but found discrepancies when applying this same theory to the murder of Elizabeth Stride, murdered on the same night as Eddowes, and that of Mary Jane Kelly. The theory encountered even further difficulties when applied to the murder of Rose Mylett, later the same year, or that of Alice McKenzie or the nameless corpse found on Pinchin Street, both of them having died in 1889. These were lumped into the same case file, an act that Holmes found profoundly intolerable.

"The obstacle," Holmes had confided to me shortly after the discovery of the deeply unfortunate Miss Coles, "is that the official force, Lestrade and Gregson included, are fixed on the idea that this must be one perpetrator. But I'm afraid the evidence points to a completely different conclusion. There is more than one person capable of these horrific acts. The hunt for a single murderer is flawed, for there is undoubtably more than one and the investigation will be forever hampered and ineffective if Scotland Yard does not admit to the possibility of multiple murderers."

"To attack a woman you'd never even met before," I mused, "to cut her throat, then defile the body afterwards in such a gruesome manner. It's unfathomable, Holmes, for even one man to be capable of such a thing. How can you imagine two such men?"

"I do not imagine," he said coldly. "I observe."

It had been a bitterly cold night, I recall, and I can still see Holmes's lean profile in the flickering firelight, his brow furrowed, his gaze deeply troubled. He had a cigarette in one hand, forgotten and burned down to a cold, ashen husk. A healthy amount of whisky in a glass sat near his other hand, equally forgotten.

"Unfathomable," I repeated.

"Yes," he said. "Unfathomable, and yet, it is quite true." There was note in his voice that put me on guard, for I have long suspected that Holmes's fierce intellect and indomitable will sheltered a sensitive nature. My fears proved completely founded, as he took to the solace of the cocaine bottle for the next two days, as I had not yet weaned him off that vile narcotic. We were both saved when the Case of the Shakespearean Spectre came to Baker Street, for which I was infinitely grateful, since I was due to be married to Mary Morstan and so abandoned Holmes and my quarters in Baker Street. But I assuaged my guilt with frequent visits and was deeply gratified to see the comfort of work replacing the drug in Holmes's life. He did not seem the worse for wear for having Baker Street to himself.

The Ripper did not commit any further crimes that year,

and our life resumed a slightly more even keel, with my buying a medical practice and settling into married bliss with Mary, while still participating in many of Holmes's most extraordinary adventures.

In 1891, the Ripper struck again and still neither Holmes, nor anyone else, could find substantial evidence that would identify the murderer. Holmes had serious doubts about whether or not the culprit was even the same person, or persons, as before. But the Ripper, or his imitator, did not strike again after that. Then, the case of Moriarty overshadowed even the Whitechapel Murders and resulted in Holmes's and Moriarty's final confrontation at the Reichenbach Falls, to the supposed death of both men.

Despite Mary's presence in my life and the solace she brought me, the three years that followed were dark for me, and it was not until 1894 that Holmes returned and I learned the truth. We did not learn that Moriarty, too, had survived until almost a decade later.

Looking over my notes, I find that this period included some of our more famous cases, including 'The Adventure of the Dancing Men', 'The Problem at Thor Bridge' and 'The Adventure of the Illustrious Client', where we were first introduced to Baron Gruner and Miss Kitty Winter, both of whom would make a further impact in our lives long after that first case was complete.

Then disaster struck in the year 1902 and we learned that humanity, already capable of descending to murky depths, could plummet into even darker waters. That was the year we discovered, much to our disbelief and horror, the blood disease that causes vampirism. We learned, too, that Professor Moriarty had become a vampire and thus survived his plummet at Reichenbach. He had used the intervening years to rebuild his criminal empire and turned his attention to the destruction of the one man who had thwarted him before, Mr Sherlock Holmes.

Moriarty's first telling blow was one of enormous personal cost for my own self, as Moriarty reasoned that he could do the most harm not by striking at Holmes directly, but at those near to him. He started with my own wife, Mary, and then used her to strike at me, infecting both of us with the disease. The transformation to a vampire broke my sanity for some time, but I recovered. Mary's personality, however, was shattered permanently. With the help of the profoundly disturbing Count Dracula and his wife, Mina, we were able to vanquish Moriarty and his horde of vampires, but Mary was forever lost to me.

Early in the year of 1903, on a dismal winter eve when neither of us had any professional engagements to force us out of doors, Holmes and I had occasion to discuss the Whitechapel Murders again. It was I who raised the subject, as the weather had fouled my mood and the Ripper seemed an atmospherically appropriate spectre. I have since wondered if this conversation bordered on premonition, as these details were destined to darken our doorstep again in a very short time.

"Holmes, have you considered the Whitechapel case any these past few years?"

At first, I thought he'd been too lost in thought to hear me, as he was scraping listlessly at his violin, making the most dismal and atrocious noises. I'd opened my mouth to ask the question again when he finally answered.

"I have, as it happens, gone over the data a number of times, and feel that a different perspective may be called for," Holmes said. "I even had occasion to discuss it with Gregson and Lestrade the other night when you were out, so it is curious that you raise the issue now. There was a fatal flaw in my reasoning. A flaw so obvious, and yet unexamined, that it has tainted that investigation from the start. Neither Lestrade nor Gregson could see it, even after I explained it. My only consolation is that every other person involved in the case has made the exact same mistake."

"What kind of mistake?"

Holmes put away his violin and filled his pipe, the briarwood one that had seen so much use. "I once remarked to you that the details that can make a case more sensational and outré are often the very same ones that lead most easily to a solution. It is the commonplace crimes, without any feature of distinction, that are so very difficult to solve."

"So you have said," I agreed. "Many times. Where is the mistake?"

"I have confused the extreme with the unusual." He lit his pipe judiciously.

"I'm sorry," I said, lighting my own cigarette. "I don't follow." The night was dreary outside, and we had nothing by the way of a case, which often sent Holmes into a black humour during which he would be foul company. But he seemed reflective tonight, though not without an air of dark cynicism. I settled in for a long explanation.

"I thought the murders extraordinary," Holmes said. "As such, I looked initially for one man. Even after I started to collect evidence that not all of the murder methods matched up, my theories all presupposed a severely limited number of killers. Two men, working in tandem, or one imitating another."

"Of course you did!" I exclaimed. "How could you not? The brutality, the macabre trophies, the audacity and sheer malice of the killings. They *are* extraordinary!"

Holmes breathed out blue smoke and shook his head in despair. "Extraordinary only in the sense that it took this long for such a thing to happen. In a city of five million, why should it be surprising that we have created or imported a few bad apples?"

"Bad apples!" I sputtered, outraged. "Holmes, really! Those murders were carried out by a monster of a man, not some wayward child!"

Holmes gave me his thinnest smile. "Ah, but we've seen real monsters, dear Watson, haven't we? The night Somersby died, remember? That warehouse out in Graveshead with the cellar?"

"Of course," I said. "I shall take that horror to my tomb."

Holmes wasn't really listening, but musing as if to himself. "When we came out of that darkened hole, out into the clean night air – as clean as London air gets, anyway – suddenly the idea of more than one brutal murderer in London, even an entire room or building of them, all having meetings and conventions and garden parties, comparing knives and methods and body counts… suddenly that idea seemed not impossible, nor even improbable, but a natural outgrowth of London itself. Don't you see that most of the official force, Lestrade and Gregson included, want – no – *need* to believe that this is all the work of one perpetrator for the simple reason that they cannot imagine more than one monster capable of this kind of misdeed roaming around London?"

"They haven't seen the same things we have," I said quietly, completing the thought. I thought of vampires crawling out of darkened, cold graves, of monsters in the sea, and our pitched battle in near darkness in that Graveshead cellar. "They don't know about the monsters."

"Indeed," Holmes said. "When one has seen a multitude of horrible things, as we have, the idea of someone, some person, crossing that unspoken boundary out of humanity and into unnatural darkness becomes easier to believe. All too easy, in fact. It just means that of the many monsters lurking out in the night, some of them may be human."

I had no answer to that and Holmes went to bed shortly thereafter. When I got up the next day, I saw that Holmes had been up early and had turned our sitting room into a fog bank of tobacco smoke in his boredom. Fortunately, Mrs Hammond nearly broke the bell pull later that afternoon in order to consult us on the matter of the Averno Spider and Holmes had the work at hand that was always his preferred antidote to any black moods that might come over him.

Next followed a quick succession of cases that culminated in the unexpected events I have laid out elsewhere, such as 'The Adventure of the Creeping Man' involving Professor Presbury and his fanciful but tragic usage of a serum from the black-faced langur. In point of fact, we had just returned from Camford the previous evening and had both of us sat up through the night, myself out of habit and nocturnal proclivity, Holmes out of a perverse fascination with the case we had just finished.

"There is danger there, a very real danger to humanity, Watson," he had murmured as he took a sample of the langur serum that Professor Presbury had used and subjected it to one chemical test after another. He had also gone through his index and had notes about the doctor in Prague, one Löwenstein, of dubious reputation, who had created the strength-giving serum. Of Dorak, Löwenstein's agent in London, and his mysterious 'one other customer', we had little information other than his letter to Presbury and I had no doubt that Holmes intended to head out there as soon as practicable.

When day finally broke and I heard the first stirrings of our good landlady below, I had just reached for the bellpull to request breakfast for us both when I heard the downstairs door fly open and feet come pounding up the stairs.

Holmes almost certainly heard them, too, but continued his experimentation, sitting on a three-legged stool hunched over the small table of laboratory equipment even when the door to our sitting room flew open and a man burst in.

"I'm sorry," Mrs Hudson's voice came from behind him. "I was just coming to tell you that you had a visitor when he rushed right past me!"

"It's quite all right, Mrs Hudson," I said. She frowned at the man, but withdrew peaceably when I ushered the man into the room.

"You've got to help me, Mr Holmes!" the man said as soon as

I had the door closed. "The police are after the wrong man, but there's no telling them that! I need someone with a rational mind, and I believe you are that man and no one else!"

He was a tall man, quite large, with a youngish, smooth face, but dark hair liberally sprinkled with grey that made me revise my knee-jerk estimate of his age several years upward. His face was handsome, with large, almost shaggy eyebrows. But his countenance was now disfigured by an expression of palpable anguish. He was quietly dressed with dark trousers and brown shirt and frock coat. He waved a newspaper with one hand while the other clutched both his bowler hat and a neat and polished Gladstone bag. The act of clutching both bag and hat in the same hand had bent the brim of the hat quite severely. The man seemed to suddenly notice this and dropped the bag, which clinked heavily onto the floor.

This finally got Holmes's attention. He set his pipette down with a frown and a sigh and turned on the stool. "Your name?"

The man seemed momentarily taken aback, as if he had not expected this question and it somehow toppled all of his plans. Then he mustered himself again. "I thought you might already know. You investigated Presbury, did you not? My name is Jekyll." He seemed to expect some recognition from us, and now looked a little peevish when he did not get it.

Holmes stood and took the newspaper from the man's outstretched hand, then went very still as he reviewed it. "Watson, I think we very much need to hear what this man has to say. In fact, I should say that this far surpasses any other concern we might have at the moment."

I opened my mouth to reply, then looked back to see the headline of the paper that Holmes held up for my inspection: RIPPER STRIKES AGAIN!

"The paper implicates a man named Edward Hyde," Holmes said to Jekyll. "You and this Mr Hyde are quite close, I take it? He is a patient, perhaps, since you are clearly a doctor?"

"Why do you say that?" the man said, suddenly suspicious.

Holmes glanced up from the paper, a note of irritation coming into his voice. "Come, now! You have come to us because you have heard of my success and methods. Is it really such a surprise to hear them confirmed? Besides, there is no secret to the matter. When I see a man with a black smear of silver nitrate, so often used in the medical profession, on his right hand, it is no great deduction to say that he is a doctor. Though, with the absence of any bulge to suggest a stethoscope, I am inclined to think it unlikely you are part of any practice. But what is your connection to Hyde, pray?"

The stranger opened his mouth to say something and then looked down at his right hand and wiped off the blemish. Finally, after a great internal struggle he blew out a deep breath and the action seemed to deflate him entirely, as if all his conviction had departed him. "No, Hyde is not a patient." He collapsed into an armchair and had to clear his throat several times before going on. "Yes, I am a doctor, but not a medical one and I have no practice. I use the silver nitrate in my chemical laboratory. This is really the first time you've heard of this affair? I half-expected, from your stories, that you would already know all about it."

"Watson has taken a few liberties in regards to making his stories more dramatic and romantic than they should be, but he has never, to the best of my recollection, implied that I have made deductions without any data. Watson?" He held out the paper to me. "Perhaps you had best read the article out loud so that we can catch up on events."

Holmes sat in his own chair and pushed a cigarette case towards our newcomer. "Have a cigarette, Dr Jekyll."

"No, thank you," Jekyll said. "I do not indulge in the vice of tobacco. Not for many years now." His bushy eyebrows, without any discernible movement, managed to somehow portray an impression of prudish, unspoken disapproval.

Holmes lifted his own eyebrows in surprise. "As you wish. There is brandy, if you would care for it."

"No, thank you," Dr Jekyll said primly. "I do not take spirits, either, I'm afraid. But perhaps a glass of water, if you have one available?"

I poured Dr Jekyll a glass from a carafe on the sideboard and returned to the paper, eager to know more, but also dreading the details.

The article ran like this:

> Some fifteen years after the many murders attributed to a monster known only as Jack the Ripper, it seems that the same killer has returned. At about midnight last night, a hideous incident occurred in Whitechapel that is likely to bring the most infamous name in history back to the lips of

every man, woman and child. Miss Eugenie 'Genie' Babington, a well-known resident of Whitechapel, was found murdered behind The Hanover public house on Adler Street. She was killed, according to Inspector Stanley Hopkins of Scotland Yard, in the same manner as Mary Ann Nichols, Annie Chapman, and so many other women. Her throat had been slit, according to the police, from left to right, with a precise, sharp instrument such as a doctor's scalpel, which was the known and preferred method that the Ripper used in the previous murders.

The public will, of course, remember that Jack the Ripper was never caught, but it seems likely that this long-standing injustice will, at last, be corrected, for one Franny Barker, a resident of Whitechapel and mother of two, has come forward and identified the man who has committed this atrocity: one Edward Hyde, a man known to the police to be of violent temper and low character. The police of Scotland Yard and the City of London Police are forming a joint task force for the purpose of tracking this murderer down and making certain that he pays the ultimate penalty in the eyes of the law.

Mr Edward Hyde is wanted by the police and anyone who sees him is urged to contact Scotland Yard. Mr Hyde is said to be short but powerfully built, with a great mane of black hair and visage that, to quote Franny Barker's deposition, 'only a mother could love, and her just barely!' He was last seen wearing a black suit, top hat and gentleman's opera cape.

Holmes gave a low whistle. "Perhaps you should explain your connection to this affair and the precise nature of your relationship to Mr Edward Hyde. I should warn you that with a witness to the murder, things look very dark for him indeed."

Jekyll, having sat for the briefest of moments, now rose to his feet again, pacing restlessly and looking from one of us to the other, his smooth face wrinkled in confusion. "You really don't know? I am the other recipient of Löwenstein's serum, through his agent, Dorak."

"Well," Holmes said, lifting his eyebrows in surprise. "That *is* interesting. But that really does not go very far in explaining your connection to Mr Hyde and this abominable murder, of which you claim that Mr Hyde is innocent."

"I do claim that, yes," Jekyll said slowly. He moved in a distracted manner, then finally sank back down into his chair again, then looked keenly at Holmes. "Would you take the case? I must know your answer before proceeding, as the explanation is of the most sensitive nature."

Holmes's grey eyes took on that distracted, introspective look that signalled his utmost attention. "If your *friend*, Mr Edward Hyde, is indeed innocent, then every effort shall be made to prove his innocence and track down the real killer. In fact, such would be true regardless of your appearance here. I am surprised, in fact, that Scotland Yard is not already here to try to enlist our aid in this matter, although that may indicate that new information has come to light, or that they already have the person they believe to be the true killer in their custody."

"No," Jekyll said. "I can assure you that Hyde is not yet in their custody. Are they likely to come here?"

"Very likely," I assured him. "Holmes is ever their first call should they find themselves out of their depth on a case."

"Which, I daresay, is often," Holmes remarked dryly. "Come, Dr Jekyll, lay the facts of the case and any evidence of Edward Hyde's innocence before us. We may not have long before we are interrupted."

Jekyll's face smoothed, as if he had just this moment decided which path to take. "Very well. To explain the connection between Mr Hyde and myself I must first explain the nature of my work. It is the langur serum, you see, that is the key. I did have a previous ingredient that was even more effective, but alas that source has long dried up. For years I sought a replacement and have only just the past few months discovered that Löwenstein's langur serum performs that duty admirably." While speaking, he took off his frock coat and laid it carefully over the back of the chair. He then proceeded to unbutton his waistcoat and collar and these, too, he laid aside.

"Brand new shirt, but no help for it, I suppose," he muttered. Then he began to pull off his boots.

"Come, man!" I said. "This is a long way, I assure you, from the Turkish bath. What on earth can you possibly be about?" I would have gone on, but Holmes laughed out loud and waved me back to my chair, thoroughly entertained by the unusual proceedings.

Jekyll reached down for the bag he'd dropped, all but forgotten until now, and began to remove, much to my surprise, a pair of heavy leg irons and manacles such as they might have used in Scotland Yard. I became aware, as he did so, of a distinctly earthy odour about the man, a dangerous whiff of something animal that was not at all what I expected from a well-respected doctor.

He started with the air of a lecturer, but there was a brittle tension about him as he did so, as if he was talking to distract himself from something unpleasant. "The aim of my research, at first, was to isolate and separate the better and more deplorable aspects of human nature." Boots removed, he laid out the leg irons at his own feet and smiled thinly. "To separate the angel and the devil within our own selves, if you will. At first, this is what I thought I had accomplished." He carefully threaded the hand manacles through the ring of the leg irons so that they should be interconnected and then started to fit the manacles to his own ankles.

Holmes and I exchanged a look and I could feel my own eyebrows rise in astonishment that was plainly mirrored on Holmes's own face. I remembered Lestrade talking of a magician that had shocked Scotland Yard with a demonstration in which he freed himself from the restraints commonly used in their prisons. Houdin… or… *Houdini*, that had been the man's name. I wondered if we were about to get a similar, private demonstration of the same skills here in Baker Street. Under different circumstances, I would have strongly objected to such a farcical display happening in my very own sitting room, especially with such an urgent case on our hands, but Holmes's grey eyes sparkled with interest and he leaned forward, so I held my peace.

Jekyll was screwing the bracket of the leg irons around his ankles carefully and precisely, and according to some private measurement, though I noticed that they were actually absurdly loose. It was not likely to be a very impressive demonstration after all, it seemed.

"It took me some years," Jekyll went on, "to realize that I was quite wrong to think of my research in terms of good and evil. These are too abstract to be so neatly pinned on the careful scalpel of science. It was the highest level of hubris and naivete to think I could accomplish so unscientific a goal. Better to say that I had managed to separate not good from evil, but *man* from *beast*. Many academics would consider us separate already, but this is another unscientific theory and quite incorrect. I choose the word *beast* carefully, scientifically, and do not intend it as a slight. Quite the contrary. It may surprise you gentlemen, and go much against the grain of our London society's sensibilities, to hear me say that the beast is disdained only by those that do not understand its nature. The beast is dangerous, yes, violent, sometimes, but it is never cruel for cruelty's sake."

That was an interesting expression, I thought, and not the first time I had heard it. Mina Dracula had said the very same thing about her husband.

"Having discovered and refined the potion that brought Edward Hyde into existence," Jekyll went on, "I have come, slowly, to feel myself somewhat responsible for his fate. This is in addition to the irrefutable fact that our fates are quite linked but I promise you that this fact is not what drives me. If I thought now, as I did before, that Hyde was an evil that I had unleashed upon the world, I would gladly end my own life in order to rid the world of it." He finished with the leg irons, still so loosely fixed that he could likely pull his unbooted feet through without too much effort, and started the somewhat awkward process of moving the turn key so that he could fasten the manacles to his own wrists.

"In my defence, Mr Holmes, there were several supreme incidents, if you will, that quite coloured my judgment against him until I learned the full truth of them. Two cases in the past, and it is quite important that you should understand that there was never any malice on Hyde's part in either of them. The first was when one of the new motor cars backfired, panicking Hyde, and he ran, in stark terror, away from the sudden noise and trampled a young girl in his haste. She was injured, but not severely; still it was quite traumatic for all concerned. Hyde does share some blame for this terrible incident, but only to the same degree that a carriage horse, running wild from a fire, might. The second was the accidental death of Sir Danvers Carew, MP, though Utterson, a close confidant of mine and the chief witness, had that all wrong, too. I say accidental, though I have no doubt that the police instantly saw Utterson's point of view and the official report will list the death as deliberate murder. But nothing, gentlemen, could be further from the truth. Hyde never laid a hand on him, merely rounded a corner and so shocked Carew that the man tried to flee into traffic. He was run over by a delivery truck and killed instantly. Utterson claims that Hyde pushed him deliberately into traffic, but this is simply not true." He finished with the manacles, though, again, I could see that they were set so loosely that they could fall right off.

"It was not really Utterson's fault, however. You see, Hyde's ferocious and, frankly, hideous appearance, which you shall shortly make the acquaintance of, makes him seem like a monster out of our worst nightmares. This causes those around him to have a natural, but spurious, reaction to the man, which goes a very long way toward explaining the terrible reputation that follows him around."

During the utterance of this extraordinary and somewhat cryptic statement, Holmes had leaned forward and locked his hooded gaze on Doctor Jekyll as our new acquaintance tested the foolishly loose fit of his bonds yet again, then finally tossed the turnkey in my direction with a rattle of his chains.

Despite my surprise, I managed to catch it and held it up questioningly.

"You'll need that," Jekyll said, "in order to release him."

"Release who?" I said, wondering if the doctor had started to exhibit some sort of mental breakdown. Did he mean to refer to himself in the third person?

"I regret this demonstration, gentlemen, but I fear that no other will suffice. Not only do you need incontrovertible proof of the connection of which I speak, but you will also need to interview the subject himself in order to prove his innocence, and he would not willingly come here for questioning. However, he is likely to panic, coming to in chains. This set, however, is much stronger than the last set, at least. They will *probably* hold. Now that I think of it, I wish I'd brought the *really* heavy set. Ah well, no help for it, I suppose." He picked up his jacket and riffled through the pocket, removing a small box, which he opened. He pulled out a vial containing a brown, viscous liquid.

"I'm sorry, gentlemen," Jekyll said, "but I have no other choice. Watch yourselves. He is likely to be *very* angry."

So saying, he drank.

Chapter 02

HYDE'S STORY

Dr Jekyll drained the vial in one long draught and then immediately began to spasm and dropped the vial on the carpet, where it cracked and lay still. Jekyll followed it to the floor, falling on his hands and knees, and he gave a long, preternaturally loud and painful groan that seemed to be dredged up from the very bowels of the earth.

Holmes and I had both jumped to our feet with this startling reaction. But what happened next was even more astonishing.

Beneath the doctor's thin shirt, the skin began to move, to twitch and bubble and roil like an overheated cauldron. I had, since my exposure to the world of vampires, seen horrible things, the fuel of nightmares, but this sudden spectacle made my blood, such as it was, run cold.

The noises coming from Dr Jekyll grew even louder, more agonized, more animalistic, while his torso expanded. I watched in horror as his hands grew to twice their size and sprouted long nails. They flexed once in a powerful grip around the chains and I now understood Dr Jekyll's careful measurements that had seemed far too loose. The shirt tore clean in half with the expansion of that broad, hunched back.

"Curious," Holmes murmured, tilting his head and stepping slightly closer to get a better viewpoint. "A conservation of mass, I see, so science has not wholly left us. More powerful body… almost like a chimpanzee's, though I would hazard a sovereign or more that the weight is the same. Almost certainly stronger."

"Holmes," I said, "don't get too close!"

When the doctor looked up, I took an involuntary step backwards, so monstrous was his face, with a protruding lower jaw and large mouth filled with teeth. His hair was a wild mane of deepest black now, with bushy facial hair that on another man would have been called mutton chops, a continuation of the black mane. The eyes had gone a deep amber, bestial, and his brow bore dark, shaggy eyebrows. While he was still a man, there was also much of the night creature about him, features that reminded me in turn of the lion, the wolf and the ape. There was an even stronger animalistic odour that emanated off him now. This newly transformed man presented the darkest, most corrupt imitation of humanity to my eyes, a display of the most atavistic and dangerous nature that man had to offer. There remained no trace whatsoever of the handsome, smooth-faced, statuesque Dr Jekyll that had been in our sitting room moments before.

This new man shook the chains on his arms, clearly alarmed, and he jumped to his feet in obvious panic. He spun, moving with alarming speed, and yanked so that his powerful muscles bulged; the metal groaned, but held. The hands were broad, blunt, with long, unkempt fingernails and I shuddered to think of the damage those hands could do as he flexed them.

"Holmes!" I said, for he was still standing less than five feet from the monster. But Holmes ignored me.

"Mr Edward Hyde, I assume?" Holmes said mildly. He slapped the paper in his hand. "If the newspaper's somewhat garbled and pithy description is accurate?"

The man bared his wild and savage-looking teeth and gave a great, barking cough that rattled the window panes. In the time that Holmes and I have worked many cases together, we have come up against many a ruffian, but there was something primeval and positively inhuman about this man's demeanour that made my hair stand up on end. I heard a small shriek from Mrs Hudson downstairs. Looking at teeth like that, I half wondered if he might not be a vampire, but the scent, animal and primitive, was all wrong for that. This was some new, unknown and fearsome devilry at work.

"Tut tut," Holmes said, completely unruffled by the man's ferocious display.

Then Hyde, if Holmes's assessment of the facts was correct and such was his name, collapsed with a sob onto our carpet. "Genie," he whispered. "Oh, Genie, what have they done to you?" The man burst into sudden tears.

I stood, astonished and perplexed. Of all the strange things that had happened in the past few minutes, this monster suddenly taken over by a fit of sobbing was, somehow, the most unreal.

His voice sounded raw and filled with emotion, exposing a grief so profoundly private that I felt embarrassed to be a witness to it.

Holmes looked at me with surprise, and not a small amount of pleasure, for which I frowned at him. It was altogether too common for Holmes to delight in a tragic twist, for nothing bored him more than a predictable problem, and he often neglected to take into account the effect that misfortunes had on those connected to the case.

Hyde, still crouching on the floor, took a deep, shuddering breath, his face hidden by the enormous mane of black hair and mutton chops. He gripped the carpet with those dangerous hands, nails scoring it like claws. Then he grimaced, wiped his tears, and stood.

"Very well," he said, his voice still raw. "The only help for Genie now is this, and for once, that milksop Jekyll actually did something right and got us here to the one person who might help us." He faced the significantly taller Holmes. "You are exactly as I imagined from the stories and yet… somehow not. Paget didn't get the jaw quite right, did he?" His voice was a deep, rusty baritone. "Tell me, Mr Holmes, will you take the case?"

"By all means," Holmes said warmly. "The return of the Ripper and your astonishing connection to Jekyll… well…" He chuckled. "You would have to throw *me* in chains to keep me away."

Hyde, visibly tense, relaxed a small bit and nodded his thanks.

"Please do sit," Holmes said. "Watson, perhaps it would be best if you locked the door. I am not quite ready to regale Mrs Hudson with all the salient details as of yet."

I made my way warily around our strange visitor in order to

turn the lock on our door. It was not a moment too soon, because I heard Mrs Hudson's feet coming up the stairs.

"Have no fear, Mrs Hudson," Holmes shouted to her. "We are quite unharmed and in no danger, I assure you."

Mrs Hudson tried the door, found it locked, and then harrumphed. It did not take vampire ears to hear it, even through the closed door. The briefest of smiles flashed on Holmes's face and I was surprised to see an answering flicker of amusement on Hyde's.

"Mr Hyde," Holmes said again, "please, do sit."

"I really didn't think he'd do it," Hyde said, finally taking a seat. He made a sad, ironic performance of rattling his chains as he did so. "Jekyll, I mean. Such a melba toast. He was terrified of turning himself in on account of the publicity. I swear that man cares more for his reputation than any real morality. He was too frightened to go to the police and too frightened not to, but I convinced him, it seems, that you were an acceptable alternative. I dared not come myself, but I needed *you* to hear my story."

"Melba toast?" I asked. My mind was still reeling from the indescribable thing we'd just seen and it seemed impossible that we three stood here making conversation.

"Melba toast," Hyde repeated. "Small, brittle, crumbles easily in your hand, insignificant. Term I picked up while Jekyll and I were hiding in France at the Opera House, though they call it *croûtes en dentelle* there, of course." He grinned at me, in case I had forgotten the alarming teeth behind that savage grin. "I will make my position plain. I know that poor Genie was murdered and I am ready-made for the part of her killer from the official point of view. The police would not listen to or believe my story, but I thought that you, perhaps, might. I know that the police will eventually put their hands on me and without Jekyll's help, there is no chance of escape for me, but that is of little matter. What matters is Genie. She was always kind to me, despite this face, and didn't deserve what happened to her. I would see her murderer brought to justice."

"Very good," Holmes said. "Perhaps if you first explain the nature of your connection to Dr Jekyll and then we can get a full account of the murder. We shall have to talk quickly, for it is certain that the police will come here soon."

"Why?" Hyde said, suddenly suspicious.

"The Whitechapel Murders are of the highest profile," I said. "They will certainly want to consult Holmes regarding them."

"Ah," Hyde said. "Yes, that makes sense."

"It is already a most exceptional case," Holmes said, "and we have hardly scratched the surface. Do you, like your counterpart, also abstain from brandy and the like?"

"By no means," Hyde said. His rusty baritone, now that he had calmed somewhat, was surprisingly warm and pleasant.

"Watson, please," Holmes said, and I, with some reservations, did as he asked. We had little time for the niceties, as Holmes had just said, but he seemed determined to mollify Hyde's suspicion and hostility and I poured three snifters of our best brandy and handed the first to Hyde.

He took the glass without meeting my gaze. Instead he spoke to Holmes. "You would try to prove my innocence?"

"Well," Holmes said, taking his glass of brandy from me, "the police hardly need my help proving your guilt. They are convinced of it already and I dare say a jury would not be far behind. However, it is my policy to follow docilely along wherever the evidence shall lead me. If you have done this terrible thing, it will do you little good to have us in your corner."

"What about you?" Hyde said, turning those amber eyes in my direction.

"You seem to be a violent and unsavoury person," I said bluntly, "and I can think of no reason to disbelieve the accusation that you have done this foul thing. However, Holmes has disproved equally believable crimes before this and I should not be surprised to see him do so in this case."

Hyde leaned back again, nonplussed. "Well, that's two honest, if unpretty, answers. I can ask no more than that."

Holmes reclined and lit his pipe. "We have seen how the elixir, which I suspect must include a component of Löwenstein's langur serum, has transformed you from Jekyll to Hyde. Jekyll believed that he had separated the evil side of his nature, leaving only the laudable morality of our better nature, but has since come to see the separation to be more between civilized and animal. Have I summarized your position on the matter?"

"That is how he sees it," Hyde said, "though I would call it the difference between a full life and a hollow one, unless you consider brandy, human warmth and contact – or anything outside of a test tube, for that matter – to be intrinsically evil and inhuman. It's a cold, hard, positively inhuman morality that Jekyll clings to, if you ask me. A hypocritical one, too, since he first invented the serum hoping to find a way to enjoy his pleasures without injury to his reputation. What kind of decency is that, I ask you?"

"You are *not* a violent murderer, then?" Holmes said. The question seemed as casual as asking for the man's address.

Hyde sat back, clearly surprised, his mane swaying with the sudden movement. "Do you know," he said slowly, "you are the first person to actually ask me that? Everyone else just assumes that I *am*."

"An impression that you do a great deal to cultivate," Holmes remarked dryly.

"People see the monster," Hyde said. "Can't convince them otherwise. Why attempt it?"

"Why indeed?" Holmes said.

Hyde opened his mouth and then closed it again, pondering. Despite the savage appearance, I got the impression that this monster of a man was no dullard, and that speechlessness was rarely a state that came upon him except by his own choice.

"I won't deny that I've been in a scuffle or two at the public house," Hyde finally said. "I like whisky and the music halls and friendly women, when I can find them, but no, I've not taken a life, especially not a woman's."

"As for not taking a life," Holmes said, "that is more than Watson and I can say, not to put too fine a point on it. Oh, I know, Watson, always for a good cause and always as a last resort, but it is true all the same."

I opened my mouth to object, but Holmes waved a dismissive hand at me.

"You and Jekyll cannot both be present at once," Holmes went on, "yet you have mentioned communication between yourself and him. How is this accomplished?"

"There is a link between us, for all that we both detest the other," Hyde said. "The change can usually be brought on with the elixir, but often it comes of its own volition, on me when I sleep, or on Jekyll when he is excited. As to communication, Mr Holmes, I can see him in my dreams, same as he can see me. Jekyll should have known that I didn't kill Genie, but he doesn't have the courage of his convictions, I think, or else he doesn't dream me as clearly as I dream him. At any rate, the dreams are incomplete and sometimes hazy, but the important things bob to the surface. I would think that each of us would know if the other had done anything remarkable like committing a murder, but I'll admit that's far from certain. Oh! And we write each other notes."

"Notes?" Holmes said. "How curious."

"Yes," Hyde said. "In fact…" He searched in his own coat pockets and produced a scrap of paper, manacles clanking as he did so. "Yes, here it is." He passed over the paper to Holmes, who took it eagerly.

"Yes, hmm," he said. "A page ripped carelessly from a small notebook, written with a blunt pencil."

"Yes," Hyde said. "I have those items here in my pocket." He offered to pass pencil and notebook over for inspection, but Holmes waved him off, then thrust the note in my direction.

Holmes read the note aloud: "'We cannot hide. Take me to Mr Sherlock Holmes at 221B Baker Street or I will expose us.'"

"Just so," Hyde said.

"Just so," agreed Holmes. "Now then, why don't you tell us your story of last night's events while we still have time? There are some details in the paper, but not many."

Holmes proffered the newspaper and Hyde snatched it away. He scanned the contents briefly and then closed his eyes and sagged in place, clearly remembering the tragedy from last night.

"There's no great story to tell," Hyde said. "It is pleasant to have company when one carouses, as I said earlier. I am very familiar with the Whitechapel area. Intimate, you might say; I find it a much more decent place than the upper-crust portions of London. Genie Babington and Franny Barker are both acquaintances that have spent time with me in public houses before, though Genie is... was... much more familiar to me. You look surprised, Doctor, but I can tell you that I am a regular at The Hanover public house and they do not mind taking my sovereigns. So it was with these ladies."

"You paid them?" I said, unable to keep the outrage out of my voice.

"Nothing so crass," Hyde said. "I was free enough to keep the drinks and food coming to ensure a pleasant time for all, and they took a liking to me for that consideration; there's no harm in any of that. We kept to ourselves and nothing much occurred until late in the evening when the three of us stumbled into the street. The plan was for us to retire to my apartments nearby and share some brandy there. Genie decided at the last minute to double back for some ale from the public house, as she doesn't always have a head for brandy. So I gave her a few shillings for the purchase. It seemed safe enough to us at the time.

"To reach my apartments, there is a short walk down an alley that communicates between the two buildings. It was there we left Genie, thinking that it was just a dozen yards or so back to the main thoroughfare and the public house. In fact, we never actually reached the rooms, which I believe the landlord will confirm, for Franny took a liking to this very same gentleman in the lobby and invited him to join us. This involved some discussion as the landlord, Grosvenor, was taken with Franny, but not so taken with my company. Seeing that Franny's campaign to convince him might take some time, I left them in the lobby and went to see about Genie. But I had hardly gone a dozen feet down the alleyway before I found poor Genie sitting in the mud and dirt with her back against the brick wall of the alley, with her throat cut and her blood all over." The mellow, scratchy voice throbbed with deep emotion. "She died right in front of me."

I found myself still looking askance at our guest, but it was clear now that Hyde was more than just a beast, however ill-favoured he looked. I wasn't yet sure if I believed his story or not, but doubt had crept into my heart as to Hyde's guilt. Still, any man that caroused as Hyde claimed was clearly of questionable character, as evidenced by his own assessment that no woman would desire his company without compensation. Yet, he also spoke well, and had clearly enjoyed some kind of education, somehow. This man was a far cry from the ruffian and low-brow murderer that the newspapers had claimed him to be.

"There is one more thing," Hyde said. "I didn't see the man that did it, Mr Holmes, but I could smell him over the stink of the alley and the iron-copper scent of poor Genie's blood.

He couldn't have been more than a few feet away and I heard a soft chuckle that sent anger and hatred through my body."

"Someone hiding in the darkness, you mean?" I asked.

"No," Hyde said. "Someone standing only a few feet away, not hiding, and it wasn't dark. Not for me. It was just that *I couldn't see him*. Like a ghost."

"Come, man!" I said. "You expect us to believe in ghosts?"

"I don't," snapped Hyde, "but I have no other explanation. I merely tell you how it was. I could hear a man, and smell him, but saw nothing."

"What happened next?" Holmes asked.

"That was when Franny and Grosvenor came following in my wake," Hyde said. "They saw Genie, and Franny screamed and then shouts and the wail of a police whistle came and I fled. I knew what people would think. I fled to the rooftops and then ran and climbed until I was near out of breath and came to in the morning as Jekyll on a rooftop in Stratford."

"The rooftops?" I said.

"That wasn't any surprise to Jekyll, I'm sure," Hyde said. "I have often used the rooftops as a way of avoiding pursuit or moving unseen. There aren't many that can climb as well as I can." He flexed his powerful arms and hands and I found the claim all too easy to believe.

"The wound," Holmes said. "Was it precise, as the newspaper claims?"

"It was," Hyde said. "As clean and nasty a business as ever I've seen."

"You mentioned, Watson," Holmes said, "that you could think

of no reason why Hyde couldn't be the culprit. I have." He took the pipe out of his mouth and, without warning, tossed it into Hyde's lap. The beast man caught it, moving with surprising speed and a rattle of chains, but he used both hands to cradle it. When he held the pipe up questioningly, it looked ridiculously small in his oversized hands.

Holmes stepped over, claimed the pipe from the unresisting Hyde, and then peered carefully at Hyde's hands, even going so far as to turn them over and take a closer look. Hyde accepted this inspection without demur and some amusement in his face.

"For someone with hands like these," Holmes said, "the scalpel would make a poor weapon. Not nearly as efficient as the fingernails, really; quite remarkable. Jekyll, being a doctor, would make a far likelier candidate, if a scalpel was really the murder weapon."

Hyde jerked in surprise, and then a barking laugh shot out from his lips. "Not likely. Not that melba toast. Scared of his own footsteps, that one. Besides, I would know."

"The dreams?" I asked.

"Exactly," Hyde said. "Something that big in his life, I would know."

"Extraordinary," I said. My disbelief must have been apparent in my voice, because he shot me a speculative look from under those shaggy black eyebrows.

"I should think," Hyde said, swirling the remaining brandy in his glass, "that we have all of us comes to terms with extraordinary, dare I say unbelievable, persons in our time, have we not? I have encountered a few of those that hunt and drink in the night before this, and I can see, or smell, rather, that you know precisely what I mean." His rusty voice was mild, almost amused, but his amber eyes slid to regard first me and then the teapot with the red ribbon and unique repast that I had left sitting unobtrusively on the sideboard. It was not difficult for me to see the implied threat. Somehow, Hyde knew about vampires and, furthermore, knew that I was one of them.

"Is a man that can be detected by scent," Hyde went on, "but not by the eye so impossible to believe?"

"Perhaps not," I admitted. Holmes looked thoughtful.

"My sense of smell is quite strong," Hyde remarked affably, "and there is nothing so distinct as the scent of blood. Now, Mr Holmes, if you would be so kind as to pour another glass of brandy, a double, for it may be a while before I get another as I can hear the sound of law enforcement down in the street. The only memories I have before five years ago are Jekyll's, you understand, but in these past five years, never has a policeman been a friend to Edward Hyde. They are familiar with me and have just been looking for some excuse to run me in, though I have done no wrong. They see me as the villain, always, and won't consider any other point of view. Wouldn't hanging the Ripper's murders on me make them happier than anything?"

I was a bit surprised, as I had not heard the police coming myself, but now I did. They were only now just pulling up to the kerb, to judge from the excited voices and booted feet in the street outside. The bell rang and then footsteps came up the stairs and our door flew open, admitting Lestrade and Gregson of Scotland Yard.

"Doctor Henry Jekyll?" Lestrade blurted out.

"Not," Hyde said, "exactly." He waved nonchalantly with a rattle of chains.

"Well, I'll be a monkey's fiddler," Lestrade breathed, his ferrety face filled with open wonder. "I have been seeking out Jekyll, him being a known associate of the man I'm after, and I track him to Baker Street and up I come and find the quarry himself, and in chains!"

Gregson, a taller man, shook his head and removed his bowler hat so that he could run his hand through thinning blond hair. "I don't know how you do it, Mr Holmes, but I have come on a completely different errand to ask you to come examine the murder scene for clues. I thought, if you had not yet read the papers, to surprise you with the reoccurrence of the Ripper killings, and here you already have the murderer in your custody! It's more than I can fathom!"

"We shall see," Holmes said. "I have, in point of fact, just been reading the account of the murder in the paper. I understand that Hyde here is your main suspect, but I should advise you that I consider it highly improbable."

"Improbable!" Lestrade exclaimed. "The noose is practically ready. He's a man of dangerous temper and numerous crimes under his belt. Besides, we have an eyewitness!"

"Eyewitness to the murder?" Holmes asked.

"As good as!" Lestrade said. "She found him over the body!"

"Very circumstantial," Holmes replied, standing up. "You also say he has committed crimes previous to this. What crimes?"

Lestrade looked up at his fair-haired companion, Gregson,

who shrugged helplessly. "Nothing serious that we can prove. He was linked to the death of Danvers Carew, but we couldn't even prove murder, let alone his culpability. But now we have him!"

"Yes," Holmes said blandly. "You have him, and I believe he will go willingly?" He turned and caught Hyde's eye. "Will you?"

Edward Hyde puffed himself up with a deep breath and looked for a moment as if he meant to rush the two men at the door, then locked gazes with Holmes for a long, drawn-out moment before finally sagging in place.

"I will go quietly," he said finally, still looking only at Holmes. "You'll work to catch the real killer?"

Both Lestrade and Gregson looked shocked.

"I will," Holmes said. "I can't promise anything, but if there is any luck and justice in the world, your stay at Scotland Yard will be a short one."

Lestrade and Gregson exchanged looks, then Gregson hollered down the stairs and two constables trod up to take possession of the prisoner. Hyde cast one backwards look, his mane wild, his eyes blazing, before they marched him out, but he did not resist.

"It would be just as well if you hurry," Hyde remarked blandly to Holmes. "I don't know how many days I can remain in jail and still retain my winning personality." I remembered Hyde's comment that he could not always control his transformation and felt a cold chill down my back.

"If I should lose my perspective," Hyde went on, "that might raise questions."

Holmes nodded his understanding. "We shall endeavour to make certain that doesn't happen."

Hyde held his gaze, then nodded, as if he were content with Holmes's response. I half expected some kind of veiled threat, a warning that he might divulge our secrets once his came to light, but Hyde made no such intimation and allowed the constables to lead him out of our apartment without incident.

"Forgive me, Mr Holmes," Lestrade said when they had gone, "but I should not give the man false hope, if I were you. It's God's own truth that you've steered us in the right direction time and time again and I would be a slow learner to cavalierly dismiss any theory that you suggest, but I should warn you that our case against this man looks very grave."

"On that, we agree," Holmes said. "All the more reason that I should see the murder site immediately."

Lestrade went on doggedly. "We had already landed on Edward Hyde as our prime suspect and discovered his connection to Dr Henry Jekyll. Jekyll would not give us any information when we questioned him this morning, but shortly after our visit, he left in a grand hurry and I took the liberty of following him. Imagine my surprise when he led me straight here. However, I have watched your front door for some time and did not see Hyde arrive, nor Jekyll leave. He is still here?"

"He is not," Holmes said. "You must have missed him going out."

Lestrade frowned, clearly not liking that possibility, but he said nothing.

"You and Gregson did not come together?" I asked.

Gregson shook his head, his habitually morose expression even more so now. "I came here to inform you of the murder and take you to the crime scene, although I should be frank and state that I agree entirely with Lestrade that Edward Hyde is our prime suspect. I had hoped that you could assist us in finding him. Never did I dream that you'd have the culprit sitting here in your study. Now you tell me that you think him innocent?"

"I have not entirely made up my mind," Holmes said, "but I consider it a likely possibility."

"Who do *you* think did this crime?" Lestrade asked.

"That remains to be seen," Holmes said. "Watson, are you ready for a ride to Whitechapel?"

Chapter 03

THE FIRST MURDER SCENE

Although Gregson had come with the express purpose of conveying us to the crime scene, we instead took a cab with just Holmes and myself, as both Gregson and Lestrade thought it best to escort their menacing prisoner back to Scotland Yard under maximum supervision.

Holmes was uncharacteristically quiet in the hansom, which I first took as the pensive thoughtfulness he used to still his mind before engaging in an important investigation, so I settled myself for a long ride in silence. We passed from a street heavy with shops and eager shoppers to a long stretch of rundown tenement buildings amidst a light drizzle falling from an overcast morning sky. The streets were wet and the hansom wheels made a hissing sound as we rolled along.

"It's the wrong shape, Watson," Holmes said, surprising me.

"I'm sorry?" I said. "What is the wrong shape?"

"Every case is a problem to be solved, Watson, a puzzle played out on a grand scale," he said, still staring out morosely at the rainy streets. Something was amiss. Usually, at the start of a new investigation, Holmes practically thrummed and vibrated with pent-up energy, the caged hound ready to be released to the chase. But now, he seemed lacklustre, despondent.

"What is required," he went on in a low voice, barely audible over the carriage noises, "is to find all the pieces of the puzzle, assemble them, and so get an idea of the big picture, if you will. But there are some factors that the worker of the puzzle can take for granted. The puzzle is best arranged on a flat surface, you understand, and can be relied upon to be a certain shape, usually one with four corners and such."

He turned to look at me finally, his grey eyes troubled, his lean face pinched. "But Dr Jekyll's demonstration has disturbed me, Watson, disturbed me more than I first realized."

"I agree wholeheartedly," I said. "We have seen some horrible things, you and I, but I don't mind telling you that the sight of that man, hunched over on the floor, is going to haunt my dreams."

"Not that," Holmes said. "It is the science of it that disturbs me, the hitherto undiscovered and unfathomable science of it. At least, we have Jekyll's word that it is science, and so understood with modern scientific methods. But I wonder." He took a deep breath, as if getting ready to shoulder a burden. "The physical transformation is one thing, Watson, but the creation of this other man, this… Hyde, a man that did not exist before Jekyll's experimentation, comes with ramifications that disturb me greatly. If Jekyll can do this to himself, what other things are possible? When I examine the murder scene that our good cabbie is even now whisking us closer and closer to, how will I be able to rule out the impossible when the impossible becomes more and more *possible* with each new scientific discovery?"

"If anyone can do it, I would bet my pension on you, Holmes."

He gave a thin smile to acknowledge his appreciation of my sentiment, even if he clearly didn't agree with it. He shook his head. "Not I, Watson. I no longer know the shape of the world, you see? The vampiric blood disease has already bent my idea of the world's shape to breaking point and now I fear that this new impossibility has twisted it out of shape completely. Also, what am I to make of this story of his, of a culprit that cannot be seen? Before our encounter with vampires, I should have said such a thing inconceivable. But now..." He lifted his hands helplessly. "The world is the wrong shape, Watson, and I find myself and my powers to be a paltry thing in comparison."

"Holmes, that isn't true!"

"I should," he continued, "in good conscience, turn this cab around. I dare not take this case. What blunders might I make anticipating witches and hobgoblins at every turn?"

I opened my mouth to protest again, then abruptly decided to change tack. "Well," I said slowly, "considering the heightened publicity of the Ripper case in the past, and seeing as how the newspapers already have hold of it, Scotland Yard is certain to spare no resource investigating this heinous crime. Perhaps you are correct to leave it to their stout judgement. Certainly young Stanley Hopkins has all the energy you could ever wish to bring to an investigation and if he is paired with someone like Alec

MacDonald… he is the strongest reasoner among them, don't you think?"

Holmes's gaze had been inwardly turned, with little regard to me, the hansom, or the streets passing by, but now it focused on me. His glare conveyed his lack of appreciation for this transparent strategy of mine. His next words came out slowly, reluctantly. "Lestrade, Gregson and MacDonald are adequate, I suppose, when it comes to chasing clues that fall directly into their lap, though they all show a shocking lack of imagination."

"Well then," I said, keeping my face as open and sincere as I possibly could, "it is only required, then, that we should make a recommendation to that effect and explain to them that you are indisposed and cannot possibly assist. Of course, I believe that Athelney Peter Jones is the senior inspector, but I'm sure that you shall be able to talk him into stepping down to let one of the other, sharper heads prevail. It wouldn't be like the Sholto case at all. He must have certainly learned from that mistake. After all…"

Holmes's face twisted in a pained grimace and he suddenly had the expression of a man who had shovelled in what he thought was a forkful of roast duck and instead been given something dredged out of the plumbing.

The hansom drifted to a jerky stop.

"Shall I turn him around?" I asked blandly.

His glare spoke volumes. Then, without a word, he pushed open the carriage door as if he was angry with it, too, and all other doors besides. I had to scramble to get out and follow in his wake.

We alit on the ground in front of The Hanover public house, the establishment that Hyde had mentioned in his account of events. The street, a narrow but well-used thoroughfare, was abuzz with activity. Not only was the place crawling with the police force, but casual onlookers, as well as several obvious members of the press, were all gathered around in the street and kept barely in check by the line of constables blocking their view of the alley across the street. The buildings around were high and cramped and several of the windows were boarded up so that that place looked a bit more run-down than some, but it did not look like a place deserving of the notorious repute that this incident would bring upon it. We could clearly see the alley that Hyde had described, which the police had blocked off. A large collection of women, all of them with sour faces and many of them holding or surrounded by children, gazed at us suspiciously.

Milling around just outside the alley was a veritable convention of inspectors. The officials at Scotland Yard, very correctly understanding the high-profile sensation this case would bring, had clearly established an 'all-hands-on-deck' policy for this endeavour. Lestrade and Gregson were already involved, as evidenced by their visit to us earlier, and to add to these, I saw the portly Athelney Peter Jones, already looking ready to tear his sparse fringe of red hair out. He was talking heatedly to young Stanley Hopkins, who was nodding and carefully taking notes, his lean face wearing an expression of great concentration. Behind them, I could also see the stout form of Arthur Bradstreet, in his habitual peaked hat and frogged jacket, and Alec MacDonald's tall, bony figure and dour face.

Lestrade had remarked some years ago that while the average person might expect the Scotland Yarders to be jealous of Sherlock Holmes's success and resent his presence as a result, this could not possibly be further from the truth. Never was this in greater evidence than when all eyes recognized Holmes and turned with looks of relief and pride on their faces. They gathered around to shake Holmes's hand and welcome him, surrounding him in a tight cluster.

"Good of you to come! Gregson found you, then?"

"We have preserved everything just as it was!"

"We have a name of the rascal, of course. It won't be like the last time, now will it?"

The men crowded round, each of them eager to get closer to Holmes to hear what he might say. Holmes was clearly ill at ease with this heartfelt praise and stood stiffly, shaking hands when each handshake was forced upon him, with his face pale and hard, though no one seemed to notice this except me.

"Gentlemen!" Jones said, raising his hands for silence. He seemed to have charge of the scene in a capable manner, making me regret my little jape at his expense in the carriage.

"Well, Mr Holmes," Jones said once he had silence enough to speak, "it's true that you and I have had our differences as to the various merits of practical and theoretical methods, but your results over the years have earned the respect of every man here and make no mistake. This is a gruesome business to be sure, but this will not be a repeat of '88 when we had no clues to go on, will it. And wasn't that an embarrassment for yourself as well as the entire force? This time, we have the name of the man and only need to lay our hands on him. In addition to a description, one of our witnesses is Hyde's own landlord, so there is no trouble finding his place of residence. Even now we have his description being circulated among the entire force and isn't he a beauty. He should not be hard to find. Still, Gregson has likely briefed you thoroughly on events while Lestrade is even now tracking down a known associate, one…" He snapped his fingers. "What was that name, Hopkins?"

"Jekyll, sir," Hopkins said quickly, referring to a small notebook. "Dr Henry Jekyll. His address is in Soho."

"That's the man," Jones agreed. "Where is Gregson? He was supposed to have returned with you."

"Finding Mr Edward Hyde was not such a great difficulty," Holmes said. "He was already at Baker Street and ready to turn himself in. Lestrade and Gregson were escorting him to Scotland Yard and will likely be back here shortly once Hyde is safely entombed. Catching the murderer, however, may be a different matter altogether."

"Wait!" Jones said, swelling up. "You don't believe that Hyde is our murderer? But he was found over the dead body, is known to have a vile temper, has had several hostile run-ins with the constables of this beat, and was known to have kept company with the murdered woman on more than one occasion. Common sense points us, in every regard, to this man Hyde!"

"So you said about Thaddeus Sholto," I reminded him gently, for I could see Holmes opening his mouth in order to make a much harsher observation, and I did not think Jones would take kindly to being upbraided so in front of his subordinates. I saw

Hopkins and MacDonald exchange concerned looks. Every inspector here had chafed at one time or another when Holmes had picked holes in their methods, suppositions and arrests, especially when the case seemed a straightforward one.

Inspector Athelney Peter Jones rose to his fullest height – which wasn't much, him being the shortest man present – and looked from Holmes's stern face to my own and back again. Then, the inspector ran his fat hand over the fringe of red hair that remained on his scalp. It came away wet. He took a deep breath and visibly mastered himself, then leaned in so that the many onlooking persons should not hear his next statement.

"Very well," he said, sucking his teeth. "You *have* proved time and time again that you know what you are doing." He thought some more. "You would not have us release Hyde?"

"No," Holmes agreed, "I do not say that."

"That is just as well," Jones said, breathing a sigh of relief, "for I do not think the commissioner would understand such a move, even in light of your recommendation. I know for a certainty that the newspapers and public would not. We need to have a suspect in custody or the city will riot in fear!"

"A fear that will be very justified if we do not catch the real murderer, Inspector," Holmes said. "Let us see the crime scene itself, shall we?"

The inspectors and constables opened a path and Holmes and I went into the alley. I felt the need to brace myself against the detestable scene we were entering. While Holmes and I have investigated more than our fair share of odious crimes, the name of Jack the Ripper has terrified many a sturdy citizen and weighed heavily on the hearts of all Londoners, and for good reason. Jones and I stopped partway to the body, at Holmes's insistence, and hung back while he looked over the scene. A knot of policemen gathered behind us, everyone watching Holmes as he went through his routine.

Seldom have I seen a more distressing sight. The body of Eugenie 'Genie' Babington was a small, discarded thing in the dirty alley, which only made the crime that much more atrocious, to have reduced a living woman to this sort of tragedy. It is a strange thing, but the blood disease that caused my vampirism had not changed the revulsion I felt at seeing such a sight.

The scent of dried blood was overpowering, even out-of-doors, both disconcerting and enticing.

If I have not spoken much of the effect that blood has on the vampire, it is because it is both obvious and subtly sinister. There is a euphoria that comes over the vampire as they drink blood, even the modest blood of livestock that I survive on. With human blood, I understand, the effect is even more pronounced and I could feel the traces of that euphoria just from the scent of it, like a man standing too long over a bucket of paint thinner in an enclosed room. Here was the ultimate temptation of my new existence, a subdued, latent murderous intent inside me. An animal madness that lay in the depths of all of my kind, and the scent of blood called to it.

"We cordoned off the scene," Hopkins said eagerly from behind us, "so as to not contaminate the evidence."

Holmes sniffed, his expression intent, and seemed to have not heard Hopkins at all, so fixed was his concentration on the evidence before him. He took a quick look at the boots of the inspectors around us, taking note, I thought, of their size and prints. He then examined the ground, laying prostrate for minutes at a time to peer through his magnifying glass at markings he found, then climbing part of the brick wall in order to peer at marks he found nearly a storey and a half up. It seemed Hyde's claim about climbing was entirely accurate.

Something had been tickling at my nose for the past few seconds, until I finally identified it.

I crouched near Holmes and spoke very quietly. "Holmes, do you smell…"

"Creosote," Holmes said, just as quietly.

"Precisely!"

"I do, but cannot account for it. I see no new road work to explain it anywhere here in the alley. Curious." Then Holmes stepped forward and examined the body itself, squinting at the ghastly wound across her neck before venturing to turn the body over.

"We did have to move the body," Jones said to Holmes. "You'll see why momentarily, I expect. Turned it over once to examine the back and then moved it back so that you could see it in its original attitude."

The most grotesque feature of the murder had been hidden by Genie herself, for when Holmes finally turned the body over, I could see the gaping hole in her back. The woman's front was covered in blood, but another large bloodstain, previously hidden by the woman's coat and dress, was smeared on the brick wall and street behind her.

"Watson," Holmes said, beckoning me forward.

I came, hastily, to examine the wound. "The kidney," I said after a moment. "Holmes, this man has taken her kidney."

"It seems our old friend Jack has gone back to taking trophies again," Holmes murmured, "or else someone wants us to think that he is the Ripper returned."

"Is it him?" I asked in a whisper.

"Well," Holmes said, musing, "someone has used a very small, very sharp, narrow-bladed knife, possibly a scalpel, first on this woman's neck, and then on her lower back. See here…" He pointed at a heavy bruise on her temple. "This likely indicates that he bludgeoned her, knocking her unconscious before ending her life."

"The amount of bleeding suggests that the kidney was removed not long after death," I said.

"So I read it," he agreed. He picked up the woman's hands, examining them both carefully. "Unmarked, which is suggestive. The blow to her forehead indicates a frontal assault and you would expect some bruises on the hands and arms as she tried to defend herself."

"Unless the blow came too suddenly to anticipate," I said, "possibly from a known associate, such as Hyde?"

"That is possible," Holmes admitted. He was looking at Miss Babington's shoes now. "Or possibly from someone unseen, as Hyde claims. Hyde himself would wear a size fifteen shoe, at least, and Jekyll not less than a size ten, yet there are, in addition to Hyde's footprints and Babington's, the prints of men's boots that are size nine, with square toes. These are all on top of many other prints as this is a much-used byway, so they are the most recent. In addition to that, there are other prints that I make to be from the Yarders behind us, but most of them have avoided coming this far. Still, if this is their idea of an uncontaminated crime scene then it is no wonder they have to call in a consultant to get results. I might have deduced a great deal more but there are too many other interfering tracks."

He looked at her head again, then examined the wall once more above her and made a soft exclamation. "Here," he said, "more drops of blood. I believe these to have likely come from the small cut on the back of her head."

"You need hardly look for the source of blood," Jones said. He and the other Yarders had come a bit closer. Holmes and I had been speaking softly to keep the conversation between the two of us, but Jones had clearly heard at least the last bit. "A throat cut like that will bleed an enormous amount of blood, more than enough to account for the blood on her dress, and the wound in her back would explain the stain on the wall."

"There are two stains on the wall and cobblestones," Holmes said, "not one." He stood up and addressed Jones and the group of inspectors gathered around him, all of which were hanging on his every word.

"I read it this way," Holmes said. "First, she was struck in the temple, a blow hard enough to knock her back against the wall, where she cut her head and then fell."

"Hyde looks to be a fearsomely strong fellow," Jones said.

"That is true enough," Holmes said. "Furthermore, the blow was, as Watson has suggested, so sudden or unexpected that the lady did not have a chance to defend herself, which does not preclude Hyde, but the angle of the blow suggests someone taller than Hyde, who is shorter than his supposed victim."

"Perhaps she leaned over," Jones said, "and he caught her unprepared that way. Or somehow convinced her to turn her back. Possibly part of a transaction, and so turning her back would be natural enough in that sort of business. After all, any woman out this late…" He held up both hands helplessly, clearly chalking up both murderer and victim as the absolute dregs of society.

"That is possible," Holmes said, rifling through the dead woman's pockets, "but there are some problems with that theory."

"Such as?" Jones asked.

Holmes showed him the few shillings he'd discovered. "This doesn't seem to be the right amount to support your transaction theory. If the man paid her, as you suggest, this would not be enough. If he were to recover the fee, logic suggests that he would take all of her money, not just retrieve his own. It's not conclusive, I grant you, but I am inclined to discard the transaction theory. Also, the signs do not seem right to me when compared with our suspect."

"How so?"

"Hyde is, as has been noted, very powerful," Holmes went on. "Certainly powerful enough to kill someone in one blow, but that did not happen here."

"A glancing blow, then?" Jones said.

Holmes nodded reluctantly. "Again, it is possible, though I do not say likely. At any rate, she hit the wall, likely became stunned, and then fell on her face. You can see a small contusion on her forehead and the corresponding droplet of blood where she fell. Then, our size nine shoe murderer leaned over and with a very sharp knife, cut her throat from behind. There is bruising on the left side of her head and some hair missing, indicating that he likely held her head in this position with his left hand while performing the cut with his right, so our murderer is right-handed. This is a slight departure from the previous murders where the victims were likely strangled before having their throats cut, but in each case the murderer has incapacitated his victim first and then done the murder."

"But they found the body face up," I said. "He would have needed to turn her over to get to the kidney, too. Your theory doesn't account for that, does it?"

"Not on its own," Holmes admitted, "which I find deeply sinister." Holmes had been combing over the dead body, the various wounds and blood splatter marks, for the better part of an hour now without showing the slightest sign of any squeamishness, but now he twisted his lips in a frown of disgust.

"*That's* what you find sinister?" I blurted out.

Holmes shook himself out of his dark reverie. "You see, I believe he cut her throat from behind, as I said, and then turned her body back over before she had completely expired."

"But why," I said, horrified at the idea, "if it was the kidney he was after?"

"He wanted to watch her," Holmes said quietly. "He wanted to watch her life ebb away."

There was a quiet, disturbed murmur from the inspectors. MacDonald swore and Hopkins' face had drained of all colour.

"B-but," Jones stammered, "as Dr Watson has pointed out, we found the body face up, just as I told you."

"He did his work to retrieve the kidney," Holmes said, "and then turned the body back over yet again."

"But why?" I exclaimed. "This is a well-used alley, if I understand that right, and he must have been worried about discovery."

"I believe he wanted to display the body," Holmes said quietly, "in order to garner the maximum dramatic effect when it was discovered. That is just a theory, but if we are dealing with someone bold, someone who enjoys the terror that is caused by his actions, someone that yearns for the attention of the public and the newspapers, and I think we are, then it is a theory that meets the facts. Unfortunately, that doesn't go very far towards either convicting Hyde or clearing him. Certainly not anything to convince a jury."

"I think you'll find that Hyde's face will do most of that work for us," Jones said staunchly. "You may have your theories, Mr Holmes, and I know better than to discount them entirely, but until we have solid, evidence that clears him and convicts another, then Mr Edward Hyde will be standing trial for the murder of Eugenie Babington. This is the real world and not one of Dr Watson's stories. I have people to answer to!"

"A jury *will* convict him, Holmes," I said. "One look at him and you know they will."

"Which is a pretty fair condemnation itself," Holmes said, "of the English justice system, but your point, Doctor, is well taken. The problem is, I don't believe he did it. If we convict him, it not only sends an innocent man to the gallows, but allows the real murderer to remain free... to kill again."

No one had much to say to that.

"That's as much as I can tell from the crime scene," Holmes said softly to Inspector Jones. "We can, I think, finally allow Miss Babington the limited grace that the coroner's office can offer her."

"A tragedy," I said.

Jones had turned to the other inspectors and constables to give orders to have the body moved, but young Stanley Hopkins was still standing, frozen, looking down at the body.

"That's as monstrous as the murder itself," Hopkins breathed. "Bad enough to commit something like this in cold blood, but to do something like this and... and... to have fun with it?"

"There are monsters loose in London," Holmes said to him coldly. "Don't let anyone tell you otherwise."

Chapter 04

WHITECHAPEL

Holmes sent two telegrams on our way back to Baker Street and by the time we arrived, it was to find Kitty Winter waiting for us.

"Surely you can't have received my telegram already," Holmes said.

"No, I never did," Miss Winter replied. "I come when I read about Hyde in the paper, and your involvement."

"The newspapers move quickly," Holmes said, somewhat sardonically, "or have taken much for granted, since I've only known myself that I was on the case for only a few hours."

"A brilliant deduction?" I asked, and Holmes snorted in derision.

Miss Winter was the head of Holmes's Midnight Watch, a covert and mostly nocturnal organization for keeping watch on any emerging vampire activity in the hospitals, morgues and graveyards. The number of outbreaks in this year were gratefully small, but it was critical to keep both the infection of vampirism and any stories from spreading in order to protect the small number of vampires that fought for England's defence, such as Miss Winter's own person, the Count and Mina Dracula, as well as myself. Because of her night-time activities, and the natural instinct to sleep during the day, Holmes was normally reluctant to contact her while the sun was up. The fact that the telegram had missed her because she was already up and out was extraordinary.

When I'd first met Miss Winter, she'd been roughened and shopworn by sin and sorrow as to seem a slender candleflame of a woman very near to guttering out. Neither she nor ourselves had known it at the time, but she'd already been infected with the vampiric blood disease from the thoroughly detestable Baron Adelbert Gruner and her luck had continued a downward plummet to the very gutters, but while her life had seemed on the knife's edge, her spirit had never dimmed. She'd lost everything at the hands of Gruner and then lost her only companions, Shinwell Johnson and then, a short time later, Nigel Somersby. However, in Holmes's employ, she enjoyed a regular stipend, which seemed to matter little to her, but also a purpose, which mattered to her a great deal. Now, she stood in our quarters in respectable dress and one of the ridiculously tiny hats that she favoured, her mouth tight and her eyes aflame with impatience.

"See here, Mr Holmes!" she said hotly as soon as we'd crossed the threshold into our own rooms. "The newspapers have it all wrong. Edward Hyde would not have done the villainous things they have accused him of!"

"Having 'it wrong', as you say, Miss Winter, is the normal state of affairs for a newspaper, at least in my experience. In this case, I am quite inclined to agree with you."

"Ah," Miss Winter said, momentarily taken aback. She'd been, it seemed, prepared for every argument under the sun, but somewhat unprepared for actual agreement. "Well… good."

"You know Edward Hyde?" I asked, surprised. It seemed that Miss Winter's taste in associates had descended from merely questionable to loathsome, for while I was willing to take Holmes's word that Hyde had not performed the murder in question, I still found him deeply unsavoury.

"I do," she said fiercely, looking almost relieved that at least someone here at Baker Street was willing to argue about Edward Hyde, even if Holmes was not. In truth, with her blazing cobalt gaze, I'd always found her more than a little unsettling, but there could be no doubt that she had always been a staunch companion no matter the danger.

"He's as ugly as sin," she went on, "and he can eat and carouse like a grizzly bear in heat, I'll grant you. I understand he fights like one, too, only I never seen that. But he's got a streak of generosity and gentleness in him, too. He bought me dinner once when I was low, after Baron Gruner cast me out into the streets."

"Of course," Holmes agreed.

"Times was hard then," she said, "and he bought me dinner and a cup and never asked for more than conversation for his trouble, not like some other gentlemen that go to Whitechapel." She let her cobalt-blue gaze drop and I half-expected her to blush, so abashed was her expression. Clearly this statement brought some unpleasant memory to the forefront, and it pained her.

"Very well," I said. "If he has your seal of approval, I shall modify my consideration of him." I made the statement as heartfelt as I could, but likely there was some reservation entrenched in my heart and she gave me a shrewd look that told me she knew it, but it was the best I could muster.

"It is just as well that you are here," Holmes said to her, "though it means I have wasted the cost of a telegram to you. If I had half the foresight that Watson credits me with in his stories, I should likely have saved the expense. It is necessary that we should mount a watch in Whitechapel during the night-time hours and your skills and senses are much required."

"Do you mean to involve the Midnight Watch, too?" she asked.

"No," Holmes said. "They would be, I fear, somewhat out of their depth."

"Scotland Yard will be increasing their night patrols, as well," I pointed out.

"It is a reasonable precaution," Holmes said, "and there is little we can do to talk them out of it, yet I fear it may do little good if our culprit can move about unseen and provide a great hindrance to our own patrol, but there is no help for it."

"You're not expecting me to play the damsel in distress to the knife, are you?" Miss Winter said. "I'm not signing up for that duty!"

"Nor would I ask," Holmes said, "not when we know so little about our enemy's capabilities."

"Are we going to try to cover all of Whitechapel with just the three of us then?"

"I am hoping for assistance from another quarter," Holmes said. "For the meantime, I would urge you and the doctor to obey your biological instincts and get some rest during the day and meet at dusk at The Hanover public house. We shall have a long night ahead of us."

"What of Hyde?" she said.

"If he tells us the truth," Holmes said, "and it is my belief that he does, then the murderer is still at large. It is possible that we might catch him before they strike again, but with the leads that we currently have, I very much doubt it. If this really is the Ripper returned, or someone like him, then he will strike again. I am also concerned that this was done in order to specifically incriminate Hyde, although they've made a poor choice of weapon in this regard. In any case, I dislike the presupposition that Hyde's proximity to the crime is happenstance, and shall be making some more inquiries into our very unusual client in order to confirm or correct his claims. If the murder was done specifically to incriminate Hyde, then there may be no further danger to the citizenry and need to patrol, but if the murders are linked to the Ripper and his previous activities, then he may continue and we must do all we can to prevent that. The best thing Hyde can do for his case is remain in custody, as unpleasant as that certainly must be for him."

"Very well," Miss Winter said, nodding stiffly. "Just don't forget him." With that admonishment, she left.

"Holmes," I said, "what if Hyde performs his transformation while in that prison cell?"

"A distinct danger," Holmes admitted with a helpless little wave of his hand. "I can hardly begin to imagine all the questions that would occur if they find Dr Jekyll there in the morning. Disastrous is the word that comes to mind and yet I hardly think it does the situation justice. However, since we are powerless to prevent it, I can fathom no course of action except to find the true murderer and so clear and free Hyde as quickly as possible."

I nodded. "Let me make a deduction of my own. The other telegram you sent was to Carfax Abbey."

"Quite right, Doctor," Holmes said with a thin smile, "we shall make a detective of you yet." The smile didn't reach his grey eyes, however, which looked deeply troubled.

For myself, I felt a cold chill infuse my bones. Carfax Abbey meant Dracula, a man that I was glad to have at our side, but one who was deeply unsettling to me all the same. It seemed that all the components of this case, even our allies, were destined to be unsettling.

It was going to be a very long, troubling night indeed.

The street in question was a wide, unclean thoroughfare with large buildings all packed close together on both sides so that the tops of the buildings seemed, even to my eyes, to disappear into a hazy, ill-lit gloom. Many of the windows were boarded up, or simply vacant, black holes looking out onto the street. The fog seemed to have a moist, unclean scent to it as it moved in silent, swirling eddies around us. Voices and music leaked out of the public house along with a yellow light spill, but the rest of the lane around us lay quiet and dismal, even if we could hear the distant sounds of horses some few blocks over. The street was by no means empty, but neither was it well-populated at this hour, with a few people that moved on the outskirts, furtive shadows hurrying about their business.

Holmes and I had dressed down for the occasion, eschewing either top hat or bowler for rough caps and even rougher coats, so as to not stand out and to make it a little more difficult for any enemy party to notice us as out of place. Holmes had considered a full disguise for each of us, but instead adopted this half-measure as we did not want any kind of makeup, costume accoutrements or the like to interfere with our movement, in case we should have to give chase in a hurry.

We met Miss Winter in The Hanover public house, where she had, in the very short time since she'd arrived, acquired any number of men, rough-looking characters in sorry clothes, that had wished to make a closer acquaintance with her. This was not surprising considering her striking looks, with fiery red hair, intense cobalt gaze, and pale, wan complexion. Despite my knowledge of her diet, which, like my own, consisted entirely of animal blood, I had never been able to shake the impression that she had the makings of a fine predator of men and women, should she ever stray from the course that Holmes had laid out for her. Better for the men surrounding Miss Winter that they not get too close and not learn what she and I knew of the world.

Despite this, the men were none too pleased with Holmes and I when she joined us and we led her back out into the street.

Miss Winter had not entirely taken up our own strategy in terms of dress and was in an emerald frock, lavender shawl and miniature black bowler decked out in pink feathers, though this last was somewhat worse for wear. But at least her boots looked sensible and I had enough respect for her speed and ferocity, which I had seen last year, to know that none of these would slow her down if the time came for action. There would be little point having that ferocity turned on me should I dare to comment on her dress or footwear in any case. Holmes had a map and small pocket lantern out. He handed me the lantern and started quietly pointing out some of the key streets that we would want to cover during our vigil.

Dracula's appearance, when it came, was as dramatic and sudden as we should have expected. Two shadows between a rain barrel and drainpipe detached themsevles and loomed up suddenly in our wake.

"Christ on a crucifix!" Miss Winter spat. "You'll give me a heart attack jumping out like that!"

"Christ has little to do with it," Mina purred, wearing a Mona Lisa smile and looking not at all chastised. (Though I have occasionally referred to her as Mina Dracula, when clarity in this account demanded that I do so, she has always corrected us in person whenever we have used either Mina Dracula or the Countess. She has also made it clear that the surnames of Murray, which she once held, no longer apply to her and the name 'Dracula', at least on its own, already has one formidable person attached to it. As such, Mina has often urged us to use 'simply Mina', so I shall.)

Dracula himself said nothing. I'd noticed before Mina's wry and somewhat off-kilter sense of humour, a stark contrast to her dour husband, if 'husband' was even the right word. I somehow doubted that any member of the clergy had said any words over them in order to consummate a marriage in the eyes of the law, but they had certainly proved their devotion to each other. The Count had been ready to raze London to the ground in order to recover Mina and punish the ones responsible when she had been taken, and she had seemed every bit as committed to him.

Count Dracula looked as formidable as I remembered him. Tall, gaunt, severe, with bushy black hair and moustache over a grim slash of a mouth. He wore a sombre black suit with a dark grey overcoat and no hat. While I had several times seen Mina in dress far less sombre than her husband, tonight she was decked out in men's breeches and shirt with a black overcoat, perhaps in deference to the clandestine nature of our mission tonight.

"I would not have come," Dracula said curtly, "for the matter seems to me a trivial one, but Mina follows the newspapers and convinced me that the matter was urgent."

"Meaning the women of Whitechapel aren't worth protecting, you mean?" Miss Winter said, her anger flaring out despite her clear awe of the two figures before her.

"The murder of a single individual," Dracula said, and made the smallest possible shrug, his face entirely impassive. "London murders a dozen people every night, or more. Women, men. I see little to make this one special."

"And yet you came," I said.

"My love," he put a hand on Mina's shoulder, "has a passion for romance, for the dramatic things in life."

Mina's smile flashed again. "It is well for you that I do." She laid her hand over the one he had on her shoulder. "At least you have avoided anything too overly dramatic in your life to compensate for my feminine excess."

Count Dracula's eyebrows may have raised themselves a fraction of an inch, or possibly not, I was not sure. His overcoat flapped slightly in the wind around his tall, gaunt frame.

"There are many unusual features to this case," Holmes said. "Most suggest we may be dealing with someone of extraordinary abilities, though if that person is a vampire or not, I cannot yet say. We must keep a keen watch." He very quickly sketched out Jekyll and Hyde's story and testimony.

"If the attacker is a vampire," Mina said slowly, "you may have chosen your help poorly. It is a peculiarity of the vampiric blood disease that it is often difficult for us to detect the scent of other vampires."

"That thought *had* occurred to me, Mina," Holmes said, "which is precisely why I explained the unknown nature of our murderer. Your sense of smell may not avail you tonight."

"At least," I said, "the problem would run in both directions. Another vampire would have great difficulty in scenting us, too."

"Precisely," Holmes said. "Our other difficulty is that this villain has a way of moving unseen."

"Unseen?" Dracula said. "How?"

"We do not know," Holmes said heavily. I could hear how it pained him to admit that.

Dracula frowned, but said nothing more.

"You shall have to lean heavily on your ears," Holmes went on. "The murderer has been detected audibly before this, after all, if we are to believe Mr Hyde's account."

"Very well," Dracula said. The two ladies and I nodded.

It was Dracula's idea that he and Mina take to the rooftops while Holmes, Miss Winter and I kept to the streets. Once agreed, Mina entered a deserted alley and climbed easily enough up a drainage pipe, making full use of the lighter weight and stronger grip that the vampire disease granted her. It took her less than three minutes to ascend five storeys and disappear out of sight onto the roof. I wondered if I myself could do much the same. Possibly. Since the disease, and the effects, had progressed slightly less than hers – she had been infected for over a decade, while it had only been a year for me – I suspected my performance would be much slower.

Watching Dracula climb was another matter entirely, reminding me that the Count had been a vampire for well over 400 years. He did not climb so much as scuttle up. He barely seemed to need handholds and ascended the wall in less than a dozen seconds like a large, ominous, cloaked spider. Then they were gone and we were left staring up a dingy, rundown tenement wall. Yellow fog lay heavily in the alley like a malaise.

London was in rare form that night, and I can seldom remember a more dismal and nerve-wracking vigil. Holmes and I each had our revolvers in our pockets, but we kept them there so that we did not alarm the few pedestrians we saw. Twice in the first hour, we saw a constable, but they looked every bit as on edge as we felt.

Holmes stepped through a stone archway, cast his gaze about in a small courtyard there, and then re-joined Miss Winter and me.

Miss Winter hugged her arms about herself, although I knew that she felt the cold no more than I.

"I feel like we're being watched," she said.

"It is a distinct possibility," Holmes said.

Miss Winter looked around, her gaze flickering from the rooftops to several dark windows on the second floor of the building to our left. "You really think that the Knife can move about unseen?" Holmes had given her a brief sketch of Edward Hyde's story, but she, like myself, was having a difficult time believing it.

"It is an incredible supposition," Holmes said, "but that is the story that Hyde holds to, and it is no more incredible than things we have seen with our own eyes."

"A poor choice of words, Holmes," I said.

He exhaled briefly in a sort of abbreviated laugh, one that had no merriment in it whatsoever. "It is at that. Nonetheless, it gives us no disadvantage to consider it as a possibility."

"I don't know about that," Miss Winter said. "Puts me in a black pit of despair just thinking about how we might be walking around being stared at by someone who I can't stare back at."

"For once, Miss Winter," I said, "we agree."

We moved then through a narrow street with a low stone wall and some tenement gardens on our right with a few rough, ill-tended vegetable gardens and many more lines hung with half-clean laundry and a series of dismal shops, their windows dark. Holmes's tall lean figure, with his rough cloth hat looking strange and out of place on his head, went first, stirring the cold, wet fog into silent eddies with his passing. Miss Winter followed, the pink feathers on her miniature bowler hat somewhat limp for the wet and cold, while I came up the rear, my hand resting in its pocket where I kept my service revolver. While the revolver was currently loaded with silver bullets, I kept ordinary cartridges in my other coat pocket, should they be necessary, since silver bullets were in limited supply and didn't offer the best range or accuracy. These had been custom-made for us with a silver bullet, but a brass cartridge on the outside and a thin wax coating on the tip, which made it possible for me to handle safely. I'd also brought, at Holmes's urging, my walking stick tipped with a heavy weight of silver on end, also shielded with a leather covering so that I did not accidentally burn myself. Contrary to Stoker's mythology, vampirism was a blood disease, not an infernal curse, so the traditional methods involving crosses, holy wafers, blessed water, or any other religious paraphernalia, had no effect. Silver, on the other hand, acted like a vitriol on the skin and flesh of the infected, including my own, so it was prudent to exercise caution.

The wind had picked up and the temperature dropped, so that the fog was replaced with tentative flurries of snow. We'd reached the end of the street and Holmes was looking into a small courtyard there while Miss Winter and I were peering down the left- and right-hand alleys when a bloodcurdling scream, part wounded animal, part bellowing charge, rang out through the night. The hollow cry echoed along the empty streets, seeming to rattle a few nearby windows that still had their glass.

Two shapes caught my eye, falling, falling, one after the other, from the top of a nearby tenement housing building about half a block away, black coats flapping in the air.

Dracula! Mina!

"Holmes!" I shouted, and he was out of the courtyard and at my side before the first of the falling figures had impacted on the cobblestones with a sickening crunch. I felt my stomach drop. Who had we just lost?

The second figure landed neatly next to the first and I strained my eyesight to make out who it might be.

But when the figure straightened and spun its frilled black cape around, I saw a man I did not recognize.

He wore a black tricorn hat pulled low, and some kind of cloth tied underneath so that I could not make out his hair colour. His eyes were hidden with silvered glasses and the lower part of his features obscured with another black cloth worn like a veil. He was about my height, perhaps slimmer, but it was impossible to tell anything else. In addition to the swirling cape, the tricorn hat had an enormous scarlet feather in it. He raised a long, narrow-bladed sword that caught the light and shimmered as he saluted us, even in the half-light. He bowed his head, then blew us a kiss, a gesture at odds with the face covering.

So astonishing was this sudden development that we all stood stunned momentarily.

It was Holmes that broke the spell, levelling his revolver and calling out, "Halt!"

The figure drew a long dagger with his left hand, flipped it neatly so that he now held it by the blade, and raised his arm to throw.

Holmes fired and the figure jerked slightly. The dagger clattered to the snowy cobblestones. Holmes had surely hit him somewhere in the upper chest region, but the man shrugged and laughed. Then, moving easily, he knelt and snatched up his fallen weapon, then touched it to the brim of his hat in a salute, as if acknowledging a touch in a bloodless and mild fencing match. There was no sign of blood or injury on his person. The rogue swept off his ostentatious hat, bowed deeply with a flourish of hat and feather, then twisted the motion into a slight sidestep in order to avoid Holmes's second shot. The man was inhumanly fast. Miss Winter and I dashed towards him, but the man spun and sped off, rapidly away from us.

Miss Winter and I reached the crumpled body still on the cobblestones.

Holmes came the barest instant after, then pointed his pistol at another figure dropping from the roof. Holmes lowered the gun. It was Mina. She caught herself on a third-storey railing, then sprung the rest of the way down to the street. She looked anxious and wild, her fangs fully protruded, her eyes ablaze with anger.

The body was Count Dracula.

"Vlad!" Mina cried, rushing to our side.

The Count's body lay face down so that I could see the long, horrible, diagonal slash in his clothing that ran across from the upper left shoulder all the way down to the right lower back; blood, black in the foggy moonlight, welled from the wound so that his back and clothes were all sticky with it. But when I hurriedly tore the cloth to get a better look at the wound, I could see that it was easily a mortal wound, long and cutting deep to the bone. Two of the vertebrae were exposed between his shoulder blades, like white, pale, vulnerable snails out of their shell.

And the wound was moving, *crawling* and writhing, the skin of his back a bubbling mass like a cauldron.

"Holmes!" I hissed. "He's been wounded with silver!" Which explained the gleam on the sword.

The Count, unmoving and lifeless – except for the horrid, bubbling movement of the wound itself – suddenly coughed and moaned Mina's name.

"I'm here, Vlad!" she said, taking his hand in her own. He was face down in the filth of the street, and made a motion as if to get up, but I held him down. The silver was still reacting, bubbling, burrowing, burning its way down into the flesh of his back, giving off black smoke foul as burning oil. We had never seen a vampire survive a wound caused by silver, which was why we used it ourselves when fighting vampires. I could not imagine the pain the Count must be in, would likely continue to be in for the last few remaining minutes of his life, which would play out in very short order on this dirty street in Whitechapel.

I had not brought anything like a doctor's bag, and so had no liniment or real antiseptics, but I had thought to tuck a few bandages and a small flask of brandy in my pocket. The brandy had been for drinking, but any hope Dracula had lay in cleaning the wound out, treating it like a vitriol injury, for all intents and purposes, and not having anything better at hand, I unscrewed the bottle.

"Hold him," I said.

Holmes moved to do so, but both Kitty, because of her diffidence, and Mina, on account of her grief, hesitated.

"Hold him!" I barked again, and they did so.

The Count's howl, when I poured the brandy into the injury, would have made the blood run cold in the hardiest person I know in the best of times, so filled with outrage and pain was it. Likely mine, too, only I was too busy. I had half-hoped that the flash of pain, unavoidable as it was, might at least have sent the Count down into unconsciousness, for his own sake, but such was not the case. I cleaned the wound as best I could with the brandy and cloth I had on hand, careful to avoid getting any trace of silver residue on my own skin. Had it been a wound with silver lodged into it, I am not sure there would have been anything that I could have done, but as it was, I was able to wipe the wound clean and stop the volatile reaction that silver causes to vampiric flesh, blood and bone. The wound smouldered now, but did not burn and smoke as badly as it had.

"How did this happen?" Holmes said to Mina.

She shook her head. "We never even saw him coming."

"He was visible enough when he jumped into the street," Holmes said.

"Yes," Mina said. "I got a look at his back after the attack, but he came to strike and escaped almost before we knew he was even there. I do not say that he was unseeable, as your Mr Hyde did, only that he came from behind, very fast. By the time we heard anything, it was too late, with the results as you see."

"You shot him, Mr Holmes," Miss Winter said. "I saw it. Shot him with a silver bullet and he just laughed at us. What kind of vampire can *do* that?" My mind was whirling, asking the same question, but we didn't have time for that now. Dracula needed better medical attention than I could give here.

"We need to get Dracula back to Baker Street," I said. There, I could stitch the wound properly and, even more importantly, allow Dracula to dine and replenish his store of blood. A vampire can sustain terrific amounts of damage, so long as the vital brain, spine and heart remain intact; we are still human, and can die if these things are injured the same as any person. However, given an ample supply of blood, we can also heal ourselves far more completely than an uninfected person, but it is not a quick process. I hoped if I cleaned out the wound more thoroughly and gave the Count time to recover, his natural healing would take care of the rest.

"Can you and Mina get Dracula back to Baker Street yourselves?" Holmes asked me. "I am more loath than ever to leave Whitechapel unguarded."

"I need no assistance," Dracula stated authoritatively, then staggered as Mina and I tried to help him up, a clear demonstration how wrong he was.

"We shall have to," I said. The idea of Holmes and Miss Winter out there by themselves with such a remarkable madman on the loose made my skin run cold, but I could see from

Holmes's expression that there was no convincing him to retreat. Miss Winter's expression mirrored my own concerns, but she said nothing. The flurries of snow started coming down in heavier and heavier clumps, and the dark, empty street moaned with the passage of the wind.

With Dracula's arm over my shoulder and Mina supporting his other side, we led Dracula in a shuffling, swaying step back towards the main thoroughfare in hopes of getting a hansom to take us back to Baker Street. Despite being a vampire myself, so much of vampire biology was a mystery to me and the fatal reaction to silver was nothing I'd ever had an opportunity to experiment with, or attempt to heal. As such, I could not guess as to Dracula's fate or if he might survive this night.

I looked back, feeling my heart drop as I saw the two lonely figures in the falling snow, Holmes saying something earnestly to Miss Winter, who nodded her head, then shook it and interjected with something I couldn't hear. Holmes nodded again and they both looked up at the rooftops, but the snow was coming down more strongly now and nothing could be seen up there but a bleak darkness. Our unknown adversary had already struck once, devastating our forces, and now I was compelled to leave Holmes and Miss Winter to fend for themselves for the rest of the night.

It was our first night of patrolling Whitechapel and already it had resulted in disaster. I just hoped all of us survived into the second night.

It was a dark and troubled ride back to Baker Street. I had to offer the cabbie a sovereign to even allow the sorry, troubled and bloody lot of us into the back. We rode with the Count prostrate on a four-wheeler's seat cushion while Mina and I crouched between the seats in order to keep our patient from rolling off his perch while the carriage rocked and bucked through the street. Dracula moaned in pain with each bump of the wheels. An awful stench came off the wound and in the brief moments when our carriage had to stop, we could hear a horrid sizzling, like a cooking steak, coming from the wound as the silver continued to burn.

Mrs Hudson, that worthy soul, opened the door at our knock and ran to get hot water and my doctor's bag as Mina and I half-carried the tall, angular form of the Count. His face was drenched with sweat, pale and with the skin so tight that he might already be a cadaver. It seemed his true and final death had come for him at last and you could see from his face, and from Mina's, that they both knew it.

We got Dracula onto the settee and I again cleaned the wound, rinsing it with cool water to remove any last traces of the silver. Dracula finally passed out from the pain, which was undoubtably a blessing, but it presented a new, unforeseen problem to my medical skills. Vampires still breathe, but our need for air is far less, and the motion of our lungs is a more voluntary process than with the unafflicted. A similar problem comes with examining the circulatory system, as the blood can run thin and sluggish through our veins. As such, detecting a pulse on a vampire patient is usually an impossible task. Such is the nature of our disease that it is all too easy for us to appear dead through the following funeral and burial, as has been documented so sensationally by Stoker's salacious book. We are not dead, or 'undead' as Stoker misleadingly labelled us. And yet, it was an easy mistake to understand, so close was the similarity.

"Is he...?" Mina said, her voice choking. She had put on a brave face during the ride, but that façade was cracking.

"I don't know," I said, which wasn't any kind of answer. Because I didn't have one.

In short, vampire though I was, and despite being a doctor for many years with experience treating extreme wounds both in the Afghan war and with Holmes, there was still much I did not know about vampire anatomy. Right now, I could not detect any pulse or breathing in Count Dracula, but the breath and pulse of a vampire is nearly undetectable under the best of conditions. If Dracula had died or merely lost consciousness, I could not begin to guess. I felt helpless in the extreme, unable to know if my patient even still lived or not. I finished cleansing, packing and rebandaging the wound with all haste, trying not to ponder the possibility that I might be treating a corpse.

"There," I said. "The bandage is done. Help me get him on his side so we can get some blood into him without putting any pressure on the wound."

I spent the next hour trying to get any sign of life out of the Count, slowly spooning teaspoons of blood into his listless mouth without any sign of response.

"We have lost him," I admitted finally, thought it was painful to say the words out loud.

"No," Mina said, but if it was reason, some arcane knowledge, or merely hope that drove out that flat rebuttal, I do not know. She took over while Mrs Hudson brought up another steaming pot filled with our secret contents from the butcher's shop. Life-giving blood.

I had taken my own cup of sustenance and then a glass of brandy to calm my frayed nerves and despairing heart. My thoughts went out to Holmes and Miss Winter, on their own in the Whitechapel streets with a murderer so cunning and savage that he had slain one of the most formidable men I'd ever encountered in one stroke. I may have lost consciousness myself, slumbering in my chair, when a slight cough brought me awake.

"He lives," Mina breathed. "My love lives!"

I felt a weight lift off my chest. I found Count Dracula deeply unsettling, but Holmes felt him to be a powerful force for good, despite the Count's grim demeanour and reputation, and I had faith in Holmes's judgement.

Barely had I had time to absorb the relief I felt when I heard the door slam downstairs and then footsteps on the stairs.

My feet carried me to the door and I tore it open, relieved beyond measure when I saw Holmes's face, haggard but alive, looking up at me. Miss Winter trailed behind him, looking somewhat the worse for wear. Whatever had transpired after I had gone, it clearly hadn't been pleasant. Through the hallway windows and the small window at the top of the street door, I could see that morning had come, practically unnoticed.

"What has happened?" I asked with bated breath.

"Count Dracula?" Holmes responded, ignoring my question, his voice tight with tension.

"He lives," I said. "Given time, I believe he will recover, but it is still too close to tell for certain."

Holmes nodded, accepting the grim news with all the equilibrium he could muster, though it was clearly a struggle.

They both followed me back into the sitting room where both Mina and the Count slept. Miss Winter collapsed as quietly as she could into a chair, the very picture of weariness and defeat. Holmes dropped his coat over the back of another chair and started pacing the room.

"Something has happened," I said, keeping my voice low. "What?"

"It is simple," Holmes said. "We have failed. Utterly and completely failed. While we were busy being so easily distracted and nearly disposed of, the Ripper has struck again and I have just come from the scene of the crime. Another woman is dead."

Part Two

A CAMPAIGN OF WAR

Chapter 05

THE SECOND MURDER

After news that the Ripper had struck again, and had done so despite our patrols, I sat heavily in my chair, holding a cup of coffee long after it had gone cold while Holmes continued to pace the room, smoke several cigarettes and drink several cups of coffee.

"It seems a strange outfit for hunting on the rooftops, does it not?" Holmes said after he had thought a moment. "A tricorn hat, in particular, is an out-of-date and somewhat flamboyant choice. But that, and the glasses you describe, also make a fairly effective disguise. Our opposition continues to present itself in a manner both sinister and jocular, an unsettling and distasteful combination."

Dracula, still in a dire condition, was now resting with Mina in my room, since I had the window carefully darkened with heavy drapes and I considered his condition far too poor to risk moving him to Carfax Abbey, even before Holmes's injunction that we must all remain here at Baker Street. Dracula's vitals had improved slightly, but this was still a very dangerous time, wounded as he was and with daylight on us. If he made it to nightfall, there would be good reason to hope.

"You have yet to tell me your part of the story regarding the murder, Holmes," I said. "What was the woman's name? How was the murder done?" I felt estranged, adrift from the case, since I'd been unable to attend the murder scene with Holmes.

"Mrs Luella Brown," he said curtly, still pacing. "But the method was very different, more like an animal attack than the knife injury inflicted on Genie Babington."

"I knew her," Miss Winter said bitterly. "She was a common enough face in Whitechapel. Everyone knew her, really, and liked her."

"She was only out on this night," Holmes said, "in order to purchase medicine for a sick child. She had just a few pennies and a bottle of cough remedy in her pocket. The bottle had the name of the doctor and I was able to see him, a practitioner in Whitechapel known for taking late-night calls. He confirmed that she had been there and used what little money she had to make her purchase." His voice took on a bitter edge. "She had come out on a night when everyone else stayed in for fear of the Ripper, and had been heading home with the medicine in her pocket when the murderer found her and we did nothing to prevent it!"

"The husband?" I said.

"Long dead," Holmes said. "She was known to several of the constables and so we were able to find her brother and deliver the news and the medicine. He has taken the blame upon himself."

"He is quite right to do so!"

"I rather think the murderer bears a greater share of the burden," Holmes said acidly. "Also the people pledged to prevent him. To wit, us." He stopped pacing, standing near the table, and beat his fist softly against the edge of it, a scowl on his face.

"Holmes," I said. "Could this be a coordinated effort? Could the attack on Dracula have been coordinated with the murder so that one facilitated the other?"

Holmes's gaze flicked over to me and then away, then back, as if weighing how much to tell me. Finally, he nodded. "Clearly, yes. We are being outmanoeuvred at every turn, Watson, and I am at a loss on how to counter it. They are organized and well aware of our movements whereas we know next to nothing about them." He stepped over and whisked his coat from the back of the chair and shrugged it on. "To that end, I need to do some research. I beg you and the others to stay indoors at Baker Street. Everyone must stay here. You too, Miss Winter."

"Sleep here?" she said, looking down with some reservation at the couch.

"You may use my room while the sun is up," Holmes said. "I doubt very much that I shall be back before dark."

Miss Winter responded to this outrageous suggestion by pursing her lips and then looking speculatively at the door to Holmes's room. Finally, she shrugged and nodded her agreement.

"Good," Holmes said. "That's settled, then."

"Are we to mount a patrol tonight, Holmes?" I asked.

"By no means," he snapped. "Right now, I have reason to suspect that it would do very little to protect the citizens of Whitechapel and possibly do them some harm."

With that tantalizing but paltry bit of information, Holmes left.

Miss Winter shook her head and then retired to Holmes's room.

Holmes was gone the entire day. The torpor of daylight was making me groggy and dull-witted and I had little to ponder except wild speculation and could make very little of the confusing and violent series of events.

I awoke when Holmes returned just before nightfall. He inquired about Dracula but would answer none of my questions, simply stating that he was still weighing theories. He yawned, but Miss Winter had not yet emerged from his own room, so he dropped on the settee and fell asleep at once. I realized that he had not slept for at least thirty hours or so.

When Miss Winter did emerge a short time later, she immediately sent some telegrams to check on the Midnight Watch and vampire activity in the city, but there was nothing there of note. Mina came down briefly then to retrieve more sustenance, but reported that the Count still remained unconscious and dangerously fragile. (We now had three teapots going, all with their own Hawthornian-scarlet ribbon to mark their contents as inedible to the uninfected dwellers of Baker Street.) We kept our voices low to avoid waking Holmes slumbering on the settee.

Miss Winter and I spent an hour with some desultory reading. When I finally asked, despite Holmes's admonition that we not discuss the case, precisely what she and Holmes had seen at the scene of the second murder, Kitty Winter shook her head.

"Mr Holmes kept me at a distance so I didn't get a good look," she said, keeping her voice low, "and wouldn't tell me nothing. I know it was a messier business than the first one, but that's about all. Thought maybe he didn't trust me."

"I would not take it as any commentary on his opinion of you," I said. "He is ever careful of arranging the facts 'just so' in his brain before detailing them to others."

"So he doesn't trust anybody?" she asked, glancing over at the settee.

I shook my head. It was more like Holmes didn't trust himself, so he was led by an overabundance of caution, lest he lay out a theory before it was entirely ready and thus prove himself wrong. He did not want to needlessly tarnish the opinions those around him had of his methods, not even those of myself and the police. Also, it added to his fondness for a dramatic touch, which I knew was a failing of his, but I couldn't say any of this to Miss Winter.

"He trusts you as much as anybody," was all I could muster.

"Hmm," Miss Winter said. She turned the page of her book, but I felt sure that she wasn't absorbing the material there any more than I was with the book that had lain ignored in my own hand for quite some time. To this day, I have no recollection what book either of us had tried to read that night. Later, we played an uninspired game of two-handed whist, but neither of us paid any real attention to the cards and eventually we gave it up for a bad job.

The inactivity was abominable. All I could think of was the horror stalking the residents of Whitechapel and how we were doing nothing. Two innocent women had already lost their lives in as many nights and standing by doing nothing while some sinister person stalked a third was almost past endurance. I had little doubt that Holmes was correct, but the necessity chafed at my pride and sense of justice. This was a stratagem I little understood, but I held my tongue. Holmes had proved time and time again that everything he did had a reason, even if he often kept those reasons to himself.

When daybreak came, it was with great relief that I read the morning papers and found that no third murder had been committed last night. Holmes, awakened by the arrival of the papers and several telegrams from Scotland Yard, devoured their contents.

"Well," he said on their completion, "that is something of a relief, Watson. The Yarders are eager for information from us and have several promising leads, but little definitive or unusual to report. Part of my activities yesterday included urging them to take a deeper look into the background of the victims and this has kept them rather busy." He caught my eye and flashed me the briefest of smiles when Miss Winter wasn't looking. I took his meaning at once. Undoubtedly, he had checked in on Edward Hyde while he was there. It seemed that Mr Edward Hyde and not Dr Henry Jekyll was still loitering patiently. I tried to imagine the furious uproar that would come from locking one man up in the evening and finding another very different man there in the morning. Such an unexplainable event eclipsed any real investigation into the Whitechapel Murders, so sensational would it be, and could well understand Holmes's anxiety regarding the matter.

Holmes again requested that Miss Winter use his rooms during the day rather than return to her own home so that she might remain on hand. Miss Winter, for her part, acted as if there were nothing unusual or improper about this suggestion and disappeared into Holmes's rooms again at the break of day, making me feel as if I alone played the part of the over-formal prude.

Our sitting room has always had something of a Bohemian air, with cigars in the coal scuttle, Holmes's tobacco in the Persian slipper, and unanswered correspondence transfixed by a jack-knife into the mantelpiece. This situation was none too improved by the number of pillows and extra blankets Mrs Hudson had pulled out of storage, which lay scattered over the settee and chairs. I was now in the process of arranging some of these to their best advantage so that I might sleep out the better part of the day. We'd likely be entertaining a theatre troupe or circus next, complete with jungle animals. With the unusual circumstances, the torpor of daylight was weighing heavily on me.

"I wonder," Holmes said quietly, once Miss Winter had retired to the other room, "if we might do something about Hyde's situation." It occurred to me that if Miss Winter's hearing was anything akin to my own, even low voices might be heard through a closed door, but Holmes was surely aware of that. Perhaps he was relying on the stupor that came with daylight, a weariness I felt even now, but if I could fight off the effects in order to quench my avid curiosity, so could Miss Winter. I shrugged inwardly. Holmes surely had his reasons.

"So Jekyll has not made an appearance," I said. "How long can that continue?"

"We have no way of knowing," Holmes said. "Have the current circumstances convinced you that Hyde couldn't possibly be the murderer?"

I pondered. "Since the Ripper's second murder was committed with Hyde in custody," I said, "he must be innocent. That much is inarguable."

"You discount my theory that we are dealing with multiple murderers?" Holmes said.

"I do not discount it," I said, thinking hard. "But I had assumed some sort of cooperation between them. Two independent murderers working with the same methods, in the same territory, on the same subset of victims, during the same period of time seems rather unbelievable."

"You have a remarkable clarity sometimes, Watson," Holmes said. "We have not, perhaps, proved every portion of your statement, but let us take that as a working hypothesis. As you recall, the second murder was a far messier affair than the first."

"You said as much before," I said. I found a better pillow for the settee and sat down. I was eager for Holmes to lay out his discoveries at the second crime scene, but I was also desperately needing sleep.

Holmes had taken advantage of the room's disarray to move

one of the side tables closer to his chair, with a blanket for padding, and now lay sprawled sideways in the chair with his long legs on the table and the briar pipe going. This was somewhat problematic, though, because of his supine position and very likely one of the burning embers falling out of his pipe would catch fire any moment and end all concerns about Whitechapel and vampires, at least for us.

"Perhaps the murderer, knowing we were on patrol, was rushed this time around?" I ventured.

"Just so," he murmured. "What of the fact that an eyewitness who got a glimpse of the murderer this time, although from far away, describes him as very tall and burly?"

"Holmes!" I said, shocked fully awake by this startling revelation. "Someone has seen him? We are finally making some progress, then?"

"Some progress, perhaps," Holmes said, "though I suspect the nature of that progress seems very different to me than it does to you. But what about Hyde's innocence?"

"Edward Hyde is burly," I said, "but no one would describe him as tall, even from a distance. In addition, he was in custody, so he must be innocent."

"So I read it," Holmes said. He sat up and sucked on his pipe again. "I do believe in Hyde's innocence and would very much prefer to have his assistance here than have him rotting in a Scotland Yard cell. But if we see Hyde as a valuable weapon against the Jack the Ripper, it is well to be sure of your tools. His story of the murder matched every detail I observed perfectly, but what of his unusual past? It will comfort you to know that

I have not taken this as gospel, but have spent a great deal of yesterday confirming the details. I have assured myself that his account is essentially a factual one. There was some trouble during their holiday in France with Hyde and an opera singer and while Hyde's behaviour was not gentlemanly there, I can detect no crime of consequence and none of the performers or patrons are much worse for the wear, despite the Parisian newspaper articles to the contrary. As to the assault on Miss Harcourt, a young woman Hyde ran over, and the unfortunate death of Sir Danvers Carew, I find Hyde blameless, though I doubt any jury presented with the facts would do the same. Circumstantial evidence, Watson, is a fickle thing."

"What of the second murder, Holmes?" I said. "You have not yet discussed the details of your discoveries there."

"It was a very different scene, Watson, yet Lestrade and Gregson, both there, insisted on theorizing that it was still the work of the same man. They cannot fathom two such brutal killers in our city."

"It is a sobering thought," I admitted.

"Indeed," Holmes said. "However, one cannot fault their dogged determination. They only want for a person to point them in the right direction. In this case, they have done a capital job of chasing down the details on the victim, which I note the newspapers have already done their best to slander, implying that this woman was of poor character."

"She was not?"

"She was poor," Holmes said, "but that is as close as the newspapers have come to accuracy. Journalism is a failing art,

Watson, if ever there was one. Mrs Luella Brown was a merchant's wife fallen on hard times, but has, in the past, both championed and donated charity money to the poor. She was very nearly a woman of the cloth, but was rescued from that drudgery through marriage to the merchant I alluded to, a purveyor of textiles that, as far as I can tell, did nothing immoral in all his life, unless you count dying at sea. As to the murder, there are some similarities. It happened half an hour after the attack on Count Dracula, or very nearly. But, as I said, this was not done with a small, sharp knife like the first murder, or with a sword, as in the attack on Dracula. This was done by an animal, a very large one, either a huge dog or a wolf. You remember, I should guess, the Baskerville affair?"

"I shall never forget it," I said with a shudder.

"You surprise me, Watson," Holmes said. "I should think with vampires and sea monsters under our cap you might long for something as simple as a flesh-and-blood hound painted with phosphorous."

I shuddered again, although what he said made logical sense. In point of fact, Stapleton and that glowing hound would be far less of a danger to me now, changed as I was. But that wasn't how I felt at all and I shrugged at both the strangeness of life and the intricacies of the human mind. "It was harrowing enough at the time."

"A fair point," Holmes said. "At any rate, the wounds inflicted on poor Mrs Luella Brown indicate a dog or wolf of similar size, if not larger. And yet, despite the savagery of the attack, there is still evidence that they have taken a trophy again. I tell you plainly that attempting to assess that with the remains spread out over a distance of a dozen feet is the fuel of nightmares. I would have liked your opinion on the matter, but circumstances being what they are, we shall have to proceed without your professional corroboration. That being said, I believe the gallbladder is missing. A rather small organ compared to the liver, the removal of which is strangely precise compared to the ferocity and swiftness of the attack. With my supposition that something not human was involved, we have to admit the possibility of an organ being consumed, but again, the gallbladder seems a poor choice for that compared to some of the more sought-after delicacies, from the animal point of view, does it not?"

"I can make nothing of it," I admitted. I unbuttoned my waistcoat and deposited it on the back of a chair.

"Nor can I," Holmes said. "But I find the location in which the attack took place very interesting. Still in Whitechapel, but some streets distant from the area where the attack on Dracula and our sighting of the man with the silver sword occurred. This is suggestive."

"Suggestive?" Mina asked from the doorway.

I stood up, feeling a bit out of place in the presence of the fairer sex without my waistcoat and in my socks. Mina paid no attention to the sorry condition of either the room or its inhabitants, but merely came into the room and claimed another red-ribboned teapot. "He lives," she said in answer to the question in my eyes. "He has not woken since we brought him here, but I have managed to get a little nourishment into him, one spoonful at a time."

"That is encouraging," I said.

"Yes," Mina said. "You were talking of the recent murder, Mr Holmes. Suggestive of what?"

"Suggestive of coordinated movement," Holmes answered. He had his hands pressed together against his face, which was a mask of concentration. "Not just cooperation, but bold, coordinated movement. One of them attacking us as a diversion in order to make certain that another could kill without interference."

"Kill with a trained dog or wolf?" I said. "It seems a uniquely awkward and unwieldy way of killing someone in a crowded city where anyone might see you. This is hardly the isolation of the moors. Where would someone keep such a hound without detection? How would they move them unseen? Why would they choose such a way of committing murder?"

"Why indeed?" Holmes said. "Do you remember when we first discovered the nature of vampirism and I said that we now had to reconsider all our ideas of what is possible with this new lens?"

"Of course," I said.

"And now," Holmes said, "we have Dr Jekyll and Mr Hyde, don't you see?"

"But you do not think Hyde is involved?"

"I do not think Hyde committed either murder," Holmes said.

"Then I fail to see the connection," I said.

"Perhaps not," Holmes replied. "At any rate, I note that it is sufficiently overcast and, of course, you have your hat and coat to protect you from the sun. Do you think you can manage to effect Hyde's release from incarceration and convey him back to Baker Street? We could use his assistance here."

"His assistance?"

"Indeed," Holmes said. "We have at least one opponent who moves about on the rooftops with ease, and our allies who can do so, or at least one of them, has been methodically and neatly – surgically, if you will – taken out of the equation. We have certainly pressed our luck having him linger in a jail cell this long without incident. I will tell you without exaggeration that I have greatly dreaded a telegram from Scotland Yard!"

I sighed. The greatest consulting detective in the world had apparently missed the fact that I'd just spent the last twenty minutes trying to arrange a place to sleep.

"You think that the police will agree to Hyde's release?"

"I am hopeful," Holmes said, "for the very same reasons that we have just outlined, flawed though they be."

"Very well," I said. "What shall you be doing?"

"Smoking," Holmes said. "Our murderer is at least a three-pipe problem and I have more than one problem concerning this case to consider."

The two constables at the door let me through without hesitation, one even opening the door for me. Their faces were tight with tension. The Whitechapel Murders, continuously unsolved as they were, put a blight on the entire force and I could tell they were feeling it.

Gregson met me partway down the stone-flagged passage and

ushered me into his office, passing through a common room with maps of London and the network of roads and turnpikes that surrounded them hung on the walls. Recent newspapers from all over the country were piled on racks or were stacked on the tables, shelves of bound newspaper clippings an echo to Holmes's own filing volumes of reference material, all of it painstakingly collected. Gregson's office was a small room, crowded by a table holding a huge ledger and boasting a telephone on the wall. Lestrade, waiting in the common room, followed us in.

"It pains me to release that scoundrel," Gregson said when I had explained my purpose, "but it is very clear that Hyde cannot have done these terrible deeds. I suppose we have no choice."

Gregson ran his hand through his thinning blond hair and looked down at the smaller Lestrade, who shrugged. The smaller detective still had his hat on and flicked the brim of it while he pondered. Both men looked exhausted. I knew that they had been working around the clock on the Whitechapel case, but hadn't known on what, precisely, until Lestrade pushed a bundle of papers across the desk at me.

"Some of the documents that Mr Holmes asked for," Lestrade said. "He has suggested that we have concentrated too much effort on the Ripper himself and not done enough background on the victims. This is everything we have, painstakingly copied from the official records and some of it added very recently. Luella Brown, Eugenie Babington." Lestrade's nose twitched in agitation and anxiety, his dark eyes were hollowed pools. I could well imagine the sleeplessness that the entire force had had to endure for the past few days. "We have compiled information here on their lives, acquaintances, family, everything we could find, as per Holmes's request." He pushed an even thicker folder. "This is the same for the original list of victims: Emma Elizabeth Smith, Martha Tabram, Mary Ann Nichols and all the rest, though I share Holmes's opinion that the first two of these are not truly connected. Some of this information is from the old files from fifteen years ago, and some we have added, as I said, very recently. Young Stanley Hopkins has done the lion's share, but we have all put in many extra hours and contributed to the file."

A man knocked on the door, which Lestrade had left ajar.

"Come," Gregson said. Stanley Hopkins entered. He was a thin man, in a dark, quiet double-breasted suit. He looked anxious. His face was youngish, making him look more like a man in his twenties than the thirty-something I knew him to be.

"Speak his name," Lestrade said, "and the devil appears."

"Is Mr Holmes here?" Hopkins said, his eyes darting around the small office as though Gregson or Lestrade might somehow have hidden Holmes in their pocket or behind the desk. Hopkins, normally a pristine and tidy person, looked a little rumpled and tired, but then, all the policemen did. A slightly musty tang suggested that it had been a while since the young policeman had had the luxury of a bath, but there was a lot of that going around at Scotland Yard, too, since the Whitechapel case had caused everyone to work double shifts.

"Holmes sent me," I said.

"Oh," Hopkins said with a clear expression of disappointment. "Does he have any leads?"

"He is following a number of lines of enquiry," I said.

"That is not quite an answer, is it?" Lestrade said. He tapped the piles of papers under his hand. "I have recently reread all the old files, as well as poring over the new ones. If there is any connection between any of these women, I cannot find it, other than the obvious fact that they all were in Whitechapel the night they were killed and most of them lived there. Holmes really thinks this will help?"

"They still seem to be attacks of opportunity to me," Gregson added. He leaned forward. In fact, every man in the office was hanging on my every word. I only wished I had better words to give these fine men who toiled endlessly and thanklessly on behalf of the city around us.

I sighed. "I do not know," I admitted. I groped in my exhausted mind for any kernel of hopeful facts I could pass on, but with the whirlwind of vampires, wild transformations and unseen murderers that dominated this case, I had little information that I could share, and even less that they might find encouraging. "Holmes often keeps his theories to himself until he has the ability to prove them."

"That," Lestrade said darkly, "is the understatement of the world." He sighed, looking even more tired. "Serves me right for asking, I suppose. Don't get me wrong, I'm glad to have you and Mr Holmes working on this case and Lord knows we can never return the favour for the assistance that he's given us over the years, but between you and me, Doctor, it is often a maddening experience waiting for your friend to produce his results."

"On that score," I said, "I can offer heartfelt agreement, but he has his ways."

"Another understatement," Lestrade agreed.

"Is there nothing you can tell us?" Gregson pushed.

"It is a complicated case," I said, shaking my head.

"I only wish that were true!" Gregson said. "From this chair, it seems woefully uncomplicated, since we know virtually nothing. If these are attacks of opportunity, and nothing connecting the victims, which is how it has seemed so far, even to Holmes, then we have precious little to go on."

"Holmes believes he may have something," I said, then immediately wondered if I might perhaps be overstating the case. The truth was, I wasn't very certain of that fact at all, and while I had seen Holmes time and time again unravel tangled knots too difficult for the rest of us, no case had ever been filled with the kind of dark collection of impossibilities as this one was.

"Well then," Lestrade said, pushing back his hat, "let us release our pretty boy criminal before he gets any prettier."

I shot Lestrade a look to see if he meant anything particular by that comment, but he was watching Gregson as the large detective fumbled in his trouser pockets. He eventually produced a small key, which he used to unlock a drawer in the desk and retrieved a large jangling iron ring. It was a heavy, cold, ancient group of keys that would unlock the cell doors.

The four of us followed another stone-flagged passage to a barred door, then down a winding staircase to a white-washed corridor with a line of doors on each side. It felt, to me, like a descent into another time, as if the cells themselves were part of an older, more sinister and primitive world. This was not the first time I had trodden these stairs, but it was never a comfortable feeling, having all that stone around us. It was a far cry from such monolithic edifices as the recently closed Newgate Prison, but no person can descend into subterranean blocks of brick and mortar, made for purposes of incarcerating our fellow persons, without some small qualms, both for the poor souls held there, and for our own chances of getting out again.

Gregson led us to the third door on the right and peered through the grating. He nodded and made way for me to do the same.

I stood to my full height in order to peer through and had to suppress a sigh of relief when I saw Hyde's shaggy mane, and not Dr Jekyll's more pleasing features. He had not changed. I let out a breath that I had been unaware, until now, that I'd been holding. The vampire body had less need for air than before the infection, but the habits of the human body remained.

"We can leave the cuffs on him, Dr Watson, if you would prefer?" Gregson said, misinterpreting my unease.

"No," I said. "That won't be necessary."

Gregson put the key into the cell door lock. The door was a serious, heavy, oaken affair with metal bands around top and bottom and it moved grudgingly when Gregson pushed it open. My understanding was that this was a temporary jail in comparison to the prisons that held inmates long term, but the door looked as formidable as any I'd seen in Newgate or the like.

Hyde, sitting on the prison cot showing his profile, seemed not terribly out of sorts for all that he'd been incarcerated for forty-eight hours. We'd made a fair amount of noise opening the cell, but he hadn't so much as moved.

"Might I speak to him for a moment alone?" I asked.

"Certainly," Gregson said, but I could see he was surprised. Then he shrugged. "We will leave the door unlocked and wait for you down at the end of the hall."

"Thank you."

The three policemen filed out. Hyde still hadn't acknowledged our presence, but when we were alone, he turned those yellow eyes fully on me.

"So," he said in his pleasant but dangerous baritone, "you are here to release me?"

"Yes," I said. "And to ask your help. Holmes has asked me to convey you back to Baker Street."

"You don't approve," Hyde said. He stood up, flexing his huge arms. "You don't care for me at all, do you?"

I sighed. "Holmes seems to think you can be of invaluable assistance."

"That wasn't an answer," he said.

"No," I admitted. "It wasn't.

"Etiquette," Hyde said, biting off each syllable harshly. "Fine society, crystal goblets and roast duck while half of London scrounges for food in the cold streets. I find nothing more detestable than a lie and etiquette is a pack of lies that perpetuates others starving, you see that, don't you?"

"I don't see anything of the kind," I said. "Society has rules because it needs to. Otherwise we're not better than…" I trailed off, somehow reluctant to finish that sentence while those lambent yellow eyes glared knowingly at me. My gaze was drawn up, irresistibly, to the high window with the dusty bars of thick iron.

Could I wrestle those bars free, if I had been incarcerated here for a crime I had not committed, instead of Hyde? The mortar looked solid, but not impossibly so. Then what? To be a fugitive from the law? What life was that?

Hyde seemed to know my thoughts well. "No better than the beasts, is what you meant. Just what I deserve, a cage, yes? But beasts aren't cruel. They don't betray or lie. The law of the jungle is harsh, but it's clean, not cruel."

"But they don't help each other, either, except when it's in their own best interests. The law of the jungle isn't exactly a byword for kindness, is it? It's a phrase that means preying on the weak, on the very old and the very young. At least humankind, as a race, has striven to improve themselves. We are, as a people, better than we were a hundred years ago and we will get better yet."

"But it's still a cesspool out there, isn't it?" Hyde shot back. "And how much do you and Mr Holmes feed off that, because if it wasn't cesspool then you and Holmes wouldn't have anything to do, would you? You have your little flat with your tea and your books and cigars and papers, all the comforts of society, but your entire reason for existing depends on that cesspool, doesn't it. Thank… *heavens*… London is a cesspool or what would Watson and Holmes, Holmes and Watson, *do* with an afternoon? No cases to solve, no stories to write." He made a ridiculous sad moue with that fanged mouth.

"So you won't help us then?"

"Oh, I will," Hyde said brightly. "What else would *I* do with an afternoon? Of course I'll help. That sounds far more fascinating than anything else going on. It's just the hypocrisy that I object to.

Besides, I owe the bastard that did for Genie." He jumped to his feet. "Also, that kind of excitement will help keep the doctor at bay. Lead on!"

"Very good!" Holmes said, when I returned with Hyde. "Mr Hyde, come in and help yourself to a cigar." Holmes went to the corner to pour a brandy out, but when he turned to hand it to Hyde I was there to take it instead.

"Allow me," I said. "Mr Hyde has recently confided to me that he finds the trappings of civilization, brandy included, a grand hypocrisy. I shall spare him that inconvenience." I lifted the snifter to my lips but Hyde snatched it from my hands before it got there.

Holmes raised his eyebrows in surprise and some amusement. It was nearing sundown and I could feel the day's lassitude leaving me. Even without having slept recently, the invigoration of night tickled at the back of my brain and I found myself alert and ready for anything. Miss Winter was awake, too, and watched us carefully, as if greatly amused.

"Brandy is one of the few things that justify the existence of civilization," Hyde said, then he drained the glass dry. "It is the *glass* that is hypocritical. Perhaps directly from the bottle, then?"

"Outrageous!" I sputtered.

His antics had generated a tolerant smile on Miss Winter's face, which Hyde clearly saw and took as a sign of approval.

Hyde flashed that feral grin at both of us before pouring himself another glass, helping himself to the cigar Holmes had offered, and settling himself into the chair nearest the fire. "So what is it, Mr Holmes, that you would have of me?"

"Whitechapel," Holmes said. "It is the key to everything and you have an intimate knowledge of the neighbourhood and its denizens that surpasses even my own, if my suspicions are correct."

"Probably," Hyde agreed. "I spend most of my time there."

"And you will help us?"

Hyde finished off his brandy and put the glass down. "No. I don't think I will."

"That's not what you said in the jail!" I burst out.

"No," Hyde admitted. "It is not, it pains me to say. I *did* need out of that jail, after all, and I wasn't certain to what extent I might owe my release to your goodwill."

"I thought you find all lies detestable!" I shot back.

"Not *my* lies," Hyde said. "What do I care about the Ripper murders? I believe that your brandy is running low and there are many other bottles calling my name." He stood up and sketched out a flourished bow. "So I shall bid you goodnight, gentlemen, lady."

"Yet another lie," Holmes said easily.

"Nothing of the sort," Hyde said.

"Isn't it?" Holmes replied. "You have been watching the clock, and the window, since you sat down. Almost as if you have your own plans for the night and I would wager ten guineas you mean to keep your own watch over the denizens of Whitechapel, only you don't plan on apprehending the culprit, do you? You plan to take justice into your own hands."

"And what if I do?" Hyde snarled. "Genie deserves better

than some delayed justice at the hands of the courts! Won't the barrister for the defence just love to parade Genie's poverty around? The newspapers have already labelled all the victims as prostitutes, why shouldn't the courts do the same? All the while it'll be some kind of show trial. The police are looking at immigrants and the poor, but what if it's some gentleman, some toff with friends on the force? No, it's going to take more than the London police to bring this man to his deserved fate." His hands flexed dangerously.

"And you call yourself Genie's friend?" Miss Winter sneered. She had been quiet until now. "You're free with that word, but you don't seem to know where her heart lay in the matter, friend, do you? Genie Babington loved the police. Her own dad walked a beat for ten years, didn't he? Brothers, too, I understand." She turned to Holmes. "Did they put that into all them papers the doctor brought back with him?"

"I have not yet had the chance to review them," Holmes said.

"You knew Genie?" Hyde said.

"I thought you only knew Miss Babington in passing," Holmes said.

"Knowing in passing is all it takes for some people," Miss Winter said. "She was powerfully proud of her father, she was. Talked about him often enough, but perhaps not to you, seeing as how you don't get along with the constables on the beat. Anyone can see that plain enough."

Hyde sat back in his chair, clearly nonplussed at this new information.

Miss Winter drove home her advantage. "If you're really

eager to strike a blow for Genie Babington, Mr Edward Hyde, you might think about working with Mr Holmes here, instead of against him."

"You have convinced me, Miss…? Wait, I know you. Miss… Winter?"

"Kitty Winter," she said. "We met briefly a year or so ago."

"I thought I recognized that fiery red hair of yours," Hyde said. "I seem to remember a long chat over dinner in a public house with a number of others present and the impression that you spoke infrequently, but when you did it showed a wisdom beyond your years. As such, I shall take heed of what you say now." He turned to Holmes. "So I guess I am at your service, after all, Mr Sherlock Holmes, for this investigation of yours." I stood flabbergasted, wondering at the ease with which Hyde had abandoned his firm position and agreed to help us. Now I felt certain that the man had just been baiting us all along.

"It is not," a strong voice said from the doorway, "an investigation."

We all turned, such was the power of command in that voice.

Count Dracula stood there in the doorway, supported on one side by Mina. He looked positively cadaverous, his skin stretched tight over too-prominent cheekbones, his hair thinner than I remembered it and untidy. He might have looked a ridiculous figure in Holmes's purple dressing gown, but for the blazing eyes.

"I say," Hyde said into the laden silence, "I do admire a chap that can make an entrance."

"I say that this is no investigation," Dracula said. "Long ago, before I was a ruler in my own country and before I contracted this disease that has cursed, but also considerably lengthened, my existence, I was a soldier."

Mina helped guide him as he shuffled carefully into the room. At a look from Mina's fierce expression, Miss Winter made room for them on the settee. I commandeered the stool Holmes had near the alchemical table for her to sit. Mina poured out a cup of scarlet sustenance from the red-ribboned teapot on the sideboard and delivered it to her husband. He took a small, careful sip, and I noted that his hand shook slightly before he handed the cup, still mostly full, back to Mina.

"It is a peculiar mindset," Dracula continued, "that of the soldier, steeled for the need to commit atrocities that most would blanch at during peacetime, for that is how wars are won. War consumes you, and well it should with so many lives in the balance, and you cannot flinch at what is required of you. Another world entirely from that of the city, from tea times and the gentle rules of society. Those rules no longer apply. I tell you, gentlemen, bluntly, that the only thing more horrible than being in a war... is *losing* one."

"Who," Hyde said, leaning forward with undisguised interest, "is this fine couple?"

"Forgive me," Holmes said distractedly. "Mr Edward Hyde, please allow me to introduce you to the Count and Mina Dracula."

Dracula inclined his head with that air of foreign courtesy that often marked him.

"Charmed," Mina said, "I'm sure."

"Count Dracula?" Hyde said delightedly. "Like from the book?"

"No," Dracula and Mina said together.

"Well, yes," Mina amended, "though I implore you to disregard what you have read, Mr Hyde. It is quite a work of fiction and Stoker does not at all represent the real picture."

"Are you a vampire, like in the book?" Hyde asked, apparently abandoning tact entirely.

"I am," Dracula said, glaring.

"You drink blood?"

"Yes," Mina said.

"And you live in Castle Dracula," Hyde went on. "In the… what was it… Carpathian Mountains?"

"Yes," Dracula said.

"Well," Hyde said with a big grin. "I guess Stoker got that much right, then, didn't he? Then you must have been Mina Harker."

"There never was such a person," Mina said. "As I said: fiction. I was engaged to Jonathan Harker for a very brief time, but that is as far as it ever went and that was, well, a lifetime ago. Dracula and I were destined for each other."

"So that part is not like the book, then?" Hyde said.

"No," Mina agreed. "Not like the book. Perhaps if anyone ever writes a biography of your own life you would come to understand it for the tedium that it truly is."

"Truer words were never spoken," Holmes added, ignoring the glare that I sent his way.

"Heaven forfend," Hyde said. "I do sympathize. There was a fellow, Stevens or some such common name, a friend of Jekyll's lawyer, Utterson, who discovered our secret and wanted to pen a tale around it. But we dissuaded him. Changed his mind and he sticks to pirate stories now."

"Dissuaded him how?" Mina asked, clearly curious despite herself.

"Jekyll made some violent threats, as I remember," Hyde said glibly. "Probably just a bluff, can't really say for sure. Reprehensible, I know, but the doctor was up for days worrying about it. When he can't sleep then I do nothing *but* sleep. It's a frankly intolerable situation." He got up to pour himself another brandy. "Anyway, it had efficacy to recommend it. A few nasty letters and dark hints was all it took and never a peep from either of them again."

"Perhaps we should have tried that with Stoker, dear," Mina said. Dracula looked in surprise at his wife.

"I say," I blurted out, unable to keep the recrimination out of my voice. "That is hardly an appropriate subject for humour."

"Quite right, Doctor," Mina said with bright solicitude. "I do beg your apology."

Dracula stood and took a step towards Holmes and the air of light-hearted banter dissipated.

"This is not an investigation," Dracula said. "This is a campaign of war, no more, no less. War against an implacable foe, and one that is well aware of the nature and necessities of war, for they have struck the first blow. We must strike the most telling one. You have now your troops arrayed before you. What will be your stratagem?" There was a clear note of challenge in the Count's voice and demeanour. I gave some thought to what the Count had said and reflected on my own experiences in the

Afghan war and thought that despite the horrors of war, there was some merit to his words and that the gravity of war had indeed found a most appropriate berth here in our humble quarters at Baker Street.

Holmes smiled his blandest smile and rose. "I am inclined, Count, to agree."

"It's the casualties of this war that concern me," Hyde said. "For we, good people, are all still present and accounted for. The same cannot be said for Genie Babington and Luella Brown."

"Quite true," Holmes murmured. "So we wage our war, but best if we keep it away from civilians if we can." He then took two quick strides and much to my surprise, threw open the window overlooking the street, letting in a wintery blast that made even the most impervious of us shiver slightly.

"Hmm," Holmes said, seeming to take the measure of both the street and the sky. Finally, he closed and resecured the window, then turned, ignoring the strange looks that passed between the rest of us and continued on in his lecturer's voice. "In summary, we are facing not a single individual, but at least two ruthless killers with an unknown agenda and singular capabilities quite equal to our own. The plan, good people, is as follows…"

Chapter 06

MAYHEM ON THE ROOFTOPS

While the remainder of us took our rest during the following day, Holmes worked around the clock. As he had outlined during our brief meeting, we would continue our patrol of Whitechapel during the night, while Holmes also reviewed his notes on the two crime scenes along with the prodigious volume of notes that Stanley Hopkins and the rest of Scotland Yard had gathered on the victims, their families and known associates.

Holmes threw back the thick curtains I'd drawn across the window for the fifth time, at least. It was late afternoon, moving towards evening, and the move cast a thin beam of wan sunlight across our sitting room, where I was trying to get some fitful rest on the settee.

"Holmes!" I chided. The settee wasn't in the direct path of the sunlight, thank heavens, but it was enough to send sharp pains through my skull. I could feel the beginnings of a headache swelling.

"My apologies, dear fellow," he said absently and a bit too loudly for my headache. He didn't sound very contrite. "You know that the fresh air helps me think." He wrestled the window open and breathed deeply. "Also, it is important that we keep apprised of the weather and the barometer is hardly the best way to predict that. In fact, there is no better method than to scent the air yourself. You remember Darden, the sailor out of Portsmouth, that explained his method to me? I have never forgotten it."

I didn't remember anyone named Darden or any story like that at all, but there was no arguing with Holmes once he had made his mind up. At least this idiosyncrasy was short-lived, for he closed the window only a few seconds after he'd opened it, apparently satisfied.

"So?"

Holmes's insistence that everyone maintain temporary residence at Baker Street bordered on sheer mania, to my mind, but none of the others seemed to find it unusual. Miss Winter, for her part, took up what seemed like a semi-permanent residence without demur or comment. Holmes, as a result, hadn't frequented his own bedroom for days now, and had taken to cat-naps on the settee, when I wasn't on it, or in his armchair. In a similar fashion, the Draculas continued to occupy my room and didn't seem in a rush to return to Carfax Abbey, though this likely rested on the fact that we had a ready supply of food and Count Dracula was still too injured to move easily about.

Hyde, on the other hand, was a different matter.

"Been cooped up in a prison cell for too long to keep sitting still," Hyde hissed, jabbing a huge forefinger into Holmes's shoulder. "If I'm idle too long then you-know-who will wake up and won't *that* be a treat?"

"Sleep causes the transformation?" I asked.

"It's not systematic," Hyde explained. "The potion is the only sure-fire method. But sometimes sleep will bring the doctor out of me, just as sometimes excessive excitement in Jekyll will cause me to emerge. But sometimes it doesn't. But I'd rather not take the chance now. I'm sure he'd be a big help to you all on the rooftops of Whitechapel!"

"Hmm…" Holmes said, considering the problem. He didn't seem to notice Hyde's hostile manner. "I will admit that you present a tangled problem. Where is it you would go? Home? It is my fear that both this place and yours are very likely being watched and you may come to harm. These are not people to be trifled with."

"Home?" Hyde said. "Furthest thing from it! I've a taste for a pint and a rare steak. Tell you what, let us see if Miss Winter will come with me and play guardian. The two of us ought to be safe enough together and we shall stick to the public places. Our opponents, whoever they might be, and however they might try to keep tabs on us, as the Americans say, won't trouble us in a public place. She can also make sure we make our rendezvous this evening so you won't worry about old Hyde going astray, eh?"

"Would she go with you?" I interjected. "Holmes, this is a bad idea."

Hyde gave me a toothsome grin. "You let me worry about that."

"I suppose if Miss Winter is amenable," Holmes said, "I can raise no substantial objection."

"Very good," Hyde said, and went and knocked on the door to Holmes's room, where Kitty Winter had sequestered herself. At her answer, he opened the door a crack and whispered his proposition into the darkened interior. I expected harsh words, or possibly thrown crockery, if such were lying about in Holmes's room but, to my immeasurable surprise, Miss Winter seemed to think it a capital idea. Hyde retreated and she emerged a few minutes later, dressed and ready to go with a wide-brimmed purple hat stolen from one of Holmes's costumes he kept around for disguise purposes.

"Some days," she said, "I feel as if I've slept enough for a lifetime and I'll admit that a nip down at the public house sounds just the thing. I've not been in such a terribly long time."

"Well then, fair maiden," Hyde said proffering his arm, "we shall do just that very thing."

"You'll meet us in front of The Hanover public house just before nightfall," I reminded them.

"Have no fear on that cause, Doctor," Miss Winter said. "I'll not forget."

The two of them headed out the door and no sooner had it closed behind them than Holmes burst out into a hearty laugh. "You really must forgive me, Doctor, for my melancholy the other day. I will confess that my melodrama now seems a small and petty thing. Puzzle pieces of the wrong shape? How often have you heard me lament on a quiet night that there is no imagination or audacity left to the criminals of London? Now... now, we have a puzzle that is audacity itself, made entirely of pieces unlike any other in the world, shapes that we didn't even know existed and I couldn't be happier. Is not the air sweet?"

"The air in here is anything but," I replied testily, for this many people in close quarters had quite overwhelmed my senses, but Holmes merely laughed and waved a dismissive hand at my pique.

"I think that I shall raid my own rooms for a change of clothes while Miss Winter is out of them," he said with a chuckle and started to suit action to word, but paused as the door opened.

"I am glad that you, at least, are in fine spirits," Mina Dracula said from the doorway.

"How is the Count?" I asked quickly, standing up.

Mina pursed her lips. "Better."

"Perhaps I should check the wound," I said.

Mina shook her head quickly. "His pride will not tolerate it, I am afraid. He is wroth enough with me that I let you do so the night of the injury. Better to say, perhaps, that he is wroth with himself for requiring it. He is not used to such things. Besides, I have been tending it carefully and making certain that he regains his strength. In fact, I have come down to tell you that we shall be joining you for patrol tonight. Or, as my husband calls it, the campaign."

"Madam," I said. "Are you certain he is strong enough? His wound was very serious. Even he is not invulnerable."

She had started to leave and my statement had caught her partway turned.

"Invulnerable?" she said, still partially facing away from us, but with her head turned back in our direction. "He is more than that. He is Dracula."

Just as Mina Dracula had said, so it was, and the four of us took a four-wheeler from Baker Street an hour before sunset. Count Dracula was quiet, mustering himself for the night of activity ahead, I think, but emanating that serious, old-world courtesy he had about him. If I should not have been concerned and looking for it, I would have missed even the stiffness he exhibited, or the occasional wince when the carriage bumped heavily in the street.

True to their words, Miss Winter and Hyde were waiting for us at The Hanover public house. We found Miss Winter sitting near the door, looking a bit green around the gills, with Hyde talking to the barkeep.

"Haven't had much alcohol since…" she winced. "Since the Baron." I knew precisely what she meant, since it had been Baron Gruner who had affected her transformation. *Since she had become infected with vampirism.*

"What little spirits I have had," she continued, putting a hand tenderly to her temple, "didn't do much. I thought perhaps that they didn't… anymore. Turns out, it just takes a lot more."

"You've both been drinking the entire day?" I asked as I carefully laid my walking stick to one side, being cautious with the leather cover over the silver head. I had my revolver, loaded with silver bullets, in my coat pocket, as well.

"Oh," Miss Winter said, "don't worry about *him*. He's fine. I'm the one with a bleeding headache, if you'll excuse me, and filled up to the ears hearing about Coleridge and Keats, I'll have you know." She shot a glance over at where Hyde was on the other side of the bar. Despite the disparaging words, there was more than a little admiration in her gaze. Several patrons left, leaving only a few of us in the place, all of them clearly wanting to get home before it finished getting dark.

The Draculas exchanged a look, not saying anything, but clearly unimpressed with their new comrades and, very likely, a little less than impressed with Holmes and I for both choosing them and allowing this turn of events to unfold.

I had brought my doctor's bag with me, but, not wishing to lug it around, made arrangements with the barkeep – aided by a few shillings – to keep it behind the counter for me. When I came back to the table, Holmes was already explaining his plan of attack.

"We shall have a long night ahead of us," Holmes said. He had a map of Whitechapel spread out on the table and had arranged two routes, one for each team, with regular stops at an intersection near the George Yard Buildings on the hour, and another on the half-hour mark near Miller's Court. The map was not overly large and he slid it from person to person so that we could all review it and memorize our routes. We did this carefully, making certain to shield the paper with our own bodies as much as possible to keep our activities clandestine.

"You look tired, Miss Winter," I said.

"Don't you worry, Dr Watson," Miss Winter said. "Kitty

Winter has struggled through worse. Night air will likely do me a bit of good. I just wish I'd taken the time to bring a little… nourishment. I've been watching him eat and drink all day, but none of that does me any good anymore." Again, she shot him that look. "A man of prodigious appetite."

"Perhaps some hair of the dog," Holmes said. He nodded at me and I handed over the red-enamelled whisky flask I'd brought for the occasion.

"This better not be whisky," she said, unscrewing the cap gratefully. It wasn't, and she drank deep before handing it back. "Thank you, Doctor."

"We thought it might be required," I said.

"Well then!" Hyde said boisterously as he came back to the table with a half-full pint. "Is the hunting party assembled? Tally-ho!"

Count Dracula insisted on resuming Holmes's previous assignment of the rooftops with Mina, this time with Hyde to increase their numbers and help look for the kind of ambush that had laid the Count low on our last patrol.

"We are likely being watched," Holmes reminded us. "Watched by a foe we cannot see. Remember both that and the man with the sword."

"The same person?" I asked.

"That remains to be seen," Holmes said, "but I rather suspect not."

"I'll know him, he gets close enough," Hyde said, tapping his nose. Then he jumped with surprising grace to grip the crossbar on the top of a street lantern at least twelve feet up. Holmes raised his eyebrows. He'd seen the traces of one of Hyde's climbs at the first murder scene, but clearly hadn't expected a performance like this. Hyde's boast about climbing had been, if anything, understated. He had to be fourteen stone, despite his lack of height, and dangled as easily from one hand as if he weighed no more than a feather. He kicked his legs up effortlessly, then braced a foot on the pole and sprung sideways, flipping neatly end-over-end, to land precisely on the grating of a second-storey balcony.

"Well," Miss Winter breathed, "will you look at that."

Hyde grinned down at us, clearly enjoying our surprise, then clambered up the side of a drainpipe with the alacrity of a chimpanzee, scaling the rest of the building in less time than would take to describe it.

"With a grip like that," Holmes said quietly, "his incarceration at Scotland Yard now seems entirely voluntary, doesn't it?" He exchanged a glance with me as the import of his words struck home. "Hyde, unlike any other occupant before him, could easily have reached the bars of the high window in his cell and, in a very short amount of time, have wrenched the bars free."

"I did have occasion to notice the bars of his cell," I commented. "They had not been disturbed."

"I would not have brought Hyde into our endeavour if I'd had any suspicions he should be a suspect," Holmes said, "but I am glad to hear that detail all the same."

The roof of the tenement building we stood next to, four

storeys up, was heavily obscured, merely a suggestion of the roofline above us. I turned to Dracula and Mina, but the two vampires had already moved away, fading silently into the darkness and fog of a nearby alley, presumably to join Hyde on the roof.

"Blast!" said Miss Winter, looking around and noticing their disappearance. "Some company we keep. The way those two sneak off! I can't sneak off like that. Can you, Dr Watson?"

"I'm afraid not, Miss Winter," I said. "Lack of practice, perhaps. In truth, I have never felt it necessary to make the attempt."

Miss Winter shook her head at me sadly. I wasn't entirely sure how to take the wordless commentary, so I busied myself examining the street around us: damp, dark, cold and silent.

It had been a remarkable but completely unnecessary performance, in my mind. Vampirism brought greater strength and reduced weight, both of these more pronounced with the passing years, so it would be a poor vampire indeed that couldn't climb exceedingly well. While Mina had not the same years or progression of the disease as the Count, she had more years than either Miss Winter or myself.

"Why be surreptitious about it?" I murmured.

"Force of habit, I suspect," Holmes said. "The combination of a military mind and a wide plethora of enemies. Learned by the Count over untold years and passed down to Mina."

Holmes, Miss Winter and I began our patrol. The streets lay cold and empty, so that our footsteps made damp echoes around us. A light snow started some few minutes later and quickly formed small pockets of crunchy sleet under our feet.

Of all the vigils that I have ever done with Sherlock Holmes, I can remember none more gruelling and taxing to the nerves. It was unnerving in the very extreme to think of being under a sinister surveillance from some nebulous, unseen foe. I kept my ears as tuned as I could for such a possibility. Voices from inside the buildings, voices and the occasional sounds of traffic from several streets over, water dripping from roofs. Once, as we passed another tenement building, angry voices, a man and woman's, came out of an open window. It didn't seem to have anything to do with us or the case, and just that fact seemed astonishing. There were still people living here in Whitechapel that were worried about their work, or finances, the daily lives of their loved ones: wives, husbands, children, not the night-time dangers of Jack the Ripper. The very idea seemed impossible. Still, they were inside, not out here in the dark street as we were.

Twice, we passed and exchanged brief consultations with the regular constabulary, but no one had seen anything. The newspapers had been running Whitechapel and Ripper editions for the past few days and no one wanted to go out after dark if they could help it.

During the first hour, and then the second and third, we met with the other team, Hyde waving an 'all's well' signal from the rooftops, though once he descended and had a brief consultation with Holmes regarding a slight alteration to Holmes's route. An hour later, the temperature had dropped significantly and the fog turned into a thin, white haze that left ice crystals on the streetlamps, windows and our clothing, though none of the heavy, wet flakes lasted very long in the street before turning to a dirty slush. Our dull vigil continued.

It was just after our fourth hour of patrol when the howl tore through the night.

The noise made my hackles rise. A wild, monstrous sound, increasing in power before it fell away. A noise like that was chilling enough on the moors, in the wild, where such a thing might be heard and that would be terrible enough. To hear such an out-of-the-place sound here in the heart of London was past all possible belief. It harkened me back, of course, to the Baskerville case, but my heart told me that I would long for such a simple answer as a huge but mortal hound covered in phosphorous. Nor could there be any doubt about what we had heard. No mere dog or imitation – this was a wild beast, loose somehow in the city, untrammelled by the laws of its people. Such a thing could not possibly be, yet there could be, as I have said, no mistake.

"Quick!" Holmes snapped. "Back this way!" We'd been moving through a narrow street with tenement houses on both sides, the roofs a jagged piece of skyline against the murky night sky. The snow had become heavier and drifts were starting to collect on the street, providing treacherous footing for our mad dash back the way we had come. We were, in fact, nearly back to The Hanover public house before we turned the corner and came upon the most startling and grotesque sight that I have ever been witness to.

The street was wider here, and the moon out and a few street lanterns lit, so coming out of the narrow, darkened alleyway into the lit street was like leaving the darkness of a cave and entering directly, without preparation, into a furious battle.

An enormous beast stood in the middle of the street with its back to us so that all I saw were massive shoulders and back, brown and furred. The beast was reared up on hind legs like a cornered bear, standing at least eight foot at the shoulder, though it did not have the barrel shape of most bears. It roared, a cacophonous, harrowing sound that painfully split my ears, and spun, quicker than anything that large should be. It clove the air with a clawed paw the size of my head.

Count Dracula, the intended target, jerked back out of the way, but just barely. A gap in his cloak, torn open by the beast, showed how narrow his escape had been.

The beast turned again, harried on the other side by Mina, and backhanded her a glancing blow. She flew a dozen feet, crashing into a shop awning, then fell limply to the street.

Holmes and I both had our revolvers out and fired into the back of the massive beast.

Both of our first shots hit, the impacts penetrating flesh and causing two small rivulets of blood to spray forth, and the creature spun and howled at us. Miss Winter, meanwhile, started circling around to the creature's left.

I got my first look at its face, a horrid, slavering, fanged and brutal visage, more like a bulky wolf than a bear, in truth. Our shots had filled it with rage rather than caused any serious injury, though we had drawn blood. The jaws of the thing were terrifying, with a short, ponderous muzzle that held teeth the length of knives. The fur ran from brown around the neck to black around the muzzle and I realized that it was wet with blood. Several bodies lay in the street, two women and a man, none of whom looked entirely familiar or... entirely intact. It was horrifically clear where the blood had come from and there could be no doubt that all three innocent bystanders were well past any effort a doctor might make. The London night air, already heavy with dirty, wet fog and the Thames's scent, was now redolent with the beast's musk and the iron tang of so much blood.

Then I noticed the trousers. Dirty, torn and shredded trousers, or at least the remnants of such, were visible around the waist, although they were mere rags below the thigh. But the overwhelming, inescapable impression was that this creature had once been a man.

Holmes and I both stepped forward and emptied our revolvers. At this short distance, we were unlikely to miss. I could see several hit home, causing more injuries to that barrel chest and torso. At least one ricocheted off the beast's skull, leaving a gash along the brow. I saw a wisp of black smoke curling from a bubbling wound – the characteristic vitriol-like effect of silver on vampires also afflicted this beast. This was something of a relief as it told me our bullets weren't completely useless. Still, the damage of several bullets and the reactions they caused all seemed paltry, insignificant things in comparison to the beast's strength and fury.

It was about to rush us when Dracula struck from behind. The beast was at least four or five times the Count's mass, but he raked that broad back with nails like talons, raining a splatter of blood from the beast's back down onto the moonlit cobblestones, to far better effect than our poor, ineffectual bullets. A small part of my brain, distantly rambling in small flashes of incoherent thought, railed at the lies and inconsistencies of folklore and legend. If this wasn't a werewolf, what else could it possibly be? Yet silver bullets, a powerful tool against the vampire, appeared to injure the creature, but not at all to the degree that I had expected. It seemed we could do very little to this terrifying new menace.

The wolf spun with amazing speed, attempting to grapple Dracula with one of his clawed hands to deliver a killing blow, but Dracula moved smoothly backwards, leading the beast a dozen feet away from us. Kitty Winter dashed in from the side, scoring her nails across the creature's exposed ribcage and then dancing away as the creature howled. Holmes was already dumping the cartridges out of his spent revolver and fitting new cartridges in the cylinder, and I hastily did the same.

Dracula returned for another blow and the monster spun to face him, clearly deciding that he was the most serious threat of all of us. It rushed him, still so fast for such a massive beast. Dracula ducked, slipped, and wove defensively, avoiding claws and snapping teeth, but only by inches each time.

The snarling wolf, towering over Dracula, was trying to corner him against the building, but the vampire narrowly dodged under a scything claw and then bounded up the wall behind him, touching various small projections on the tenement wall at five, ten and fifteen feet up in one smooth series of movements.

The werewolf, by contrast, leapt straight up to land on the

second-storey ledge right next to the Count, who ducked yet another attack from those snapping jaws.

Holmes and I both finished loading and snapped the cylinders on our revolvers shut, then rushed to get a better vantage point to try to make a telling shot, but it was hopeless. Both the werewolf and Dracula were three storeys up now, and climbing, the werewolf attacking constantly, Dracula still trying to stay one step ahead of those fatal blows and succeeding, but just barely.

"Blast!" I said, the sudden helplessness filling my heart with despair. "How are we supposed to contend with something like that?" Holmes and I were both waiting for a clear shot, but the whirlwind melee made it just as likely that any bullet we sent into the fray would hit our ally instead of our foe. I had never felt more helpless.

Kitty was helping Mina to her feet and I was relieved to see that neither woman had come to serious harm, though, of course, the night was far from over. Mina, clearly still reeling from her impact against the building, was leaning heavily on Miss Winter's supporting shoulder as they both limped over. Mina's dark eyes, watching the fight, were very wide and filled with fear.

"Hyde be damned!" I snapped. "Where has he gone? Wasn't he with them?" I stared at the part of the building near us, trying to gauge how quickly I might ascend myself, for all that the fight was very likely to have moved onto the rooftops by the time I got up the first storey. Nevertheless, I took a step in that direction, but stopped when Holmes put a hand on my shoulder.

"There he is," he said, pointing up.

I looked up to where Dracula's retreat had just about reached the level of the roof. Dracula neared the ledge just as the werewolf had closed the distance with a spectacular leap from a ledge to a cornice, and was about to grab his fleeing quarry with a great hooked claw.

But Holmes wasn't pointing at them, he was pointing at the roof, where a bulking shadow rose up on the very precipice.

Hyde.

With a bellow, he dropped onto the werewolf.

Hyde, for all his bulk, was still dwarfed by the monster, but the werewolf, intent on rending Dracula, never even noticed him coming. Hyde landed on the werewolf's head and shoulders, dislodging the beast so that both figures tumbled into a spiralling fall.

"Look out!" Holmes cried, for they were falling directly towards us.

The four of us scrambled out of the way, but even while doing so, I saw Hyde grip the beast's shoulders and tuck his head into the furred chest while they fell. If it were luck, or some innate acrobatic ability of Hyde's, I never found out for certain, but it was the creature that struck the cobbled street first, with Hyde on top. Their combined weight hit the street with all the force of a cannon shot, and there came a sickening crunch.

Chapter 07

THE BEAST

For a long instant after the impact, everyone in the street was too stunned to move.

Then Holmes and I rushed over to the two fallen figures, ready to put the muzzles of our pistols to the beast's temple and fire if there were any sign of life. Hyde, shaken and clearly stunned, slid off the werewolf's body, rolled weakly, and lay gasping on his back.

"Stupidest… damn… thing… I… ever… done," Hyde gasped. "Was it marvellous?"

"It seems to have ended the battle very thoroughly," Holmes said, his eyes still on the unmoving beast.

"Are you alright?" I asked Hyde, shocked. It seemed impossible that he could have fallen the way he did and not sustained enormous injury, but he stood carefully and shook himself out, testing his legs and then shaking his arms. He winced a little, but nodded. "I'm not broken anywhere that I can find. Beastie broke my fall."

"That," I said, "was incredibly foolish, but also, without a doubt, the bravest deed I have ever witnessed." I held out my hand.

Hyde took my hand, but very carefully. "I'm still a little woozy," he said. "And I've a headache like a freight train went through my skull, but it's nothing a pint and a shot wouldn't clear up."

Dracula dropped down neatly from the building and moved to Mina's side. "Are you injured, my love?"

"A little battered and shaken," Mina said, "but not seriously injured."

Dracula, with a little nod of thanks to Miss Winter, took over the duty of helping Mina stand steady.

"Watson," Holmes said with a tight voice.

I turned and looked at the beast. It was… moving. No, that wasn't the word. Shimmering? No. It was *transforming*.

Had I not seen first-hand some days ago the remarkable transformation of Dr Jekyll to Mr Hyde, I would have disbelieved my eyes now. The flesh crawled, writhing and twisted as if it were a living thing independent of the body, and it made the gorge rise in my throat just to look at it. The impossibly tall creature diminished, shrinking substantially in height, though it gained mass elsewhere. The facial features, tooth and fur and muzzle, twitched and fell inwards and somehow reformed into a brutish, bearded, if entirely human face.

An obese man now lay in the street, remarkable if only for his almost complete nakedness and the great rolls of fat he possessed.

I rushed to examine him, checking first for a pulse. It was there; weak and thready, but there.

"Holmes," I said. "This man is alive. But he won't be much longer if we don't get him inside."

The streets had been deserted on account of the Ripper attacks, but now, the howling and the thunderous crash had finally drawn the few remaining patrons out of the public house and prodded others to look out of dirty windows. A constable's whistle sounded somewhere in the distance.

"God," Hyde said in a quiet, stunned voice, staring with wide eyes at the unconscious man who had just transformed before him. "Makes you want to throw up just looking at it. Is that… that is… is that what it looks like when I change?" He seemed too bewildered to realize what a shock his statement would be to the others besides Holmes and I, who did not know his and Jekyll's secret. He looked dazed still and was clearly not thinking straight yet and I determined to check him for a concussion next.

"Very much like," Holmes said, his voice heavy with meaning. "Remarkably so, in fact." He gave me a significant look and I understood the import of his words at once. For all that this beast had looked nothing like Hyde, Holmes clearly suspected that the extraordinary change had a similar scientific explanation behind it. The effect had looked remarkably similar, prompting all sorts of strange thoughts in my feverish brain, for the events of the evening had a surreal and otherworldly weight. As little as a few years ago, I would never have believed in vampires or shapeshifters, a statement that would have been even more true of Holmes, the pure logician. But now, we had had both those truths thrust forcefully upon us and had to, and Holmes continued to emphasize this, reassess the world in the light of those new possibilities.

I completed a brief survey of our ragged, motley crew. Hyde did, as I suspected, have a concussion and Dracula, Mina and Miss Winter had all suffered minor contusions and lacerations, but I was relieved, particularly in light of Mina's impact with the awning, to see that none of them had been seriously injured. I did my best to arrange and shelter the remains of the poor trio of persons that had, apparently, been in the wrong place and the wrong time and lost their lives for it.

I returned to the unconscious and nearly naked man who had been our assailant. All this time a crowd had been gathering, but, possibly on account of Dracula's glower, they had not drawn too close.

Holmes was examining the man. Despite the hideous fall, there was not a mark on him and though he continued to remain unconscious, despite his state of undress in the cold street, his breathing was steady now, as was his pulse. The pale, ponderous flesh looked white and unblemished.

"Hmm," Holmes muttered, fingering the remnants of the man's trousers. "The clothing was quite expensive and torn this way very recently – see the fraying?"

"So the man was well dressed before this transformation?" I said.

"Precisely," Holmes said. "I also detect the scent of beer on his breath, despite having presumably transformed twice, and possibly something… unusual." He kept his voice low.

"That seems an understatement," I said.

Holmes gave a thin smile. "The evening has certainly been eventful. The transformation and lack of clothing have robbed me of a great deal of my data, but present their own evidence, too. See here." He had to strain enough to roll the man so that I could see the unmarred back. "No sign of the injuries that we inflicted. None."

The police arrived and Lestrade, taking charge of the scene, immediately began to field a deluge of stories from the various onlookers. Shockingly, it had all happened so quickly that none of them had seen any part of the actual altercation except through fogged windowpanes. Though they talked of the ferocity of the wild man's episode and the enormous racket he had made, none of them seemed to have gained a good enough look to mention a great beast that stood on its hind legs. One man, a smallish bar worker, maintained that the man had a huge crowbar and began to help the police search the street for it. Another man swore there had been a huge mastiff in the fat man's possession. When a grey-haired harridan, louder than the rest, suggested that the man had been wearing a giant pelt, but that it had been carried off by that same mastiff, the rest of the crowd began to echo this same fabrication.

The unfortunate victims were identified as Mr John Shannon, a plumber, along with his wife, Ruth, and sister, Helen. The three of them were well-known and well-liked at The Hanover. Holmes spent a short time reviewing their remains before covering them again, his expression solemn.

Dracula, Mina and Miss Winter had all slipped away at our urging, though Holmes had a brief conference with Hyde before the official force arrived. Holmes and I explained to Lestrade that the three of us, Holmes, Hyde and myself, had stopped the man ourselves. It gave me a twinge inside to tell such a lie to Lestrade and the official force, especially since we had been forced to make it something of a habit as of late, lest we find ourselves explaining some of the more bizarre elements of our case to them. I found myself feeling both guilt and a profound envy. Lestrade moved in a world without beasts, without monsters and men and women that drink the blood of others.

Lestrade gave Hyde a speculative look, but accepted our story readily enough, that the man had given us a terrific fight, but since he did not fit any description of the culprit, we let Lestrade know only that we wished to question him, as he may have valuable information. It seemed that any link to the second murder, which had all the markings of a savage beast, would be very difficult to link to this unimpressive figure of a man. Nor did we have any evidence to connect him to the more precise Ripper murders.

Several of the gunshots had been heard, as well, though this was attributed to the naked man again and the crowd began to look for a discarded revolver in the street along with the crowbar. We could certainly not admit to having done the shooting ourselves as we would then have to explain why we had shot an unarmed man in cold blood and how we had missed with every shot, since the man was clearly unharmed.

"The man shot at you?" Lestrade asked us, eyeing us keenly.

"There were certainly shots fired," Holmes said, "though you can see that we are not injured. It was very dark and he was… quite wild, possibly not in his right mind."

"Thank the Lord you were not injured," Lestrade said warmly.

"It was," Holmes admitted, "a very close thing."

"This is our Ripper, then?" Lestrade said. "I'll admit…" He eyed where two constables were drawing a blanket someone had provided around the prostrate man. Another had been sent to get the paddy wagon and a stretcher. "He's not the picture I had in my mind."

"There is no sign of a knife," Holmes said. "Nor did we see one during our scuffle. I am not entirely convinced this is the man."

I looked a little askance at Holmes at this. Certainly the man presented a serious threat and we knew him to be responsible for the Shannons' murders, if nothing else. There was a problem in that it certainly did not seem to match the description Holmes had used of the surgical knife that had been used on Genie Babington. However, Holmes had described the second murder scene, the death of Luella Brown, as being one of particular violence, and the beast we had seen could certainly be responsible for that.

"Well," Lestrade said, "there is no understanding the modes and methods of a lunatic. Perhaps he may not have done for Genie Babington, or perhaps he did and has altered his methods."

"My fear," Holmes said, "is that this man was in league with the Ripper and this is yet another distraction, perpetrated so that the Ripper can continue to stalk prey uninterrupted by either your patrols or ours. I urge you to send patrolmen throughout Whitechapel looking for any kind of disturbance."

Lestrade agreed and this was done, though that left us with precious few persons to keep the onlookers at bay.

Holmes drew me aside. "We shall have to proceed very carefully," he said to me in hushed tones. "There is no help for it, we shall have to let the police arrest this man, but there is a great deal of danger."

"You think this man may resume that bestial form?"

"It is certainly possible," Holmes said. "After all, we have already seen how little truth there is to the vampire stories. We already know that the stories about the werewolf's change during a full moon, if they are even applicable, are wrong." He pointed at the sliver of moon in the sky. I hadn't even thought to check if it were a full moon, though the beast and transformation fit the werewolf legends well enough. But tonight's moon wouldn't be full for weeks.

"As such," Holmes continued, "imagine the carnage that should occur if things go awry. Without Dracula, Mina, Hyde and Miss Winter I do believe tonight would have gone very differently. I should hate to repeat it without them at Scotland Yard." He pointed to where the paddy wagon had pulled up and two constables were pulling out a litter to lift our new prisoner into the back.

"Lestrade! Holmes!" Gregson called from across the pavement. He had not arrived with the others, or with the paddy wagon, but had rather just run up to the gathering crowd. "Mr Holmes!" The tall, blonde detective seemed frantic to a degree I had not seen in the law professional before this day. Lestrade, deep in conference with two patrolmen, made his way over to us just as Gregson pushed his way through the crowd.

"It is as I feared," Holmes said. "The Ripper struck again while we were distracted, yes?"

Gregson nodded. "Precisely, Mr Holmes!"

Holmes turned to me. "I shall require you to ride back to Scotland Yard with the paddy wagon so that I can examine the crime scene." I was bitter at being kept from the examination of yet another crime scene, but realized that Holmes, as ever, had reasons for his request.

"Take Hyde with you," Holmes said. "He has a familiarity with the man's methods that may prove useful to you in keeping our prisoner docile."

Hyde, listening to Holmes, looked a little startled, as if he had not, until just now, considered the similarities between himself and the fat man who had become a werewolf.

"I have some laudanum in my bag," I said. "That may prove useful."

Hyde nodded. "Just the thing, I should say. Lots of it, probably."

I turned to Hyde. "Will you come?"

"Aye," Hyde said, "I'll come." He looked over at the paddy wagon.

"I think," I said, "that it is time to confide in Lestrade. We'll need to keep our man drugged, and that will take some explanation, but we also need to warn Lestrade of the very real danger. He and the rest of Scotland Yard are pulling extra shifts to help patrol at night. They are stepping into the same mire that we are. Invisible men, horrifying transformations, and I don't just mean Hyde and the werewolf!" I smacked my own chest with an open palm to indicate what I meant. I realized that this was a point that had been bubbling up inside me. Reconciling myself with the representatives of the police department, the men I had known for years, was an action I needed to take for my own sense of redemption as much as anything else.

"We can trust Lestrade," I finished lamely. "The police need to know the danger they're in, too."

Holmes pursed his lips in thought. "You're not suggesting the entire police force?"

"No," I said. "Just Lestrade, perhaps Gregson. They can keep a secret."

"Start with Lestrade, then," Holmes said, "as Gregson is going to lead me to the crime scene. You'll have to try one and delay the other. I'll need to see the latest murder and you'll need to find a way to make certain our prisoner does not wake up for the time being. We must interrogate him later, too, but one problem at a time, perhaps."

"I hope you won't hold it against me," Lestrade said as we rode back to the station in the paddy wagon, "but it chafes me to have drawn prisoner detail when Gregson and the others are back there investigating the crime scene!"

I sighed. "No, I quite sympathize. Prisoner duty wasn't my first choice, either."

Hyde, having administered the laudanum, was now also drawing blood from the patient, showing himself to be quite competent with the tools of a doctor's trade, which I suppose should not have been too surprising.

"You're taking a sample of the man's blood?" Lestrade asked.

"Yes," Hyde said. "The doctor will have questions that only blood can answer."

Lestrade shot me a quick glance, but I shook my head.

"You mean Dr Jekyll," he said. While he'd now apparently dismissed Hyde as a suspect for the Ripper murders, he had not forgotten the connection between Jekyll and Hyde. How much it would have astonished him, I'm sure, to have heard the full story.

But Lestrade shrugged and turned to me. "Does Mr Holmes have a theory to explain this little series of events? Probably does, but hasn't deigned to share it with you, either, eh? I bet it's a pip!" The springs on the wagon were rickety, squeaking with every bump and doing very little to smooth out the rough ride. Lestrade, Hyde and I were riding back with the unconscious fat man, now swaddled in a spare coat and blanket the constabulary had produced.

"He has shared… some of it," I said slowly. "It is… rather remarkable." Hyde was looking at me with a narrowed gaze, but didn't say anything.

"Remarkable, you say?" Lestrade said, catching my eye. The stoat-faced man twitched his nose and gave me a beady stare. "I am all attention."

"It is, in fact," I said, "more than remarkable. It is several remarkable facts piled one on top of the other, so that the whole mess of it becomes entirely unbelievable, yet I know it to be true. Now that it comes time to tell you…" I lifted my hands helplessly, "I honestly despair of being able to make you believe in even a small portion of it."

Lestrade said nothing, only shifted his gaze from Hyde to the still-unconscious fat man, and then back to me.

I took a deep breath. "I shall start, I believe, with vampires and werewolves."

Lestrade sucked in a breath and I half-expected him to dismiss my statement and laugh, but he did no such thing. He leaned forward, a little precariously with the motion of the paddy wagon, his eyes locked on mine. Hyde kept watching me, perhaps wondering if I planned on spilling his own secret along with my own.

"Over the past year," I said to Lestrade, "some of our cases have moved from the world of simple reality that I've come to rely on London for, and strayed into what I can only describe as legend. The first of these has been vampires. While the blood disease that causes vampirism seems to be a matter of science, it still can produce startling results." While talking, I had been fiddling with my walking stick and now pulled off the leather covering, revealing the solid silver head beneath.

Lestrade's gaze flickered over to the cane. "Are you," he said softly, "going to tell me that this man here is a vampire or a werewolf and demonstrate with silver?"

I paused, surprised that Lestrade had anticipated my line of thought, at least to a point. Though, in fact, I had no idea if the legend of silver harming a werewolf would turn out to be valid or not. Certainly most of the folklore surrounding vampires had proven spurious, at best. I'd seen silver have a damaging effect, but it hadn't done much to stop the creature, which seemed far more terrifying and indestructible than anything our supernatural experience had led us to expect. Also, it went completely against my ethics to inflict something akin to a vitriol wound on an unconscious prisoner. My purpose here was to try to keep our prisoner sedated, not awaken them through torture.

I steeled myself, convincing myself that the next step was a necessary one.

I put my naked hand on the silver head of the cane.

The effect, and the pain, was instantaneous. It felt like burning flame shot up my hand and arm and when I turned my injured palm up for inspection, I could see smoke smouldering out of the wound I'd inflicted on myself. The sound of sizzling and a burning stench filled the back of the wagon.

"Christ!" Lestrade cried out.

Hyde, thinking quickly, had already torn open my doctor's bag and pulled out salve and the fixings for a bandage. "Here," he said. "Give it here."

I'd inadvertently dropped the walking stick and Lestrade picked it up gingerly, tapping his finger tentatively on the tip with no result. A little of my blood was still on the silver head, bubbling and adding to the stench. Lestrade wiped it off with handkerchief and the smouldering stopped. He tested his own finger on the silver again, with no result. While Hyde assisted with applying a bandage to my wound, Lestrade repeated the experiment with the silver head of my cane a few more times, his jaw clenching as he did it. He then retrieved the leather cover from the floor where I'd dropped it, fitted the covering over the silver head.

Lestrade handed the covered stick back to me, his eyes narrowed. "You are telling me, Dr Watson," he said slowly, "that you've been bitten by a werewolf?"

"We are finding," I said wryly, "that the old legends are riddled with errors. We, as yet, know little about the werewolf except that this man is one, or something very much like it. We are, however, far more intimately familiar with the vampire." I could feel the throbbing ache in my incisors that adrenaline always brought about and had no doubt that my fangs would now be showing and flashed Lestrade a smile that must have looked predatory indeed.

Lestrade jerked back as if I'd struck him, banging the back of his head unnoticed against the paddy wagon wall. The silver stick dropped from his hands. His eyes were wide as saucers and all the blood had drained from his face. He stared, his mouth open. The wagon turned sharply to the left so that we all had to brace ourselves or be dislodged. A sharp crack of a whip came from somewhere outside, and raised voices, which then started to fade with distance, as if we had just circumnavigated some kind of traffic accident and then left it behind us. The cry of a newspaper boy drifted in, and then it, too, faded.

"Well," Lestrade finally whispered. "This does explain a great deal." He nodded at the man still lying there. "And him?"

"This man was a giant wolf when we fought him," I said. "He clearly isn't now, but the rest all needs to be discovered. We have, however, seen a similar change before this…"

"Hideous," Hyde said, shivering. "Truly hideous."

"Which gives me some hope that Holmes will be able to shed

some light on the science of this phenomenon, so that it does not stay shrouded in mystery."

"Well," Lestrade said. "If there is any man for fathoming the unfathomable, it's Mr Sherlock Holmes."

He shot a glare at Hyde. "What about you? Are you a mermaid?"

"Only in the bath," Hyde said, with great gravity. "Though I do, of course, drink like a fish at every opportunity. Reputation to maintain among the other denizens of the sea, you know."

Lestrade snorted, then took a very deep breath and turned his gaze back to me. There seemed to be a great deal more to say and I still wasn't completely certain that Lestrade believed me or understood all the ramifications of the things I was telling him, how completely his world had changed now that he was aware of the dark things within it.

The paddy wagon came to a halt and Lestrade, all business again, hammered on the doors to have the constable driving unlock them since they'd been barred on the outside.

The constable flew the doors open and Stanley Hopkins was there with him. They brought out a stretcher and I checked the prisoner before they moved him, concerned as I was with how much guesswork might have gone into Hyde's estimate of the proper dosage, but the man seemed to be deeply unconscious still. The constables transferred him into Scotland Yard and then a prison cell without any great difficulty and it was only then, after I had a moment to realize that any immediate danger seemed to be well and truly over, that I breathed a deep sigh of relief.

"I shall take a cab back to Baker Street," Hyde said, after we locked the man in. We stood, just the two of us, in the dank, poorly lit hall outside the cell. "If I'm to adhere to Holmes's injunction that we are being watched and are only truly safe at Baker Street with the safety of numbers, then I'll need some things from Jekyll's lab. Also more of this laudanum."

"What for?" I asked.

"We'll need to examine the blood, of course," Hyde said. "And I'm not the man for that. That's where the laudanum comes in. We'll need Jekyll. The drug will help with that."

"I'll be staying here until the prisoner wakes up," I said. "Perhaps he'll tell us something of the phenomenon himself."

"Very good," Hyde said. "Have you any money?" He grinned as I handed some over, a dark expression, for all that he was our ally in this endeavour.

We went upstairs, where Hyde departed and I sought out Lestrade in his office.

"We need to keep the prisoner under observation," I said, "so that we know the second he wakes up."

"I'll arrange it," Lestrade said.

"Is there any news from the murder scene?" I asked.

"Only a little, but what news has come will twist your gut, Doctor. It is not *one* murder scene, but two."

Holmes had told me as much, but that didn't make it any more pleasant to hear.

"Two murders," Lestrade went on, "but not two women. There is one woman and one man murdered this time."

"One woman and one man?" I said, frowning. "Are we certain it's the Ripper? That doesn't match the previous murders."

"Who else could it be?" Lestrade said with derision. "Come

now, Doctor, as if there could be two bloody madmen running around Whitechapel."

"Were they both murdered in the same way?"

"Here we come to the end of my knowledge," Lestrade said, "for Gregson has sent a short note and that is all. You'll have to depend on Mr Holmes to give you the details, I should imagine. In the meantime, I have some things to show you, Doctor. In fact, it's something I should have shown you and Mr Holmes a long time ago."

I arched my eyebrows at this intriguing statement and watched Lestrade as he riffled through a file drawer and pulled out a battered folder marked with a large red 'X'. He then crossed past me, as I settled into the chair in front of his desk, and closed the door. Then he turned to face me, regarding me carefully.

"Will you tell me the whole story?" he asked.

So I did. Or at least a brief sketch of our dealings with Count Dracula, Mary's transformation, Mina's abduction, the Midnight Watch, and our battle with the vampiric Moriarty. I left out a few details, such as the affair with Baron Gruner and Kitty Winter's own vampiric transformation, as I did not feel it necessary to put her at risk.

When I finished, Lestrade sat in thought and then said, "You are not the first person to talk to the police of vampires."

"Am I not?"

"No," Lestrade said. "I should like to call in young Stanley Hopkins, as this was originally his discovery. But before I do that, I have a question. I see now, as I think on it, how carefully you have kept your secret, and I understand the reasons for it.

I should not have been so quick to divulge such a thing were I in your shoes. Yet you have not asked me to keep it a secret."

I shrugged. "You are a friend, Lestrade. I did not think I had to."

"Nor do you," the policeman said. His ferrety face showed a flash of pleasure when I used the word 'friend' and then grew serious again. "Yet you did not tell me until now, when it became important to tell me for the good of the force and the city, and I quite agree with your reasons for waiting until the appropriate moment. I shall do the same and treat the preservation of your secret as sacrosanct. I will tell Hopkins that you have experience with and an understanding of vampires, but no more, for while Hopkins is a good man, the more people that know, the more danger you are in."

"I thank you," I said gravely. "That is exactly the approach that I would ask of you."

When Lestrade opened the door and called out, Hopkins came bustling over and into the office and then stopped, seeing the marked file folder on Lestrade's desk.

"You have changed your mind, then, Inspector?" he said with excitement.

"I have," Lestrade said. "Dr Watson and Mr Holmes have presented me with incontrovertible proof of the existence of vampires."

Hopkins opened his mouth and Lestrade cut him off.

"I'm afraid that is a story we are not at liberty to share, but it does bring us back around to your unusual discovery. It is that which I would like to share with Dr Watson now."

"By all means," Hopkins said eagerly. I always felt a bit of amusement that Lestrade and Gregson so often referred to Hopkins as young, for while the man was ten years their junior, he had now been on the force for well over a decade and was closer to forty, I thought, than thirty. Still, he was lean, with a boyish face and excited quality that made the moniker fit too perfectly to be avoided, it seemed.

"Hopkins here uncovered a police report that may interest you," Lestrade went on, "which has its own curious chain of events." He slid the folder in my direction and I opened it and saw a large quantity of papers, which seemed to be several weathered police reports from years ago. In addition, there were a few portions that had been blotted over with ink so as to become completely illegible.

"One of the reports concerns the first series of Whitechapel Murders," Hopkins said, talking very quickly. "A private detective had been engaged to assist in the matter, hired by an unnamed noblewoman. The detective's name was Sebastian Greene. Greene, according to his reports, discovered some evidence that proved to be too outlandish to be considered. He believed he had found evidence of creatures that could walk the London streets at night, preying on others and completely undetected. In short, vampires."

I took a deep breath and nodded.

"Here's where it gets even more interesting," Lestrade said. "There is a record of a visit to the police commissioner from another noble, a man described as 'tall and curly-headed' that came to object to Greene's involvement and wanted him removed from the affair."

"There is no record of this nobleman's name?" I asked.

Hopkins shook his head. "Redacted." He leaned over my shoulder, flipped one of the pages back, and pointed at one of the ink blots.

"I didn't know that Scotland Yard was in the habit of redacting records," I said, surprised.

"We're not," Lestrade said bitterly. "The commissioner refused, because while Greene had his outlandish theories, he also promised to give Scotland Yard a great deal of useful information and they were desperate for any kind of lead they could get on the matter. Of course, once they got some of that lauded information, it all appeared, to them, to be purest poppycock."

"However," Hopkins said, "Greene disappeared a week later and was never seen again."

"So we have a mysterious noblewoman that hired him," Lestrade said, "and a mysterious nobleman that wanted him fired, and no idea of the identity of either. When Greene disappeared, we thought little of it. After all, the man believed in vampires and was jumping at every shadow. I did not meet the man myself, but the impression conveyed by the officers dealing him was not one of stability and sanity. He talked a great deal about the danger of cities, a common enough topic, particularly with the Whitechapel Murders and the spectacle the newspapers made of them. It was thought, when he disappeared, that he had likely fled the city and besides, we had the actual Whitechapel Murders themselves to worry about at the time and one missing detective was not considered significant."

"The talk of vampires was not likely to improve that impression," I said.

"It did not," Lestrade agreed. "It was the reason that most of his testimony was thought to be worthless and discarded. I only tripped over it last year, buried in the records, by accident. I think there were copies of the record that got destroyed, but these were overlooked. I started reading them out of curiosity and was a little bit shocked to find the man's statement both lucid and well thought out. As you can see, they are voluminous and, I assure you, painstakingly thorough. I tell you the man was nearly Holmesian in his careful attention to detail. While the final conclusion of vampires seemed outlandish at the time, I was still struck by how careful and close his reasoning was. I thought of showing these to you and Mr Holmes, but… well, I know Mr Holmes's opinion on ghosts and bogeymen. I thought of it as a curiosity and there seemed little reason to dwell on such details when the Ripper murders were so long ago. Now that the Ripper is back and you tell me in such a convincing manner that vampires are not so outlandish after all, well, I think perhaps you had better take these so that Mr Holmes can have a look."

"I will," I said, "with gratitude."

There came a knock on the office door and Hopkins opened it to find a breathless constable there.

"The prisoner," he said. "He's awake!"

Lestrade and I rushed down to the level in which the cells were kept. I, for one, dreaded every step and expected to hear that bestial snarling and see the cell door burst asunder. I'd pulled my pistol out of my coat pocket, too, an instrument I'd never expected to need while in the very heart of Scotland Yard. But there was no need.

The man, now properly clothed in rough attire provided him by the police, looked more innocent and ordinary than he had any right to. When the constable that Lestrade had set to watch him opened the grate and stepped out of the way, Lestrade and I both peered in to view the heavy-set man fumbling with the sleeve of the woollen shirt he now wore.

"Don't look a right proper Ripper, does he?" the constable said.

"Open it," Lestrade told the constable sharply, clearly not pleased with the man's commentary. The constable hastily produced the key.

"Perhaps we should consider…" I started, but the constable had already inserted the key in the lock and snapped it open. I yanked the cover off my silver cane and adjusted my grip, images of a pitched battle in the Scotland Yard basement rampaging through my brain. But the man only sat there, plucking at his sleeve as Lestrade and I entered the cell.

"I don't think this is my shirt," the man muttered plaintively. "This one's missing a button. Where are my clothes?" He spoke in such a mild, quiet way that it was hard to associate him with the beast that had caused such destruction and I had to remind myself that I'd seen both the destruction and the transformation myself.

"You were found without your clothes," Lestrade snapped. "And I don't mind telling you that you are in some very serious trouble indeed. Murder is the charge! Perhaps you had best start with telling me your name and what you've been doing in Whitechapel the past few evenings."

I cringed inwardly, but tried to keep any expression off my face. It was hard to imagine this man committing the Ripper murders and we had no real evidence that would convince a jury, despite what we'd seen with our own eyes. There simply wasn't any part of the murders that we could sufficiently connect with this inoffensive person.

"My name is Fleete," the man said sullenly, glaring at them out of piggy eyes. "George Fleete." He leaned back, sharpening the glare. "My head hurts! What did you do to me? What have you done with my clothes?"

"You'll have to remember that yourself," Lestrade said. "They weren't with you when we found you."

"Found me?" Fleete said. "What you mean is some constable got free with their nightstick on the wrong man. I've done nothing. You might be used to pushing nobodies around, but that's not going to work with me. Wait until Mother hears about this! You're in a great deal of trouble."

"One of us is in trouble, sure enough," Lestrade retorted, but Fleete let loose with a derisive little laugh and did not look at all impressed.

"You have no idea what you're getting yourself into," Fleete said. "Mother will see you ruined, or worse." His voice darkened at the word 'worse' and his face looked positively maniacal. If there was so much as a scrap of fear or uncertainty in the man, I couldn't see it.

"What do you know about the Whitechapel Murders?" I blurted out, infuriated by the man's demeanour.

"More than you ever will," Fleete said to me.

"What does that mean?" Lestrade asked, but the man merely flashed a grin and refused to say more.

"What about sightings of a monstrous dog?" I said, trying a different tack.

Here Fleete looked shocked, but only for the briefest of moments before he put his guard back up. "I don't know anything about any dog," he said.

For some reason, he hadn't expected that question. Was it possible he had no memory of his transformation or any actions he took as the werewolf? That would certainly match some of the legends and fairy tales about werewolves. He had been surprised but had recovered quickly and now had a cagey expression.

"Three people were murdered," Lestrade said harshly. "Perhaps you know something about that? Do the names of John, Ruth or Helen Shannon mean anything to you?"

"No," Fleete said and he looked like he meant it.

When pressed on these answers, Fleete simply shook his head, unwilling to say more on either matter. He was, however, more than willing to talk about more mundane things. Mother was Madam Clementine Fleete, who lived with him on Sherborne Street. He had no real profession but had come into a great deal of money left to him from his father, who had been a shipping magnate with affairs in both England and India. He made a little gambling, he said, but seemed to find the idea of a profession demeaning. The man did not deny visiting or drinking in Whitechapel in general, and The Hanover specifically, but blandly denied having anything to do with any murders, though he repeated the boast that he knew more about them than we would several times. More than that, we could not find out.

In a moment of desperation, while the man was answering Lestrade, I contrived to insert my own meaningless question about the crossroads of his home, which was merely an excuse to punctuate my question with a jab from my silver-headed stick into the man's exposed wrist. I hated to inflict injury on a helpless prisoner, but needed to puncture the man's shield of complacent normalcy and get some real answers.

Fleete merely jerked his hand back, looking irritated and angry at my rudeness, but there was no sign of the characteristic reaction that silver generated in both vampires and the beast that he had transformed from.

After an hour of this fruitless interrogation, Lestrade and I were at our wit's end and had gathered very little information for our efforts.

I left an hour later after making Lestrade swear to continue to hold him. I also convinced Lestrade into boarding over the window of Fleete's cell in order to prevent any accidental exposure to the moon when night came again, though I felt distinctly foolish insisting on this point.

With my notes on Fleete's interrogation and the folder on Greene that Lestrade had given me, I hailed a cab and gave them the address for Baker Street.

Chapter 08

MADAM CLEMENTINE FLEETE

It was a dull, overcast and grey morning, which matched my mood perfectly and also took the sting out of still being awake after the sun had come up. Still, I was glad for the protection of my great coat and a large hat. As the last traces of morning fog slid by the carriage windows, I considered what I had discovered about Fleete and decided that, all in all, my report was likely to be a great disappointment to Holmes. Despite revealing my most shameful secret to Lestrade, I had discovered nothing about the prisoner's transformation, motives, or connection to the Ripper murders. I did not know how he had become a werewolf, or why, or any idea of what kind of control, if any, he might have regarding his condition. While I was able to convince Lestrade to the extent that he could post a watch around the clock on the cell and bolster the door and bars of the cell, I was by no means convinced that these measures would be enough to contain the beast should the man be able to effect his transformation again.

Was he truly a werewolf, like the legend? Certainly the legendary vulnerability to silver seemed to be overstated. What else was false? Did the phases of the moon have any connection? Lestrade had taken my advice to block out the cell window so that the moon could not shine in, but we had very little idea if this would accomplish our goals. Certainly some part of the legend was false since it hadn't been a full moon last night. In addition to knowing nothing about the beast, we got next to nothing from the man. His bland normalcy had to be an act and yet it had been an extremely convincing one. The man seemed to have no knowledge or concern about the Shannon murders at all, which hardly seemed possible, and yet neither Lestrade nor I had been able to shake the man from his unbelievable story. The Ripper murders had turned the city upside down and now we had our first real lead and it seemed impossible that we should thwarted by this blasé individual. Holmes, under a great deal of pressure himself, would have nothing but scorn for my effort here and he would be quite right to feel so. The situation was completely untenable.

Although I did not have Holmes's intricate knowledge of the streets of London, no Londoner could occupy the city for as long as I had and not develop a passing familiarity. As such, Sherborne Street, the location for Keystone Manor, where Fleete claimed to live with his mother, was present enough in my mind that I couldn't help but notice when the cabbie actually passed it. Perhaps I need not return to Baker Street empty-handed after all.

"Cabbie!" I shouted. "Turn around!"

The cabbie had to drive me a good distance along Sherborne Street before we found Keystone Manor, a good-sized house of white stone standing back a little from the road with an iron gate and fence guarding the perimeter. A double carriage sweep, with an immaculate front lawn, stretched two curved arms down to the road from the house to the gate. A bit of wooded thicket could be seen behind the place and a winding road, probably leading to a stable, lay on the left. From the sounds of voices and bustling coming through a few second-storey windows, it seemed a busy household. Two grooms were polishing a four-wheeler in the drive.

"Excuse me," I said to one of them. "Is this the Fleete residence?"

"Aye," the groom said warily.

"Is Mrs Fleete in?"

"Madam Clementine Fleete is engaged," the man said. "Who are you?"

"My name is Dr Watson, working with Scotland Yard," I said.

The man looked deeply unimpressed, but went to the front door and conferred with someone inside, though the door was propped open and he did not enter. The sun dulled my sight enough to ensure that I could not make out the figure he spoke with. After a few words, he turned and gestured grudgingly for me to approach the front door.

Walking up the white stone porch, I found an imposing figure waiting for me just inside, a beefy, red-haired man with a nose that had once been broken, wearing a butler's uniform that must have been custom-made. I held out my visitor's card, but he declined to take it.

"We know who you are, sir," he said in a soft, whispery voice startling in such a large man. "Madam has been expecting you." I could feel an expression of surprise spring onto my face, but managed to wrestle it into submission after a few seconds. I tucked my card back into my jacket pocket.

The towering butler led me through a cool hallway laid with Moroccan tile that seemed to run the length of the house and held enough windows on either end to satisfy the requirements for a greenhouse, should the Fleetes decide to repurpose it.

"Please wait in the library," the butler said, gesturing to a large doorway to my left, and departed without waiting for any acknowledgement on my part.

The library was another impressive room, airy, expansive and by no means limited to books. Gallery might have been an equally fitting word and several tall glass cases lay in between the shelves and formed a sort of columned wall running down the middle so that it seemed more a museum showroom than a room dedicated to reading. The room did not have a door, such as seemed proper to me in a real library, just the open doorway, and a small, scarlet-enamelled table lay just inside. There were several small tables and comfortable-looking chairs dotted around. On the table nearest to the doorway lay a silver platter with ivory-inlay handles that held a single visitor's card. Looking behind me, I could hear voices in the house, possibly upstairs, but no one near me. I flipped over the card and felt my hackles rise.

The previous visitor had been one Lord Arthur Holmwood. When I flipped the card over, I saw that there was a faint reddish mark on the back. I sniffed at it, wondering about blood stains, but it was something more innocuous, like wax.

Of course, Dracula had told us his story some time ago, when he'd first engaged Holmes to track down Mina after she'd been kidnapped. Holmwood was connected to both them and to Van Helsing. There had been some time when both Dracula, and to a lesser degree, myself, had been thoroughly convinced that Van Helsing had been the Mariner Priest, the villain responsible for transforming both my wife and I into vampires. The process had been devastating enough to me, but it had cost Mary both her sanity and her soul, and then, her life. But Moriarty was eventually revealed as the Mariner Priest and was now dead, for certain this time. While Moriarty had embroiled Holmwood's friends Quincy Morris and Dr Jack Seward in his plans, no connection to Holmwood or Van Helsing had ever been proven. But his name set my brain on fire now. This alone had been worth the trip! I could hardly contain my excitement and was already dying to flee the property so that I could fill Holmes in on the news.

As it turned out, I had some time to contain my excitement. Madam Fleete may have expected me, but that knowledge didn't seem to generate any promptness on her part and it was well over an hour before she was properly motivated to make an appearance.

In the meantime, I idled about the room, perusing the shelves. The books were a predictable and uninspired collection and I soon found myself looking at the glass cases instead. Many odd and obscure objets d'art lay on translucent shelves in the cases, though there were no labels of any sort, such as a museum might boast, so that many of the items displayed might have been some kind of antique tool, or might instead have been fossilized cow dung, for all that I could discern. I'd whiled away most of that hour before tripping over the item that shook me every bit as much as Holmwood's card had.

It was tucked into a case in the corner, on the bottom shelf so that I had to crouch to view it properly. A plain figurine of an unidentifiable greenish stone, cracked and in poor repair, clearly ancient. The edges of the thing were roughened and indistinct so that I had to squint, even with my keen eyesight, to make out the almost unfathomable, unknowable shape. Despite the worn edges, it had a strange angularity, so that the thing almost seemed to fold in on itself, for all that it wasn't terribly intricate. It was a monstrous beast, nothing found in nature, I was sure. Perhaps bat's or dragon's wings, I couldn't be sure. A feeling had crept over me while I stared at it, a feeling both indescribable and profoundly unique. While I didn't know the subject, or the artist, I had seen this distinct and disturbing style before on a diadem – and it had cost Lucja Nowak her life.

A diadem belonging to the Esoteric Order of Dagon.

"Mr Watson," a woman's voice said behind me.

I jumped and stood up quickly, too flustered to even bother correcting her to 'Dr Watson'.

Madam Fleete was a black-eyed, hard-looking, blocky woman with artificial brassy ringlets piled above a stern, weathered face with a blocky nose almost as impressive as her butler's. To compensate, perhaps, she was sporting a great deal of makeup including bright carmine lipstick. She wore a gleaming pink dress with gauze and taffeta cascading in all directions. Madam Fleete did not seem to be an overly large woman herself, but in this ensemble, she was of prodigious size. Three maidservants followed in her wake, attempting to keep the material from touching the floor and, in one case, attempting to pin portions of the taffeta lace explosion back. They trailed like attendant rowboats following a ponderous steam trawler. Just watching the bouncing pink waves Madam created every time she took a step was a nearly hypnotic exercise and I had to tear my gaze away and regard her weathered and hostile face.

"You have George, I assume?" she said. "Worthless man. Well, you can keep him. We certainly won't miss his presence here at home. You! Stop that!" This last outburst was at the maid desperately pinning the material back, or up, or down. It was difficult for me to ascertain the maidservant's actual goal. Whatever it was, she retreated before Madam Fleete's verbal assault, hovering a few feet away but ready to dart in again at a moment's notice.

"He's in the custody of Scotland Yard," I said. "I'm afraid he's in a great deal of trouble."

"George has a knack for getting into trouble," she said. "It's really his default condition. What would you have of me?"

"I was hoping for information on his activity and character," I said. "He has been less than forthcoming."

"Petty and low," she responded promptly. "He drinks, he

gambles. He squanders money. It is no great mystery. Likely he was too drunk to understand your questions."

"It must be rather more than that," I said. "He has become embroiled in a murder investigation. It is rather more serious than the activities you mention."

"Well," she said, "that is rather more than his petty endeavours to date. I suppose I must congratulate him. At least the term 'petty' no longer applies."

"Madam, this is hardly a matter for levity."

"I suppose not," she said, though her tone didn't sound very chastised. "I hardly think that he would be involved in anything like that. Still…" she shrugged, which sent another rippling cascade of pink taffeta about her person. "There is very little I can tell you about George that is not a matter of public record. He sleeps here, but spends very little of his waking hours at home. He often travels to India and is gone for months on end. I'm afraid my son and I are not very close. We have hardly spoken of anything significant for years and what conversation we do have is not only trivial but commonly vulgar."

"You have not noticed any peculiar behaviour from your son in the past few weeks?"

She snorted and walked over to one of the small tables that held a brandy service tray. One of the maids rushed over to assist, but Madam Fleete paid no attention and poured out some kind of yellowish liquor and sipped at it judiciously. "George is very much like a train line to the most squalid parts of London. He leaves early and comes home late, usually in a worse state of repair. As far as I know, he continues to do so, as he has for years, excepting trips to India, but he has not taken that trip for months. I would be very much surprised if he were involved in murder, as that would represent a serious departure from his busy drinking schedule."

She set her drink down and turned her black eyes full upon me and I suddenly realized that while not an attractive woman, she did possess a pair of wondrous, enchanting eyes worthy of a queen.

"He is useless," she said casually, "but also harmless. You really should just let him go."

I found it difficult to respond and was suddenly reminded of my first meeting with Count Dracula, who had frozen me in place with a look.

Then I shook my head and managed to blurt out a response. "I… I don't think that's possible."

"Ah well," she said, as if the matter were of no consequence. "Now, all of these questions are much more appropriately addressed to George, whom you have in your possession, and I have a busy social calendar, as you can see. Good day to you." She set down her glass, still half full of whatever liquor she'd been drinking, and swished mightily out of the room.

I was stunned, to say the least. This woman had just been informed that her son was suspected, at least, of murder, and seemed not to have the slightest care for either her son or the murder in question. Even more than that, the Whitechapel Murders had generated fear, unease, curiosity and often, a barely expressed fever of Schadenfreude, and Madam Fleete seemed to be immune to all of these despite the fact that her son often frequented Whitechapel. She hadn't even asked if it had been the Whitechapel Murders that her son might be connected to. Nor had I thought to ask after the butler's odd statement that Madam Fleete had been expecting me, but it was clearly too late to do so now.

Filled with bewilderment and confusion, I left.

A most interesting development had precipitated at Baker Street when I returned.

"Look who's here," Miss Winter said with a sneer when I entered our sitting room. She nodded over at the laboratory table where Holmes and Dr Jekyll were both poring over the results of a chemical test. Jekyll's gaze flickered over to Miss Winter at her comment and I saw a flash of disdain cross his smooth face before he composed himself again. Then he picked up a small journal and made some notes in it, referring to the results of his chemical test as he did so. Hyde had clearly been successful in transforming back to Dr Jekyll.

Miss Winter sneered again at the doctor, in case he had missed the first one, and closed a book of poetry she had been reading.

"Oh yes," Miss Winter said, seeing the question on my face. "I know about Jekyll and Hyde. Hyde told me himself, though I'll grant you it's a story I'd not have swallowed had I not seen his change and Fleete's change before that. Two in as many days." She shivered. "Hyde seemed to think that we needed Jekyll here, but I do not find it much of an improvement."

Jekyll sniffed disdainfully, but didn't otherwise comment.

Clearly, these two were not fast friends and I wondered what that said about Miss Winter's relationship with Edward Hyde.

"Watson!" Holmes said. "Come, tell us what you have learned."

Dracula and Mina were nowhere to be seen, but then it was the middle of the day now. I felt a burning need for rest myself. It also made Miss Winter's presence and wakefulness surprising.

I very quickly gave them a quick sketch of what I'd done and seen since we'd parted company last night, though Hyde, had, of course, told them most of what had transpired with George Fleete. I was particularly eager to convey the connection to Lord Arthur Holmwood.

"A red mark, you say?" Holmes asked. "On the back of the card? With the scent of wax?"

"Yes," I said.

"Did Madam Fleete wear lipstick?" Holmes asked.

"Yes!" I said, snapping my fingers. "A very bright shade that matched the colour on the back of the card!"

"Interesting," Holmes said. "And suggestive. It may give us some clue as to her motivation for her involvement, if she thinks so highly and amorously of Holmwood. Her using the card as a proxy also suggests that the original is not available to her. Perhaps her affection is unrequited."

"That seems a great deal to infer from one lipstick smear," Jekyll said dubiously.

"Well," Holmes said, "it is a working theory and now we shall have to be on alert for facts that corroborate or contradict our theory. At any rate, the name of Holmwood tells us a great deal."

Both Miss Winter and Jekyll looked blank at this exchange. Evidently neither had read Stoker's fictionalized account of Dracula's trip to England so the name of Holmwood meant nothing to them. In point of fact, Jekyll had never heard of Dracula or Stoker's book. Hyde's knowledge seemed not to have transferred over to him and Miss Winter had given him a brief explanation of vampires, but that was all. This caused a rather long digression as no one had even seen fit to explain the presence and nature of vampires to Jekyll, for all that he now shared the room with two of us.

I also wondered, in passing, if either Dracula or Mina were conscious enough to hear Holmwood's name from my rooms upstairs, but I heard no sign of any disturbance and concluded they must be sleeping and pressed onward.

I then told Holmes of the figurine I had seen and gave him the rest of the details from my visit, including Madam Fleete's strange behaviour. Just discussing the figurine – and the diadem that it reminded me of – made my flesh run cold. I could see that the story had a profound effect on Holmes, too, for his face grew tight, and then pensive as he mulled over any possible connection.

Finally, the doctor shook his head. "All of this is very interesting, but hardly the point. It is the transformation that is important. I have spent the last few hours examining blood samples from both last night's assailant and Miss Winter. There are a great many similarities between them. The vampire's transformation is one long change, over years, possibly decades, while my own and the werewolf's is something a bit more sudden and impermanent."

"That seems a superficial commonality, at best," I said. "More semantic than scientific."

"So I would have thought," Jekyll agreed. "Except for Hyde's discovery." He held up his hand. "What do you make of that!"

I looked at his hand, seeing nothing out of the ordinary. "What am I looking for, Doctor?"

Jekyll looked at his own hand and his excited expression went suddenly blank and then he sighed. "I nearly forgot. The transformation itself healed our injury, but I have Mr Holmes's assurance that it happened."

"Hyde tested his own reaction to silver," Holmes said. "It gave him a rather large wound, same as it would deliver to a vampire or, as we have seen in our encounter, a werewolf."

"I tested it on Fleete, the prisoner, while he was in human form," I said, "and saw no such reaction."

"Nor does silver interact with my flesh," Jekyll agreed. "You see the linkage now?"

"It does seem very similar," I agreed. "But why?"

"We don't know!" Jekyll said. "But I've done some tests on his blood and it seems that Fleete has somehow been ingesting a potion similar to the one of my own making. I even detect traces of the wolf serum, whereas I used a distillation from the black langur, the very same as Professor Presbury from your 'Creeping Man' adventure, Dr Watson, and from the same source in Prague. It is similar in effect, too, and accomplishing a similar reaction with the human body, but using a few different ingredients and with a cosmetically different result. It is also probable that, like

Hyde and myself, Fleete has very little memory of his actions as a werewolf."

"Come now," Holmes said. "Evidence suggests that the beast we fought was exactly that, a savage beast with less than human reasoning. That hardly describes Hyde. Also the results that you call cosmetic, the physical differences between Hyde and a werewolf, are hardly trivial."

"Trivial enough!" Jekyll declared. "Trifles!"

"You could tell all of that from a blood sample?" I asked, astonished.

"Well," Jekyll admitted, "there is some guesswork here, I'll grant you. This is why we need more information from George Fleete. This Madam Fleete and her connections are of no consequence."

"Stopping the Ripper is the highest priority," Holmes corrected. "Understanding Fleete's transformation, while chemically fascinating, is merely a necessary step towards that far more important goal."

Jekyll's mouth became a tight, compressed grimace. It was obvious he did not at all agree with Holmes on this matter, but he said nothing.

"The two murders, then," I said, "what did you discover examining the murder scenes?" It chafed at me that the breadth of activity had necessitated our splitting the investigation and I was anxious for the details.

"Two victims," Holmes explained, "one woman, one man, as I said." He had a map on a nearby table that he pointed to. It had several pen marks on it. "It is very clear, after Jones's murder during the attack on Dracula, and this double murder while we fought with Fleete, that the group of people perpetuating these murders are not only watching us but arranging these assaults on our forces while other operatives commit the murders. Look at this here, where I have marked both murders sites from last night in red, and our fight here, near The Hanover public house. All the sites are within Whitechapel, but carefully spaced so that they could commit their murders uninterrupted by our patrols." Here he referred to a small notebook. "The woman murdered last night was named Lila Emmet. There is no sign of a struggle and the victim was knocked senseless first with a blow to the head, just as with Babington, likely from a stout cudgel. Then her throat was cut, as with many of the original Ripper murders, from behind, from left to right with a very sharp, short knife, possibly a scalpel. The victim was known to the constabulary and while the newspapers have mistakenly accused every victim of being a lady of the night so far, they will actually be correct when they make the same accusation of Miss Emmet. However, there were footprints in the light snow, both hers and from our size nine men's boot with square toes, the very same as I discovered near the murder of Genie Babington. The position of the prints and the blood indicates that she was attacked from the front, but there is no sign that she defended herself or even saw the attack coming, just as with Miss Babington."

He tapped the other red mark on the map. "Here, we have the other murder. The victim was one Ben Roberts, a tanner and remarkable in that he is the first male victim. Again, the throat was cut and again the victim put up remarkably little resistance."

"The Ripper killed one and then another in short succession?" I asked.

"I believe we are meant to think that," Holmes said, "but that is not how I read it. There are some curious differences. The first is that the attacker's boots are a full size larger than the attacker's prints from the other crime, and lack the distinctive square toes. Further, there are signs that he approached his victim at great speed, as the toes made a far more distinct impression than the heels. The second is that while the throat was cut by a very sharp blade, I do not believe it was the same blade that ended the life of Miss Emmet. Here the tracks got a bit muddled, but I believe the attack was committed from the front and from a short distance away. There is no sign that Roberts was incapacitated first, either by a blow to the head or strangulation, such as has been done with most of the other murders. So now our short knife has become a longer blade, and our attack of stealth is now looking more like a quick slash with great skill and speed."

"The man from the rooftops!" I said. "The one that attacked Dracula!"

"Just so," Holmes agreed.

"Neither of these two methods matches the second murder, does it? The savage animal attack that killed Luella Brown."

"No," Holmes said. "So now we have three separate attackers that not only work together, but often provide distractions so that the others can commit their atrocities uninterrupted. We have the first murderer, who is likely the original Ripper, capable of moving unseen, who does his deed with a scalpel and killed Genie Babington. Then we have our savage animal who murdered

Luella Brown and never did any man fit the evidence as well as George Fleete fits ours. It was during Jones's murder that Dracula was attacked and injured by a man possessing incredible speed and a long, silver sword.

"Then we have the double murder, the first matching the methods of our original murder, our original Ripper, the second committed by someone with a longer blade, moving very fast. There can be little doubt that this is our rooftop assailant. At the same time, our enemies arranged an impressive and murderous distraction which cost the Shannons their lives and, I suspect, was meant to cost at least some of us ours."

"If they're working together," Miss Winter said, "then they must know something of each other."

"Indeed," Holmes agreed. "Probably a very good deal."

"Fleete hinted he had some knowledge of the murders," I added, "but he would say no more. If there are two or more murderers cooperating in this grisly endeavour, to what end?"

"That, Doctor," Holmes said, "is the most important question and one that suddenly becomes even more important when we correlate any connection to the Esoteric Order of Dagon."

"The what now?" Miss Winter said. I realized that we had never told her that particular story, it not having any real connection to vampirism. Jekyll, too, of course, looked blank.

So Holmes sketched for them a brief explanation of the 'Adventure of the Innsmouth Whaler', which I have laid out for the reader elsewhere, and which details our encounter with the Esoteric Order of Dagon, one that I would almost as soon forget. Of course, Holmes, in his retelling, did not ascribe any supernatural abilities to the aquatic monsters that seemed to both rule and serve the Esoteric Order of Dagon, but I could not be free of such concerns, as much as I would have liked to be. The sea beasts I had given the diadem to had seemed possessing of unfathomable knowledge and I still saw them in my dreams. Still, both Miss Winter and Jekyll were interested and concerned at Holmes's story.

"Well then," Kitty said. "If the good doctor can't get anything out of Fleete by normal methods, then we need to *squeeze* it out of him."

Holmes took out his briar pipe and packed it carefully. "I believe that I have a stratagem that could prevail where the police have failed on that front. It will take some time to arrange, but I believe I can have the tools at our disposal by tomorrow morning. In the meantime, I shall spend the day doing a little research on the Esoteric Order of Dagon and Madam Fleete and that figurine. Watson, do you feel up to joining me just after supper time? That should give you the day to catch up on your sleep?"

"Certainly," I said.

"In the meantime," Holmes said, "I must ask the rest of you to once again keep yourselves here in Baker Street."

Holmes had looked over at Miss Winter, perhaps expecting some objection from that quarter, but Miss Winter shrugged and, with shocking abruptness, stood up and left the room, entering Holmes's room and shutting the door behind her with a loud bang. I couldn't for the life of me tell if this was some display of anger on her part, an appalling lack of social etiquette, or perhaps merely the soporific effect of daytime getting the better of her.

The truth was, the more time I spent with that woman, the less I understood her.

"Stay here?" Jekyll said. "That will be quite impossible. There are things I need at my lab." He stood in order to lock his gaze with Holmes, seeming ready for a contest of wills on this matter.

"I'm afraid I insist," Holmes said, still tending to his pipe. He now lit it and exhaled a thin stream of blue smoke before turning his gaze fully on Dr Jekyll. "Both you and Mr Edward Hyde are still wanted for questioning by the police. As you can see, I have many of the amenities that your lab can offer here, certainly for all the tests that you earlier said you require."

Dr Jekyll opened his mouth to protest, but Holmes went implacably on. "You also told me that you had brought quite enough of the ingredients that you need to either provoke the change to Mr Hyde or maintain your own person indefinitely and we have already sent for a change of clothes for either Hyde or yourself. Unless there is some other errand that you need to run. If so, tell me what you need and I shall have it delivered with the utmost urgency."

"No," Jekyll said, taken aback. "No other errand."

"Good," Holmes said. "It is a safety precaution and shall not last too much longer, I promise you."

I looked keenly at Holmes, well aware that his story about either Hyde or Jekyll being wanted for questioning by the police to be a lie, and a very curious one at that. Why should Holmes require such a falsehood? Still, I said nothing.

Holmes left shortly thereafter and I settled in for another afternoon sleeping poorly on the couch. I had seen no sign of

Dracula or Mina, but could hear the occasional sound of movement from my room and wondered how long Dracula's recuperation would take.

Dr Jekyll did not take to his imprisonment gracefully and it was difficult, with my sensitive hearing, to get any real sleep while Jekyll grumbled and banged vials and glass retorts around on Holmes's long lab table. If the mumbling involved was any indication, Holmes's table was a poor and completely inadequate substitute for Jekyll's much more robust lab across town. Despite this petty and mumbling diatribe, I managed to get some sleep.

Part Three

THE CULT STRIKES BACK

Chapter 09

THE ESOTERIC ORDER OF DAGON

I awoke just before dusk and had just started stretching out the kinks in my back that everyone, vampire or not, acquired from sleeping on a couch when I saw a note from Holmes stating that he would be returning shortly and requesting that I check on Fleete at the police station.

Our nocturnal household was just rising and Mrs Hudson had arranged ample sustenance for our little band of mostly blood-drinking investigators. In this short period while Dracula recovered and Holmes firmed up his campaign of war, that same campaign was nearly brought to ruin when Mrs Hudson revolted, ready to have us all thrown out on our ears. It seemed that blood from the butcher's shop was a macabre and grotesque regularity that she was willing to suffer in small quantities for my own person, but when it became necessary to quadruple our supply, she was quite at her wit's end. In addition, having strangers sleeping in the bedrooms at night while her lodgers sprawled on couches was the last straw. Her first obstreperous objection came from Dracula and Mina in my room, but this was smoothed over by Dracula himself, who thanked Mrs Hudson for her accommodations in such a charming manner that he quite won our landlady's heart and soul. A day later there was another near row on account of the fact that Miss Winter, Holmes, Jekyll or Hyde were all taking turns sleeping in Holmes's bed during the night.

"Highly disgraceful!" Mrs Hudson railed. "Like the hot swapping berths on a dirty ship and that's not the kind of establishment that I run, gentlemen!"

Of the two affronts to decency, I believe the sleeping arrangements far outweighed our macabre diet, by Mrs Hudson's reckoning. Particularly when a woman was involved. Mrs Hudson sniffed her disdain and disapproval at Miss Winter constantly when she thought Miss Winter could not hear her. Mostly Miss Winter ignored this, but occasionally the passive tirade would become tiresome to her and she would fix Mrs Hudson with a glare that sent our landlady scurrying from the room.

The first two days, Mrs Hudson showed a clear admiration for the smooth-faced, handsome Dr Jekyll, but he spent one morning regaling her with the fascinating properties of a particularly corrosive chemical compound that he had created, and how he'd sold it to the government as a useful tool in both warfare and interrogation to fund his other work. Mrs Hudson had been appalled and had since refused to speak to him, referring to him once after that as a 'dried-up shell of a man'. She would have nothing further to do with him. Hyde she loathed on sight and he did little to discourage this, often badgering her with leers and off-colour jests to amuse himself. I do not believe Holmes shared Jekyll and Hyde's secret with our good landlady and their constant appearance and disappearances, unexplained to her, added a great deal to her distaste for both persons. It made for a rather trying time for all of us.

I completed my toilet and hastened to Scotland Yard where Lestrade greeted me with some surprise.

"I just let that Alu-something fellow down to see the prisoner," he said. "I got the impression that you and Holmes were both busy elsewhere. It was irregular, but he had a note from Holmes and… well… your friend is a hard man to say no to."

"Alu?" I said, a sinking feeling settling into my stomach.

Seeing my alarm, Lestrade grabbed another set of the heavy keys and we both hastened down to the cells. When we reached the bottom, we encountered a constable coming our way from the direction of Fleete's cell. The corridor was lit only by dim gas lights so that even with my eyes, I could not make out Fleete's cell door some dozens of feet away.

"Why are you not with the visitor?" Lestrade snapped.

"He said to leave him alone with the prisoner," the constable said with a small quaver in his voice. "I don't mind telling you, Inspector, that man makes my flesh crawl."

The next sound I heard made the hackles rise on my neck. In my time with Sherlock Holmes I have heard some terrible noises, such as the howl of that great hound on the moors during the Baskerville case or the coughing death rattle of

Charles Augustus Milverton, but the blood-curdling scream of despair and fear that rang out was worse even than those memories. Lestrade, the constable and I dashed down towards Fleete's cell where we could see that the door hung slightly ajar, the heavy iron ring of keys dangling from where the key in question had been left in the lock.

The door swung outward and Count Dracula's lean form appeared in the half-light.

"Come, Doctor," Dracula said. "I believe we have what we need here."

I rushed past Dracula to make certain the man still lived, chastising myself harshly for allowing a prisoner to be tormented so, and found that Fleete was very much alive, but unconscious with his head on the table. I assured myself that the man still had a pulse and seemed to be breathing unimpaired, but I was still rattled when I left the cell.

Dracula had already left the corridor and I hastened to catch up with him, but Lestrade put a restraining hand on my arm.

"Be careful, Doctor," Lestrade whispered. "I know you and Holmes have occasionally bent the laws in your pursuit of justice and likely the world is a better place for it. But there are some thresholds that a man simply cannot cross and still remain the same person." He looked at the stairway that Dracula had just ascended and shivered. "Be careful about taking the dark path."

I felt precisely the same sentiment, but only said, "I hear you, Inspector. I just hope it's not too late."

"What in the world did you do to that man!" I railed at Dracula. We were in a hansom rattling our way back to Baker Street. "Lestrade was white as a sheet when we left, to say nothing of the prisoner!"

"Merely frightened him a little," Dracula said. "I did him no injury and he will be recovered from his fear when he awakes. Mostly. More than most as I hardly think the man can keep three facts in his head all together. He is an imbecile."

"What did you discover?"

"The man has truly little memory of what he has done," Dracula said. "It is as Dr Jekyll surmised. When the werewolf is awake, Fleete himself is asleep, very much like Hyde and Jekyll." He glanced my way. "Do not be surprised. I have had little to do except lie and listen and my hearing is quite keen, as you should know, Doctor. I also believe that Jekyll is correct when he says that Fleete's changes come on him as a result of a chemical stimulant and have nothing to do with the phases of the moon. This should be a great comfort as it means that no change will come on him while he is imprisoned as he has no access to the chemical compound. Even more telling is that while I deduced this from Fleete's statement, he himself has not reasoned it out fully. He suspects he transforms into some kind of beast, but has not the courage to face the facts or investigate further. He is also completely mistaken about the origins of his curse. He believes that he was cursed by a shaman in India after offending their church, but in fact I believe it is his mother that is somehow responsible. He is aware that 'Mother' is a fearsome person with arcane and esoteric knowledge, particularly of Eastern drugs and medicines. She receives curious packages, including herbs and remedies from strange ports and strange persons, but has not associated this fact with his curious condition. In fact, he most often forgets this condition, mostly because he engages in as much drink as is required for the task on a very regular basis. He is also aware that his mother belongs to a secret organization about which he knows little, but again, has not connected this fact to anything else of significance. But there is another person of her acquaintance that also belongs to this secret society and *he* is the reason that I have pushed myself out-of-doors, when I would have rather recuperated another evening. He is why I took it upon myself to interrogate the prisoner and came here to this squalid official building."

"Holmwood," I said.

"Yes," Dracula agreed. "Lord Arthur Holmwood."

When we returned to Baker Street a short, rotund person was waiting in our sitting room.

He had curly blond hair, worn rather long and so sprayed over with hair pomade that I at first mistook it for a wig. He wore a long sapphire-blue jacket and a pale green waistcoat, both sporting enough oversized, shiny brass buttons to flag down a ship passing in the night. He peered at us through a pair of wonderfully dark, magnetic eyes. The room was empty except for Dracula, the man and myself.

I looked around behind me and amended that judgement. Not *us*, then. Dracula hadn't entered the room with me but had slipped silently away, presumably up to my rooms to inform Mina of what we had just discovered. I kept trying to compensate for the lack of scent that one vampire held for another, but it was simply uncanny how *silently* that man could move.

"Your landlady said I could wait," the blonde man said, seeing me look around and perhaps misinterpreting my discomfort.

Holmes was still absent and Miss Winter was presumably still sleeping. I could hear Jekyll's soft voice down below with Mrs Hudson, though his words were too low for me to make out. That seemed a strange pair of companions for tea or dinner, the tall, prudish scientist and the Scottish matron. Regardless, that left me alone to face our new visitor.

"You are Dr Watson, are you not?" the man said, levelling an accusatory finger at me. He bustled over to my side and drew me to sit with him on the sofa, then proceeded to draw out a cardboard tube from a voluminous jacket pocket. From this, he produced a series of foolscap sheets. He hooked a smaller table with his foot and dragged it over so that he could spread out the first of the papers in front of me.

"This one?" he said, jabbing a finger at the paper.

It was a series of artistic renditions of many pieces of jewellery and ornamentation, all drawn next to each other so that it was such a jumble that it took me a second to focus my gaze on the artifact he indicated, a gaudy and clunky but malformed piece of gold that looked as much melted as formed.

"I don't know what you mean," I said, more than a little taken aback by the fellow's strange dress and manner.

"This one, then?" he said, pointing at a different drawing.

My blood, vampiric though it was, ran cold.

"Yes!" I said. "The diadem! That's it precisely!" Here, rendered in a close, cramped picture, was the very same diadem that had belonged to the Esoteric Order of Dagon, the same one that I'd thrown into the sea to appease the strange sea creatures that had served the Order, all so that Holmes could return safely to land. To this day, Holmes gives no credit to the threat they posed to his person, but I still maintain that he had been in some of the gravest danger of his career. Still, with the diadem gone, we had very little of evidence so that the entire episode almost seemed a dream. That is, until I'd run across that figurine in Madam Fleete's house that had given me the same feeling.

"Ah," the man said, a long, drawn-out sigh as if he'd been holding his breath for a long time. "You are one of the very few people outside of Innsmouth to have ever seen it and lived to tell the tale and the reports conflict so much it was difficult to be sure." He made a small notation next to the drawing.

"Now," he said, putting that one sheaf of foolscap aside and pulling another from the bundle. "That was the easy part. There will be more guesswork with this one." The new sheet of paper was blank, but he also produced a charcoal pencil and, in a series of quick, competent strokes, drew another, strange but not entirely unfamiliar figure onto the paper.

"Was this what you saw?" he said, looking at me intently with those dark eyes.

"The figurine?" I said.

He nodded.

"It is the same incomprehensible figure," I said. "Something of a squid, a bat and a monstrous man. But it was both not as clearly defined as you have it here and somehow more frightening. The face less fully formed, the wings more of a suggestion in the shadows than this."

The man swept aside his first drawing, discarding it carelessly on the floor. A man after Holmes's own heart. He pulled out another sheet and drew the figure again, this time smudging the pencil lines with a small cloth to make them less distinct.

"Yes!" I said, warming to the task and sudden, impromptu collaboration. "The wings should be larger yet. The head, too, so that it does not quite fit the body, which, too, was indistinct. The figurine was incomplete at the bottom."

"Perhaps a hazy suggestion of water?" he said, smudging a few more lines to implement his own words.

"Yes," I agreed. "I had not realized it was water represented there, but that does look more correct. Very much so. I think that is very close."

"Well," Holmes said from the doorway. "That appears to settle that. Watson, I see you have made the acquaintance of Mr Bertram Tolliver who specializes in the very topic we are wrestling with."

"You are an archaeologist with the museum?" I ventured, shaking Tolliver's hand.

"Very much like that," Tolliver said, giving me a broad wink. "The seediest kind of archaeology known to man. I'm a newspaper man for the *Daily Telegraph*."

"Tolliver is familiar with the Esoteric Order of Dagon," Holmes said, discarding his coat on a chair. "A specialist in his field. He was very excited to come speak with us when I related our story."

"The Esoteric Order of Dagon has a presence in London, then?" I asked.

"No," Tolliver said. "But there are other orders of a similar nature, a bit like different schisms of the Church, each splinter with their own pagan deities and though they cooperate occasionally, there is often bitter infighting between them, as well."

"Other orders?" I asked, shivering at the idea that this kind of cult, and the supernatural elements upon which they were based, could possibly be plentiful enough to fulfil the picture that Tolliver described.

"Oh yes," Tolliver said. "The Church of Starry Wisdom, the Chorazos Cult, the Cult of the Bloody Tongue, the Black Brotherhood, the Brotherhood of the Beast, the Brotherhood of the Black Pharoah – they have a lot of brotherhoods, you see."

"Which of these do you suspect as being involved?" Holmes asked.

"None of these," Tolliver said. "Each has its own pagan deity, you see, such as Hastur, who is a monstrous sea creature, but also a man dressed in yellow and sometimes, a place. Or Nyarlathotep, who is often a man with black skin, who is not a man but a bat-winged monster, depending on who you ask."

"These could be bat wings here," I said, pointing at the place where Tolliver had drawn such.

"Yes," Tolliver said, "but the other features don't match, in as much as you can correlate any data from these kinds of cults. Information, facts and data seem to have a malleable consistency in their hands. A by-product, perhaps, of believing that reality itself is malleable and of little importance compared to their objects of worship."

Holmes snorted softly in derision as he puffed on his pipe. "An anathema to any proper way of thinking."

"Yes," Tolliver said. "Atrocious, isn't it? I'm afraid all of my information is likely to be taxing and stressful to a logical, orderly mind, Mr Holmes, but I shall do the best I can to cudgel it all into a rational shape for you."

"You said that this shape isn't worshiped by any of the cults you mentioned?" I prompted.

Tolliver shook his head emphatically and picked up the rendering. "No, this is above all of those. I would call this one the master pagan god of the mythos, if such words as 'master' or 'mythos' did not imply an element of organization. He is sometimes called Great Tulu, Dread Katulu, or Kutulu in other parts of the world. In the western world, Cthulhu is most often used."

"Is this Cthulhu worshipped here in London?" Holmes asked.

"There are rumours," Tolliver said. "I knew a man that swore to me that an organization called the Cult of Cthulhu was operating here in London, but he expired in an opium den before I could get the full story. Expired with such convenient, or inconvenient timing that I have long been certain that he was silenced, possibly by this cult, but was never able to discover more. I suspected this cult of having some traces in London, but have never been able to catch a whiff of where or who might be involved. That was part of the reason I rushed over."

"Well," Holmes said, giving me a significant look when Tolliver wasn't watching. "We shall have to keep the location of our information secret for the moment. It may be that our patron of the arts has only stumbled into this work of art and has very little connection with the cult you mention, but rest assured that if we discover any trace of this cult we can steer you in the right direction." I knew what that look meant. We could hardly divulge Madam Fleete's name to Tolliver without imperilling our own investigation, in addition to the necessity of keeping so many secrets ourselves that should be devastating if they made their way into a public newspaper.

"Isn't that always the way," Tolliver said morosely. "Even private detectives are not so dissimilar to their official counterparts on this matter. The flow of information goes only one way and hardly a scrap will come to me." He seemed more saddened by something abstract than by either Holmes or myself.

"Perhaps we can do better than that," Holmes said. "We might even be able to make a gift to you of the figurine for your trouble if the original owner can be persuaded to part with it."

"Well," Tolliver said, shrugging. "One can hope." Tolliver seemed to be a man who had seen much of the world, perhaps too much, and many of those things both strange and terrible. It had not left him with a grand opinion of people in general.

Dracula, Mina, Miss Winter and finally Jekyll all entered the sitting room, but it fell to me to attempt sketchy, half-ignored introductions, which no one paid the slightest attention to. Both Holmes and Tolliver were far too engrossed in their subject.

Dracula and the others, for their part, did not interrupt and were content to listen to the discourse between Holmes and Tolliver as he spoke of the Cult of Cthulhu and other similar groups and their many and varied works. Clearly Holmes, and the others, were convinced enough that this subject had more than a little to do with the current Whitechapel Murders. I knew with a certainty that I was.

Holmes had more questions and Tolliver had an expansive knowledge on his subject and they spoke for two hours, with Holmes taking notes while Tolliver expounded on the various cults throughout the world, all linked very loosely, on these strange objects of worship that had only the most nebulous of connections to each other and were similar only in that none of them were remotely human. While some of the cults had presence and history in many parts of Europe, including England, it seemed that the greatest concentration was in America.

It was when Tolliver mentioned a time when one of the original branches of the Cult of Cthulhu collected the body parts of Norman invaders during the eleventh century that I could no longer remain silent.

"Could some version of this cult be responsible for the Ripper murders? Whoever is perpetuating this crime has collected several grisly trophies such as you are describing."

"Ah, Watson," Holmes said. "As always, you cut directly to the core of the matter."

The others leaned forward and Tolliver himself sat back in his seat and stared at me completely flummoxed.

"Well I never," he said. "That is to say, I was so curious to hear what you had to say about the figurine that I dashed over here at Mr Holmes's request and never considered why he asked me what he did." He frowned. "Yes, it is quite possible."

"What possible use could they have for such trophies?" Mina asked.

"There are a great many rituals that could require such trophies," Tolliver said at once. "Ceremonies to demonstrate their obeisance to their pagan god, to curry their favour."

"To what end?" Mina asked.

"To a great many ends," Tolliver said, "in their mind. The grandest would be to allow their gods entry into our world. You see, they believe that their gods are magical, powerful, nearly omnipotently so, except that their very existence, the unreality of it, you see, bars them from our mundane world of flesh and bone." Tolliver seemed to look at Mina more closely, as if he hadn't really paid any attention to her before this. "Forgive me, I did not mean to frighten you by speaking of such tragic and misguided actions from the minds of the medically insane."

I had starting lighting a cigarette and nearly burned our sitting room down by spilling the cigarette and lighter when Tolliver spoke the word 'frightened' to Mina. I saw the flash of a smile behind Holmes's pipe, too.

Tolliver pressed on, seeming not to notice the ripple of reaction around the room. "You have to understand, madam, that these cultists are not sane in any true sense of the word. Why, believing they can bring figments of their imagination to life, it's purest drivel, of course. I'd just as soon believe in goblins and ghouls."

"Yes," Dracula purred, "nonsense to the core."

"I am sorry," Tolliver said. "Forgive me…" He had clearly not caught her name.

"Madam du Beauvoir," Holmes lied easily, "and the Earl du Beauvoir, of course."

"Yes," Tolliver said. "Charmed, I'm sure."

"Thank you, Mr Tolliver," Holmes said. "You have given us a great deal of invaluable information and even more to ponder. I should like to consult you again should we encounter anything further requiring your expertise during our investigation."

"Of course," Tolliver said, standing up. "I am quite at your disposal."

Holmes caught my eye and I escorted our eccentric scholar to the door and down the stairs. "Thank you again, Mr Tolliver," I said warmly.

"Yes," Tolliver said, only belatedly realizing that he was being dismissed without having got any real information out of Holmes. His expression was filled with deep yearning as I ushered him into the street and closed the door behind him. I almost felt sorry for the man, but then pondered a newspaper getting hold of the true stories of even just half the people present in the room upstairs. It was a thought that made me shudder.

When I returned to the sitting room, Holmes was just closing the windows again, clearly having indulged himself in another examination of our balcony and room. It only now occurred to me that with someone unseen murdering people, and very likely part of the surveillance that hung over us like a Greek tragedy, Holmes knew precisely what he was about.

"Holmwood," Dracula said, when Holmes had satisfied

himself and I had closed the door. "Holmwood is at the heart of this matter and possibly Van Helsing behind him."

"There is that possibility," Holmes said, and sat down again while Dracula related all that the man had learned from George Fleete.

"We are behind again," Holmes said, once he had digested this. "But closing the gap, for while our enemy knows a great deal about us, we are finally learning something about them."

"What is our next step, Holmes?" I asked.

"We cannot afford to neglect tonight's patrol," Holmes said. "I will tell you that Tolliver's information paints a very grim and serious picture, particularly the supposition that they are collecting trophies for some mysterious ritual. Now, we have two fears. The first is that they may strike again tonight in order to murder some innocent and collect another trophy, if that is their aim. The second, particularly in conjunction with the double murder and trophy collection enterprise of last night, is that they *do not strike*, which may be an indication that they have completed their trophy gathering. That may bode well for the denizens of Whitechapel, but there is the concern that all of London may pay the price."

"How so?" I asked.

"It's their goal you fear," Mina said.

"Yes," Holmes said. "While Tolliver may dismiss their goals and ceremonies as pagan rites of little significance to the outside world, once one discounts their profane and barbaric nature, I cannot do so quite so readily."

"What do you believe their purpose could be?" Dracula asked.

"I cannot theorize without data," Holmes said, "and I have very little on this matter. We are not even certain that Madam Fleete, George Fleete, or Lord Arthur Holmwood, are connected to this Cult of Cthulhu, only that they are connected to each other. But it is a promising hypothesis. We also know that this organization, or Madam Fleete, possesses some dangerous and arcane knowledge. This, combined with the supernatural elements of our opposition, makes it very unlikely that their goal is anything less than a threat to all of London, at the very least."

Dracula frowned. "We cannot patrol Whitechapel and keep both Holmwood's and Fleete's estate under day and night surveillance. To say nothing of the difficulties daytime surveillance presents to some of us."

"Perhaps we can enlist Lestrade and some of the other detectives in our cause," I suggested.

"I am inclined," Holmes said, nodding at me, "to reluctantly agree with you, Watson. We have let them into our confidence a small degree. Do you believe that you can convince them to assist us in this matter with what little information we can give them?"

"They would do so," I said confidently, "if you asked them." My friend still didn't seem to understand the high regard that everyone in law enforcement, from the lowly constable to the detectives and chiefs, held him in.

"Very good," Holmes said. "It is a danger for them and I hate to put them in such a position with only partial information, but there is no help for it. Lestrade, at least, is aware of the existence of both vampires and werewolves now. We shall have to trust him to arrange efforts on that front. At least there should be a modicum of safety during the day. I insist that we handle the surveillance at night. If we devote a team to each establishment, that will only leave one team to patrol Whitechapel, which is the best we can muster. We shall let Scotland Yard work the day shift."

"I believe," Dracula said, "that Mina and I are very likely best suited for watching the two houses unobserved." Mina nodded her quick agreement.

I wondered a little at this, for I should never have sent my own wife, should she still be alive, on such a treacherous mission alone. But of course, Mina was hardly a helpless and shrinking violet.

Holmes shook his head. "I must stress that the enemy is watching us, undoubtedly waiting for an opportunity to strike. As such, we must always be on guard and even you and Mina, despite your individual skills, must not be alone. Our enemy certainly has methods of moving undetected that we do not know the full depths of and it is entirely possible that they have methods of detection of similar prowess. We shall watch in two-person shifts."

Dracula nodded. "As you wish."

"Watson," Holmes said, "you must stress this to Lestrade, too. Their daytime surveillance must also be in two-man teams."

"I will make certain of it," I said.

"You've been going out alone," Miss Winter observed with a little bite in her voice. "At all hours without Watson or anyone else to keep you safe."

"I have taken some risks during the day," Holmes said, "but

they have been calculated ones, I assure you, and I shall be more careful in the future now that our enemy has become even bolder."

"How have your investigations gone, Holmes?" I asked, for Holmes had been particularly close-mothed and cryptic about this case and the lack of information was driving me to distraction.

"I have discovered a few interesting things about Madam Fleete and Arthur Holmwood," Holmes said. "Madam Fleete has been a widow for many years. Her husband provided a son and then promptly died before George was even two months old, so he never knew his father and has lived under the thumb of his very strong-willed mother his entire life. In addition, the manner of the father's death is somewhat suspicious, though I can prove nothing. The widow was left with extensive financial resources."

Holmes consulted a small notebook and continued. "Lord Arthur Holmwood, although he's now known as Lord Godalming since he inherited the title, is equally wealthy. The Godalming fortune is old money and there is little left after the death of Arthur Holmwood's father except for Arthur himself. Arthur is fairly well known among the others of his social circle, but in the past few years, he has withdrawn, and few have seen him."

"The Stoker book says he remarried," Hyde said cheerfully, "found happiness years after the tragic death of Miss Westenra. You know, after the blight of darkness fell off him."

"I think Stoker meant you, dear," Mina said brightly.

"Yes," Dracula agreed. "You are most certainly correct."

"He is not married now," Holmes said.

"Arthur was a stiff man," Mina said. "I never really got to know him very well, but Lucy adored him before she was taken ill. It's hard to imagine him married."

During the investigation of the Mariner Priest, Holmes had done a serious investigation into the story behind Dracula. That included Jonathan Harker, Abraham Van Helsing, Arthur Holmwood, Dr John Seward and Lucy Westenra, as well as Mina and Dracula himself. He had found that all were real, but very few of the people were as Stoker had represented them. By the end of the affair, Dr Seward and Quincy Morris had both attempted to murder us, but these had been pawns of Moriarty, used because their association with Dracula made them handy tools. Both men were now dead. Jonathan Harker, whom Mina had never married, had also died, but in a rather mundane traffic accident several years before. Holmes had even taken the precaution, vampires being part of the equation, of visiting his grave. There had been stories that Van Helsing, Holmwood and Seward had all travelled to Australia together and there vanished, but these rumours were proven partially untrue after Seward's assassination attempt and death. However, Holmes hadn't been able to get any leads on either Van Helsing or Arthur Holmwood at the time.

Holmes summarized that early information for the others, then launched into his more recent investigations.

"Holmwood had been missing in Australia long enough that his estate, with his father gone, was in disarray and he returned last year in time to set it right. But our Lord Arthur Holmwood has become a great recluse and I have been told that no one gets in to see him, which makes his visit to Madam Fleete all the more interesting. I need time for a few other information-gathering expeditions, but I suspect that the time will come to interview Lord Holmwood."

"There are other ways of bracing the lion in the den," Dracula said, "that do not require sending in a calling card first."

"Very true," Holmes said. "We shall, I think, have to make use of them very soon."

Chapter 10

TRAITOR IN OUR MIDST

We began surveillance on both the Fleete residence and Lord Arthur Holmwood's estate day and night, a task that stretched our poor forces thin as we also reassumed patrols over Whitechapel in the evenings.

George Fleete was something of a problem, too, as any evidence we had to implicate him in the Ripper Murders was hardly the kind that we could trot out before an English jury. That Fleete could be dangerous, there was no question. If Dracula was correct and Madam Fleete possessed the chemical ingredients to transform him into a werewolf, it could possibly be used on nearly any person. In which case, George Fleete seemed a singularly useless and odious man, but also an unknowing tool for Madam Fleete, which put her into a particularly dangerous light. Any woman capable of perpetuating such a crime on her own flesh and blood was an amoral and serious adversary indeed. Lestrade was willing to charge Fleete with the death of the

Shannon family and keep Fleete indefinitely, even if he had no real evidence to convict him.

Lestrade was also, as I had predicted, at his wit's end regarding the Whitechapel Murders and under such pressure from his superiors, with so few leads of his own, that he was more than happy to follow Holmes's explicit but cryptic instructions to the letter. He posted detectives outside the Fleete and Holmwood residences during the day with orders to be as discreet as possible and to send a telegram to Baker Street with reports of any unusual activity. Lestrade didn't even balk when Holmes refused to give him particulars about why he suspected the residents of these homes.

The net result of their daytime surveillance, our night-time surveillance and our patrols all bore the same fruit. That is to say: nothing happened. While it was heart-warming in the extreme not to have to bear the burden of another murder victim, Holmes's warning about the Cult of Cthulhu, or whatever organization might be behind these atrocities, drawing close to accomplishing some unknown, unnatural and ultimately dire goal weighed heavily upon us all.

The four of us, Holmes, Miss Winter, Hyde and myself, trudged up the stairs in Baker Street just as the morning broke as the very picture of weariness. Dracula and Mina had their clandestine ways and had not shared a cab with us on the return. Just as likely they were already up in my room in slumber.

Holmes, leading the way, took two steps into our sitting room and froze. I half-expected some gory mess from his sudden and stiff demeanour, for I could see that he had gone as tight as a piano wire, but when I stepped around him to view our room, I could see nothing amiss.

"Holmes," I said. "Whatever is the matter?"

"Stay where you are," he snapped at all of us. "I wish for no contamination of the crime scene."

"Crime scene?" I said. "I see nothing amiss."

"That," Holmes said firmly, pointing at the small end table next to the couch, "was not where I left my pipe."

"Mrs Hudson has been cleaning, then," I said, wondering if the strain of the case was starting to get to my friend.

"When Mrs Hudson cleans," Holmes said, "she cleans. Scourge that she is, she will occasionally, as much as I prefer otherwise, put my pipe in the rack, but she never picks up my pipe from one table only to leave it on another. That is not where you left the newspaper, either, and the lid on the teapot is askew. Nor was the door to my room open. Again, Mrs Hudson takes care to close it after any intrusion she feels required to make. No, someone has been in our sitting room, possibly through the entire place, and has not taken any care to hide the fact. Possibly, that indicates sloppiness, but I think it more likely to be intended as a taunt in our direction." He knelt and examined the carpet. "There are far too many of our own prints to read much here, but see how there is a mark among the ash that Hyde carelessly allowed to drift off his cigar last night."

"Sorry," Hyde said with a stiff yawn. "Did they touch the brandy bottle, do you think?"

Holmes barely glanced at the sideboard. "No."

"So that's safe, then," Hyde said, crossing behind Holmes to pick up the bottle and pour himself three fingers' worth into a glass. Before he could raise it to his lips, however, Miss Winter had stepped over and taken it from his hand only to upend the contents down her own throat. Hyde, rather than being irritated or offended, only grinned at her. She responded with a curiously intimate bump of the side of her hip against his. Miss Winter was possessed of extraordinary strength, but of course, was not trying to cause injury and the equally strong, perhaps, bulk of Hyde did not move much. I had a half-instant of shock and speculation before propriety made me tear my gaze and my thoughts away from such speculation. It was clearly no business of mine, but my innate curiosity and, honestly, my surprise, continued to clamour in the back of my brain while I watched Holmes examine the room. He finished with the sitting room and then examined his own room and finally disturbed both Dracula and Mina, as well as Mrs Hudson downstairs, before he was satisfied. Miss Winter, Hyde and I had all seated ourselves and sat in companionable and semi-exhausted silence. The sun was showing stronger outside the curtained window now and I was nearly passed out on the sofa when Holmes returned.

"It seems our opponents, knowing that we are drawing closer to them, have decided to investigate us in a less passive manner," Holmes said. "They have seen the blood in the teapot and carefully examined the chemistry lab. If they did not know that at least one of us was a vampire before, they will likely conclude it now. Also, they may or may not be able to ascertain something of Hyde and Jekyll's dual nature and certainly know that we have come to an understanding of George Fleete's condition."

"Who?" Miss Winter asked. "This Cult of Cthulhu?"

"That remains to be seen," Holmes said. "It is our unseen opponent, our elusive assailant with the square-toed boots, that committed our first murder. He was the first in the window and, without the interference of many other tracks such as we had at Miss Babington's murder, I can now tell you that he is smallish in height, but active and values silence, since his boots appear to be rubber-soled. The rest you can tell from the relatively small prints and the healthy stride."

"Of course," Hyde said with a wry lilt in his voice and a small smile that indicated he was willing to take Holmes's word for it.

"But I think there was another man, too," Holmes went on, "who is, perhaps, a match for Dracula's attacker on the rooftops. Pointed toes on this man's boots. Tall, well over six feet and equally active. Of course, we can also infer that from the fact that they both climbed up the building and came through the window without any difficulty. Also, they came in while Mrs Hudson was downstairs and she heard nothing."

"The bastard that did for Genie is the one with the square toes?" Hyde said. Miss Winter, too, had stiffened at the idea.

"Mrs Hudson!" I said, belatedly realizing that she'd been in hideously intimate contact with danger and we had known nothing about it.

"She is fine," Holmes said.

"Unnerving thought," Hyde said. "Being spied on so closely. You had said they were watching us and we knew that they can move unseen, but to have them be right here, in this room, handling the things in this room… well, it turns my stomach, if I'm honest."

I could not help but agree. The fact that someone had been here, in Baker Street, moving unseen, impervious to repercussions or retribution, was a startingly discomforting one. I looked around, wondering if he might possibly still be here? It was ridiculous, after seeing so much and being on this case, with all its unnatural elements, to be rattled by something as relatively unthreatening as this. After all, he hadn't injured anybody, as he had in Whitechapel. He hadn't taken anything that we knew of, or destroyed anything. But it was unsettling all the same to be invaded so effortlessly.

"He is not here now," Holmes said, seeing my gaze and easily divining my thoughts. "After all, there are a great many persons here now with exceptionally keen hearing and smell. Nor do I believe he is a vampire, so the difficulty that vampires have scenting each other is not a barrier here. No, he deliberately waited until everyone had left to break in." Even the phrase 'break in' seemed poorly chosen, since a man that cannot be seen had no need to break anything. He could simply walk in the front door. Someone might investigate the sound of a door opening, but since there would be nothing unusual to see, what would come of that?

Holmes had finished his examinations and now seemed to have nothing further to say and so settled himself down for a nap on the couch. Despite being unnerved by the violations to our residence, I did the same on the other couch. (There was an additional one in the sitting room now, brought in after Holmes had laid his injunction for all of us to stay together.) There was a cot in the corner for Hyde, but he instead pulled a book off the shelves, seemingly at random, then poured himself another drink, and settled down to read in one of the chairs.

I am an old campaigner and as such, have occasionally been woken from a sound sleep by a violent call to action, and despite the fact that I now sleep mostly during the day and stay awake at night, I do not feel that this aspect has changed much. But on this occasion I was not in my best form as I woke to an enormous bang and was so disoriented that while reaching for gun or walking stick, neither of which was at hand, I flailed to such a degree that I landed in my rumpled night clothes, looking, I'm sure, quite dazed. I saw Holmes on the couch opposite me sitting up with much the same dazed look.

The bang, which still echoed in our ears, was followed by a hideous screech of purest anger. A woman's screech, though there was nothing of fear in it. I had the incoherent notion that the Ripper had struck again, this time on our very doorstep, and we had slept through the butchery of another innocent victim. But no, this was not a screech of pain, or the sound of a victim. In fact, I started, as my senses came back to me, to feel real fear not for whoever had made the screech, but for whoever the screech had been aimed at.

We did not have to wonder long on this score, for the door to Holmes's bedroom was yanked open and a large, naked form came flying out. It landed on the floor and rolled awkwardly – or perhaps bounced is a slightly more accurate term – to a stop when it impacted heavily against the couch that Holmes was now sitting on.

"You… were… not invited," a voice hissed from the doorway of Holmes's room and I looked up to see Kitty Winter, rather indecently resplendent in a short, clinging nightshift and with her wild candle-flame hair all awry. I might have blushed were I not too stunned and still sleep-dumb to process what had just happened.

Jekyll, for it was he on the floor, groaned, rubbed his head and tried to sit up, but he seemed to be having some trouble.

Miss Winter slammed the door with such force that it shook the entire apartment, making the glasses and chemical beakers rattle and causing plaster dust to sprinkle down on us from the ceiling.

"Well," Jekyll said ruefully. "Not exactly the worst situation that Hyde has left me in, but it ranks up there, I think, in the top ten."

Holmes, with ultimate care and precision, picked up a shawl with two fingers and dropped it adroitly in the naked doctor's lap, providing the barest minimum of decency.

"Hyde?" I said. "If he forced his way in… under our very roof!" I could not form a decent sentence so great was my outrage.

"No," Jekyll said, rubbing his head. "Hyde was, if my puerile dreams are any indication, extremely welcome. It was I that was not."

"Oh," I said. My flash of anger drained away to be replaced by chagrin and embarrassment.

Holmes, for his part, made a non-committal grunt and rolled over, promptly going back to sleep.

Dr Jekyll sighed wearily and began to try to find some clothes.

I looked unwillingly back at the door to Holmes's room, remembering the beautiful and angry vision that I'd just seen there and felt another emotion twist in my stomach. Envy. Jealousy. A deep, unfulfillable ache for the bond, however tenuous, that Hyde and Miss Winter now seemed to share. My Mary was gone twice over. Moriarty had murdered her heart and soul when he'd made her into a vampire, for the woman that had emerged had shared nothing with the woman I had known. Then I had murdered her body. I had saved my dearest friend, for Mary had been about to kill Holmes when I'd shot her, preventing her foul deed, but I'd killed her body nonetheless. I wondered how much truth might be hidden in between the lies of Stoker's book about Dracula, for Holmwood, too, had had to murder his Lucy after she had risen and begun to prey on children as the Bloofer Lady. I wondered, too, if the lure of human blood, a temptation and a yawning pit of darkness that lay in my nightmare, might one day consume me. Would Holmes ever have to end me as I had ended Mary, as Holmwood had ended Lucy?

I pushed that fear as best I could to the back of my mind and went about helping Jekyll to find some clothes.

While the rest of us were still trapped in Baker Street, Holmes went out yet again, refusing to elaborate on where he might be going.

"I hope to have some news when I return, Watson," was all he would say.

I spent a dreary afternoon, much of it sleeping, while Jekyll fiddled with the chemistry table and took more notes in his notebook. When I awoke by late afternoon, Hyde was with us again, having changed spontaneously, I gather. Which meant that Jekyll, of course, was nowhere to be seen. Hyde and Miss Winter were on the other sofa looking at a book together. Whatever row Miss Winter had had with Dr Henry Jekyll didn't seem to extend to Edward Hyde, or perhaps they had worked it out. I could not seem to tear my mind away from wondering more about my comrades in arms than the mysteries surrounding our enemies – Madam Fleete, Arthur Holmwood, the Cult of Cthulhu and Jack the Ripper.

When Holmes finally returned, he seemed in such excellent spirits that I pressed him for some kind of news.

"I have broken the case wide open, Watson," he said. "Come, I will tell you all about it. Get everyone gathered around and we shall all raise sherry glasses to the final conclusion to this case, which is bound to follow shortly now that I know all there is to know about Arthur Holmwood, Madam Fleete and the Cult of Cthulhu."

This was soon done, since everyone was in earshot and just as curious, naturally, as I was, to hear any news. Holmes, good as his word, insistently passed out the sherry glasses and poured each of us a bit of sherry from the sideboard. Once everyone was settled, he lifted his glass.

"To the Cult of Cthulhu!" he sang, which seemed a strange

toast to me, but I tasted the sherry and found it fine, if very sweet. My tastebuds had changed in some peculiar ways on account of the vampiric blood disease and while I required blood for nourishment, I was still capable of drinking and enjoying many other things. Sherry, however, was no longer one of those. I set my glass, mostly still full, on the table next to me. I noticed that Miss Winter, Dracula and Mina had all done much the same, and likely for much the same reason.

Holmes had lifted his glass, but had not so much as touched it to his lips. He set it down now, with exaggerated care, his gaze locked on the one person in the room who had downed his in an instant.

Edward Hyde.

"I'm afraid you will have to forgive my subterfuge," Holmes said. "In fact, I have not cracked the case wide open as I stated. But I have discovered a rather curious fact. One that I have suspected for some time." His gaze was still locked on Hyde's face. "You see, we have had a spy in our midst for some time now. A spy that I'm afraid must be dealt with if we are to successfully stop the cult. He has been giving information to the enemy, making it easy—"

"That… taste," Hyde said. "You bastard, Holmes! You've drugged me!"

"I have," Holmes agreed. "I am not the dedicated scientist that Jekyll is, but I am no amateur, either, and have combined your regular transformation potion with enough sedative to suit my purposes. I had to be quite careful with the dosage."

"Mr Holmes!" Miss Winter snapped. "This is really too much!"

"You… bastard!" Hyde said. "You've got the wrong…" He collapsed on the rug.

"Well," Dracula said, putting his glass down carefully, untouched. "You have a peculiar way of treating your allies, Mr Holmes. You had better be right about this."

Mina looked ready to chew nails. She had only had a tiny sip of hers and showed no ill effects, but she took a step forward and hurled the rest of her drink full in Holmes's face.

"Hyde is a friend," she snarled. My every instinct made me want to step in between Holmes and Mina, but Holmes's calm demeanour restrained me.

"It is a fair accusation," Holmes said, pulling out a handkerchief and mopping the sherry from his face. "I do not blame you for it. I only ask that you wait and hear all the details before pronouncing judgement on me."

"Hyde would never betray us!" Miss Winter said. She immediately crouched next to Hyde to check on him.

"I quite agree," Holmes said. "Hyde is not the culprit at all. However, he does share a great deal with the actual culprit. I had hoped the change would come at an opportune time and spare me these theatrics, but alas, this was not the case. I had a need to produce Dr Jekyll at the precise moment that I needed him, without giving him any warning, and I was not certain that Hyde would cooperate."

I could see the ripple of information and thought go round the room, almost a tangible thing, as everyone, myself included, realized the import of Holmes's words. It was Dr Jekyll that stood accused. I could hardly believe it.

Miss Winter, not entirely mollified but now willing to let Holmes proceed, it seemed, took a step back. When she did, I could now fully see the change coming over Edward Hyde.

It was, as before, a profoundly disturbing sight. The skin bubbled and twitched, like a bubbling cauldron but also like a thing with its own life and energy quite apart from the man underneath. The body shrank, elongated. Hyde's grotesque face recoiled and Jekyll's smooth one emerged. The clothes Hyde wore had been very loose, possibly for this very reason, but even so the ridiculousness of the too-short sleeves and truncated, but now exceedingly roomy dressing gown was a thing that would have been comic on the large doctor's frame under any other circumstances.

"There," Holmes said. "Let's get him up off the floor, shall we?"

When Dr Jekyll came to we had his wrists and ankles tied to the chair so that he could not move. He woke slowly, but when he looked up and saw our faces and felt the bonds, I could see the anger and then fear creep into his eyes.

"What is the meaning of this!" he snapped, but there wasn't much force in it.

Holmes took some time lighting his pipe before he spoke. "You said before that the potion administered to Fleete was very similar to your own, with the exception that wolf serum was used in place of the black langur. But 'similar' is not quite the proper word, is it, Dr Jekyll? You might have more correctly said *identical*. Having examined the compound myself, and being a first-rate chemist, I can attest that it is quite unique in the annuls of chemistry and quite the mystery. I do not believe that anyone could possibly create it without your help. Since we know that Madam Fleete was giving the potion to her son, and especially since I have uncovered no great faculty for chemistry in the lady's background, it follows that you gave her the serum, and in fact, produced it for her."

Holmes raised a hand. "No, don't bother denying it. I can see from your face that I am quite correct. I would still dearly love to know the complete formula."

"If you've tied me up to wrest that out of me," Jekyll said, "you've made a grave mistake. I'll not share it with any man!"

"As you will," Holmes said. "That is not my main purpose. My question to you is: why?"

Dr Jekyll sighed and ceased struggling with the bonds on his wrists, which were too well tied to afford him any real hope regardless. He hung his head and sighed again. "I've been worried, all this time," he mumbled, "that Hyde would tell you, for it was possible that he could have seen the answer in his dreams. Also possible that he knew nothing about it at all and I had no idea which it might be."

"Tell us what?" Mina said.

He looked up and his shoulders bowed, as if shouldering a great burden. "The Cult of Cthulhu," he said.

Holmes leaned forward, his eyes glittering. "What of it, Dr Jekyll?"

"I was a part of it, some years ago, just before I made my breakthrough and brought Hyde into existence."

"What year?" Holmes asked.

"I joined in 1896," Jekyll answered, "then made my breakthrough in 1898 and then Hyde came into being and I left the cult a few months after. You see, they presented themselves as a scientific organization, and so they were, at first. Ancient tomes and forbidden knowledge, the earliest progenitors of science, you understand. They held a treasure trove of untold knowledge in various private libraries and only by joining the cult, if they would have you, allowed access. It was well worth the price, too, or so I thought at the time."

"You were not with them," I said, "when the Ripper first terrorized Whitechapel, then?"

"No," Jekyll said. "But I heard both Madam Fleete and a man named Griffin talk about it, mostly Griffin. He is quite proud of it. It sickened me, but really what had that to do with me? I was determined to mine their library for my own purposes and so I did. I was with them for two years, no more, but the information I gathered there was invaluable to my work. Suffice to say that I would have never made my breakthrough without them. Then *he* came and twisted the science to perverted ends, and used less scientific means to get there. He's mad, I tell you. So I left. But before I left, Madam Fleete convinced me to make a version of my serum, only she never told me who she'd planned on using it on. I never imagined her giving it to her own son."

"*He* came," I repeated. "Who is he?"

"Van Helsing," Dr Jekyll said, "of course. He came and indoctrinated people, Madam Fleete worst of all, and it truly became an organization for evil."

"Ah," Dracula said, realising the news was a thing he long suspected. He stood and paced, restless and wolf-like, while Mina looked up at him with a moue of concern.

"Van Helsing," he seethed. "I should have known. What of Holmwood, was he a part of this?"

"An integral part," Jekyll said. "At first, he was the glue that kept the organization together, for he was a man of charm, when he put his mind to it. In fact, I think Madam Fleete was quite enamoured with him, but that came to an end."

"Ah," Holmes said, clearly making a mental note of the fact that his theory on the lipstick had some weight to it. "How?"

"I am not certain that Holmwood ever returned the woman's affection," Jekyll said. "I was not close enough to either of them for that kind of confidence, but he was gracious enough about it in public and I believe she had hopes. Until Van Helsing started working his changes on the man."

"Changes?" I said.

Jekyll shuddered. "That poor man is hardly a man at all anymore, and more mad now even than Van Helsing. He came with Van Helsing and is entirely his creature, some kind of hybrid vampire that I don't understand. He has the powers of a vampire, is hideously strong, stronger and faster than any of you, but has no weakness to sunlight or silver. From your description, I am almost certain that it was Holmwood that so seriously injured you on the rooftops of Whitechapel."

"Oh, Arthur," Mina said sadly, almost to herself. "You deserved better."

"How?" Dracula said to Jekyll. "How was this accomplished? Not even Moriarty was capable of this."

"You do not understand," Jekyll said. "You cannot hope to match these people, Mr Holmes. You may be, as Mr Watson's stories claim, the world's greatest detective, but that is a paltry measurement compared to the forces that Van Helsing has gathered around him. He sees Count Dracula as an unholy prince of darkness with magical powers and has collected powers of science that far surpass any magical power Dracula or the like might possess. You must not align yourself with these vampire creatures, Mr Holmes!" The man's face twisted with the weight of his impassioned plea. I do believe then that if Jekyll had had the use of his arms and legs, he would have prostrated himself on the floor and begged Holmes to change his course.

"How dare you!" Kitty Winter cried and stepped, with lightning speed, across the room and smote Dr Jekyll full across the face. He looked shocked and suddenly terrified.

Miss Winter had moved too quickly for me to intervene before, but now I interposed myself before she could strike again. She let out a little cry of rage at the bound man, but let me put both hands on her shoulders and firmly push her back. Jekyll did not know, even now, the level of restraint she had used. I'd seen Miss Winter open another vampire's throat with a similar blow.

A wave of uncertainty drifted slowly through the room. Dracula's face remained impassive, but somehow tighter than before. Mina's face had become a picture of concern, her wonderful dark eyes wide and regarding Holmes avidly. Miss Winter's own expression was a mask of fury; I could feel a pit of concern equal to Mina's that Holmes might, no *should*, distance himself from us and everything we represented. We, the infected, the *vampires*, the creatures of the night that fed on the blood of life, we could not possibly represent the service of light. Surely Holmes would come to the same conclusion.

Dracula and Mina had barely reacted to Miss Winter's outburst. They were still watching Holmes as if, in the back of their minds for this past year, they had expected and awaited this crisis of morality.

I turned my head, too, still keeping Miss Winter in check.

Holmes had risen, pipe still in hand, but otherwise taken no action. Now, he looked down at the terrified doctor and… chuckled.

"For such a brilliant mind," Holmes remarked casually, "you have a negligent lack of understanding about morality. Perhaps this is why your experiments along those lines have had such unusual results. There is a group of people out there, extraordinarily gifted people, systematically murdering London citizens. These people, emotional outbursts aside…" Here he flickered a glance over at Miss Winter, who actually tempered her anger with an expression of shame. If she had not been a vampire, I would have expected a blush to match her red hair.

"These people here," Holmes continued, "stand against them, as do I. Where do you stand, Dr Jekyll?"

"I…" Jekyll looked confused. "I don't know. I only know that both Van Helsing and Holmwood frighten me."

"What of the man with the square-toed boots?" Miss Winter said.

"Griffin," Jekyll said at once.

"You mentioned him once before," Holmes said. "As being proud of the Ripper's actions."

"Yes," Jekyll said, nodding. It seemed that once his secret had come out, he was more than willing to divulge the rest. "Yes, he's frightening, too, but not in the same way. I don't know where he's from for certain, but he sounds like he's an Englishman."

"Sounds like?" I asked, curious at the phrase.

Jekyll sighed. "Don't you see? All your guesses are true, Holmes."

Holmes pursed his lips at the offensive term 'guess' but did not interrupt.

"The Ripper can't just move without being seen," Jekyll went on. "He is completely invisible. Standing, talking, running, murdering someone in Whitechapel, it doesn't matter. He is not visible to the eye. In the meetings where he was present, he had to wear a great cloak and hat so that we knew he was there. Even dark glasses and bandages underneath to try to pass among the normal people. Or at least he used to. I understand he's made a pair of invisible trousers and shirt now so he can travel unseen without being completely exposed to the elements. And an invisible knife, of course. I gather that making himself invisible was something of an accident, though of course Griffin won't share any part of the formula and would not accept any 'amateur', as he put it, to look at his work. Or the results, I guess." Here an involuntary giggle burst out of Jekyll's lips and I started to wonder if the strain of our interrogation, or perhaps his involvement with this entire affair, might be too much for him.

"You'll never stop him," Jekyll went on. "Even if you manage to topple Van Helsing and the cult, Griffin is an independent entity, working as it pleases him. No one knows where he lives or sleeps, not even Van Helsing. The only method of contact that Van Helsing has for Griffin is an arrangement to leave notes at a statue next to Holmwood's gate. Messages written using a code or cipher so that even if you intercept them there is no hope of gaining information that way. They have no way of finding him, or stopping him, even if they wanted to."

"Griffin is not part of the cult?" Holmes asked.

"He is," Jekyll said, "and he isn't. Griffin doesn't believe in the return of Cthulhu any more than I do, but they offered a certain kind of protection. And he committed the early Whitechapel Murders. All of them, or so he claims. Now, I believe that you are quite correct, Holmes, in speculating that he has assistance this time. Certainly Holmwood and, of course, Fleete, though I would guess that George Fleete is mostly guilty of abominable stupidity and lay the murders at Madam Fleete's doorstep."

"To what end?" I said. "Why so many murders? Of what purpose are the trophies?"

"Required for their foolish ceremony," Jekyll said. "The primary purpose of which is to bring their pagan god into existence. Or to drag him, or her, I suppose, here from a strange place that somehow transcends existence. They are quite vague and filled with contradictions. But they meet and hold pagan rituals in Holmwood's country home in Wimbledon. But it is a strange sort of distasteful worship. This was ultimately why I left. Suffice to say that this pagan god of theirs, if real, would upend the regular world order and enslave mankind so that the entire world would be subservient to the most favoured of Cthulhu, which is to say, the cult members. They would, in effect, rule the world."

"You believe this?" Holmes asked. I stared in shocked surprise at the question. How could anyone believe such foolishness?

"No," Jekyll said, "of course not. In fact, I don't think most of them believe it, either."

"If you left the cult, as you say," I asked, "why are you still making a version of your potion for them?"

"I'm not," Jekyll said, "but she already had a substantial supply from me before that. Also, the more of the potion that she gives to him, the stronger and less predictable the results. There may come a time when he no longer needs the potion to transform."

"You say you have left the cult," Holmes said, "but you have been reporting our movements and actions to them, haven't you?"

Jekyll nodded, defeated. His large, smooth face was twisted into a grimace of pain, but there was actually a note of relief in his voice. "Yes. I've had no direct contact but Griffin slipped me a note through the window when I was here working and everyone else was asleep. He demanded I give them what information I could. I burned the note and started writing some reports in my notebook, with a plan to leave them outside the window, but you have been too watchful for me to deliver more than one. I believe you scared him off, though, since you clearly were wise to his intrusion."

"He should have changed his boots," Holmes said, "or done a better job of hiding his footprints. He has become so used to people that don't trust their observations that a trained observer takes him unawares."

Dracula paced. "Your report of the goals of this cult has left me, if I am truthful, a bit perplexed. They are not the goals of any sane person."

"On account of destroying the world and all, with us in it?" Miss Winter said tartly. It seemed that close proximity with Dracula and Mina had somewhat eroded the awe with which she held them.

"In my experience," Dracula said, "when someone is filled with destructive dreams of overturning the world order, it is because they themselves are located near the bottom. When we look at our members of the Cult of Cthulhu, we do not find ditch diggers and fishmongers. We have lords and ladies, some of them with extraordinary powers. This Griffin moves unseen and seems to indulge his whims as he pleases. This ability to indulge themselves seems true to, at least some degree, most of them. If they do believe, why take such a risk? If they don't believe, what is their true goal?"

"A very excellent question," Holmes said and looked at Jekyll. "You said that you do not think that most of them are actual believers in the cause. Are they there, like you, simply for the pursuit of knowledge? Knowledge forbidden or lost in most other places?"

"I would surmise so," Jekyll said. "At least with Madam Fleete and most of the others. I think Griffin just wants to carry on killing with their protection. Holmwood I do not understand except to say that he is Van Helsing's entirely. It is Van Helsing that frightens me, because he is the true believer."

"This is hard to believe," I said. "How can a doctor, a man of science, throw in with superstition? For that matter, even if he did believe this nihilistic dream, what benefit can he see in it?"

"It is because of…" Jekyll's gaze shifted to Dracula, standing grim and foreboding. "Him," he said tentatively. "When Van Helsing lost Mina to him, and Lucy Westenra, so he claims."

"That is a lie," Dracula said at once. Mina nodded in agreement.

Holmes blew out more smoke. "I investigated the allegations of the Count being involved in Miss Westenra's death when he first brought me his case. Stoker's claim is quite erroneous as I was able to establish with certainty that Miss Westenra met her death before the Count was in our country."

Dracula shot a sharp glance in Holmes's direction, but then nodded, as if to himself. Holmes had told him that he'd investigated his situation, but apparently, the extent of Holmes's discoveries still surprised him.

Holmes did not notice Dracula's look. "I say 'her death' because she was transformed a full week before the Count's arrival in England. It was three days after, three days in which she murdered several children, when her body met destruction. Stoker's claim that Holmwood staked her is essentially correct. This has always been a thread of the case that has bothered me, as it certainly seems to indicate *some* vampire was involved, but I have never been able to establish who. The best theory I have is that Moriarty did so himself, possibly to orchestrate the conflict between Van Helsing and Dracula, though I have never been able to corroborate it. Moriarty, if it was he, covered his tracks too well."

"Mr Holmes," Mina said with a crafty smile. "Are you sharing a *guess* with us?"

"Come now," Holmes said with a wry smile and a glitter in his gaze. "Let us keep this conversation civil without resorting to name calling. Let us call it the balance of probability."

He turned to Jekyll. "There is one other point I would like clarification on. How do you know of the secret messages?"

"I found one," Jekyll admitted. "Found one that Griffin had apparently read and discarded. I thought it might give me a way to find him, or rather, let the police find him, for I don't mind telling you it is an unnerving idea, him being around. But it did me no good."

"You join a murderous cult," Miss Winter sneered, "that you alternately assisted, abetting murder, and then betrayed. You claim to be both intelligent and moral, but your actions hardly bear that out."

Jekyll glared impotently at Miss Winter, but had no retort for her accusations. Nor could he, to my mind. Our benign Dr Jekyll was revealing himself to be an odious man with little character. A sharp contrast to my first impression of the man.

"The message," Holmes said. "Did you retain it?"

"I did," Jekyll admitted. "I have it in my notebook. But understand, it is not a recent message. I purloined it before I left the cult. It is nothing but a jumble of fabricated symbols. I doubt that even you can make anything of them. They are not even grouped like words, as far as I can see." Holmes leafed through the notebook and found what he was looking for, a long ribbon of paper folded over several times. Looking over Holmes's shoulder, I could see only a wild confusion of meaningless symbols, none of them even organized into words or paragraphs, and felt the situation to be hopeless.

Holmes, however, showed no sign of dismay, but got up and went wordlessly to his bedroom. He returned with a small bundle of wooden shafts, most of which looked like the cut-off ends of broom handles. I had seen this bundle before, but had never really paid them much attention among the many oddities that Holmes kept about and I had no idea as to their purpose. He untied the bundle and dumped them absently on the table, then picked one out seemingly at random. I saw Dracula and Mina exchange confused glances. Jekyll and Miss Winter each looked equally curious, as was I.

Holmes used a bit of sticking plaster to affix the end of the paper ribbon to one end of the rod at an angle and then carefully wound the ribbon around the rod in circles so that the edges of the ribbon lined up exactly. I could see nothing accomplished by this, as it still looked a jumble to me and apparently was equally unsatisfactory to Holmes, for he grunted softly and pulled the ribbon free at once. He repeated this procedure twice more with different sized rods and then I heard a small sigh of satisfaction. Looking over his shoulder again, I could see that the strange characters now lined up perfectly.

"Scytale," Holmes murmured. "A simple elegant device but easily circumvented if you know the trick. You only need one of the same diameter as the original." Rotating the paper-covered rod, he copied down the lined-up characters.

For a long moment, Holmes studied the new arrangement of characters.

"Substitution cipher, I would guess," he murmured. "Not an overly complicated one, either. If the original language is English, then this should not take long." He retrieved a pencil and several pieces of foolscap. "From the arrangement, I should guess that the dots denote the spaces between words and that two dots indicate the end of a sentence. Really, they would have been far better off omitting this kind of structure and leaving things a bit more jumbled." He started taking notes, copying several of the characters.

"This is not nearly so difficult as the book of code that Moriarty used during the Birlstone case, Watson. I believe I noted then that I can read many ciphers as easily as I read an agony column. This is not quite so simple as that, but neither is it very complicated. I begin to think that we overestimate Van Helsing's intelligence if this is a product of his."

He noted a small group of characters that he'd copied over onto the foolscap: .

"These are the most frequently used characters in this message, in order," he said. "The most common letters in the English language are E, T, A and O, in that order, followed by N, R, S, H, D, L, F... well, the list goes on and it is a quite useful one to commit to memory. Now this message isn't so long that we can rely on this order of frequency, but it gives us the basis with which to form a few hypotheses. There are several one-letter words in this message, which can only be A or I, so that supports our supposition on the letter A and gives us I. There are a couple of other words which offer us clues, since they use the same characters together. Since these are most likely to be E, T, or O, this cements our theories on these letters. In addition, this character appears very often at the end of words, which is almost certainly an S. This word, >⊓□, appears twice, which is mostly likely 'the', or possibly 'she'. Either way, we have our H with a fair degree of certainty. Now that we have so many letters deciphered, it would be a strange thing if we should not be able to solve the rest." So saying, he filled in the remaining words with alacrity.

"There, Dr Jekyll," Holmes said, "is your jumble of fabricated symbols."

> *You are needed for the next meeting. I wish to impress*
> *on the others the need for action. Be glad for the Rippers*
> *time will come again. Use the south tunnel entrance.*

Dr Jekyll hung his head, shaking it sadly. "A very impressive display of cryptography, to be sure, but it changes nothing. You have not been listening, Mr Holmes. These people are beyond you. What extraordinary gifts your vampire accomplices here possess are completely eclipsed by Holmwood, who has all of their strengths and none of their weaknesses. They have a version of my formula and are capable of making a dozen beasts such as the one it took your entire team to capture in Whitechapel. They have Griffin, a force you cannot possibly take measures for. Van Helsing may be mad, but he is also ruthless and cunning and, mark you, your equal on the playing board. You are playing a game you cannot win, and you are playing with inferior strategy and inferior forces, for stakes you still do not entirely fathom. You cannot hope to win."

"We shall see," was all Holmes said.

"This is all very interesting, Mr Holmes," Miss Winter said, "and certainly we needed to stop this bootlicking weasel…" here she kicked Jekyll's bound feet and he yelped, then sank back down into his seat, his face both sheepish and frightened. "… but what is our next step now that we know?"

"Our next step, Miss Winter," Holmes said, "now that we have properly identified the cult and its goals, is to strike back. The message I decoded, as old as it is, makes a reference to tunnels. I believe this may refer to an underground tunnel that allows them to leave their home clandestinely. We know from Jekyll that they meet at the Holmwood estate. Tunnels would allow them to arrive and depart without being observed."

"Tunnels," Dracula said. "Tunnels we could use, as well, in order to gain entrance, once we locate them."

"That," said Holmes, "shall be our very next step."

Chapter 11

WE LOSE ONE OF OUR OWN

U nfortunately, the next blow in this terrible war was not to be ours.

We had been gearing up to beard the lion in its den, so to speak, and interrogating Jekyll for as much information on Holmwood's estate in Wimbledon as possible when the doorbell rang.

"Blast!" Holmes said. "This is no time for company, invited or otherwise!"

Never had he been more correct. Jekyll was still bound to a chair in the centre of the room while Holmes had drawn up, from Jekyll's testimony, several sketches of the Holmwood estate complete with several notes on where, precisely, we might be able to climb one of the walls and enter, from the limbs of a tree, a third-storey window. I had laid out several firearms, including my old service revolver, a similar revolver of Holmes's, and a hunting rifle that Holmes had procured last year, though I had yet to see him use it. We had several boxes of ammunition set out on my writing desk, Holmes's pocket lantern and a dark lantern on the floor. All were present: Dracula, Mina, Miss Winter, in addition to Holmes and myself. In short, no one could possibly enter the room without being filled with all sorts of questions that it would be difficult to answer.

Dracula had moved to the door of our room, listening for any feet upon the stairs.

"She will turn them away, of course," I said, for Holmes had given exactly those instructions to Mrs Hudson.

There was a loud voice at the door, a familiar one, and Mrs Hudson's protestations, and then, alarmingly, the sound of boots on the stairs. Dracula shot me a warning glance and I scooped up the two revolvers and the boxes of ammunition. Miss Winter did the same with the rifle and, relieving me of the handguns, took all the armament to Holmes's bedroom while I dumped the boxes of ammunition into a desk drawer. Mina had followed Miss Winter out of the room, carrying the lanterns. Holmes snatched a dagger off the desk, a small, jewelled, sharp and absurdly expensive article that had been given to him by a noble client, with which he opened his mail, and swiftly cut the cords around Jekyll's ankles and wrists.

Dracula exchanged a glance with Holmes, who nodded, and Dracula removed his hand from the door and stepped back. Holmes had just picked up the map and folded it in half when Inspector Gregson blundered into the room.

I have known the burly blond detective for many years and worked with him on many a case that involved some grisly and dismaying crimes, but never have I seen the man so distraught.

"H-Holmes!" the man stammered. "It's terrible, horrible; tell me you will come!" He seemed oblivious to the rest of us, staring openly at Holmes as if my friend's help was the last scrap of hope in a dark and doomed world.

"What has happened?" Holmes said, folding the map one more time, longways, and sliding it into his jacket pocket.

"He didn't show up for his shift," Gregson said and I realized with a shock that the hardened inspector had tears in his eyes. "It wasn't like him, not like him at all; you know how he is. Never missed a day with all his years on the force. Not a one, and you know how rare that is. It's a hard job that we do, I know you understand that, too, but he never complained."

I crossed to the sideboard and poured out a healthy three fingers of brandy. "Here, Inspector," I said. Miss Winter, Dracula and Mina were all staring at Holmes and I, the unspoken but plainly visible urge to eject this intruder and obstacle to this evening's endeavour, but I knew Gregson too well to consider that now. I shooed Jekyll out of the best chair and ushered Gregson into it, then handed him the brandy.

"Here," I said. "Drink this and tell us what has happened."

Gregson gratefully accepted the glass and drained half of it in one gulp, wincing a bit as the fire of the brandy bit. He looked not only in the grip of utter despair, but also lost as I had never seen him.

"His landlady found him," he said. "Found him and reported it to the station."

"Inspector," Holmes said, and I could see him fighting the impatient urge to shake the man, but I could also see concern and worry in Holmes's clear grey eyes. "Who, Gregson? You must gather yourself and give us a clear account."

Gregson took a deep, shuddering sigh before he lifted his gaze and said, "It's young Stanley Hopkins. He's been murdered."

Holmes took charge then, altering our plans on the fly. He gave quiet instructions to the others on the other side of the room, pitching his voice so that Gregson couldn't hear while I consoled the inspector, but I had no difficulty overhearing.

Holmes sent Dracula and Mina out to the Holmwood manor, telling them that the rest of us would be joining them shortly. After they left, he told Miss Winter that she must take out Jekyll in a cab.

"But," Holmes said, "after we leave, first give him this," and handed over a small glass bottle. "It's our last vial of Jekyll's potion, but we have need of it. He will be much more useful to us as Hyde, and more trustworthy. Watson and I shall look at the scene of Hopkins' murder and see what we can discover and then join the four of you."

Miss Winter made a face, but took the potion without comment.

Holmes and I ordered two cabs, one for Gregson, Holmes and I, and another for Miss Winter and, hopefully, Hyde. Dracula and Mina were already gone, proceeding to Holmwood's home using other, more mysterious methods. I wondered, not for the first time, what those might be. Perhaps they simply moved along the rooftops. I'd seen them do so on more than one occasion.

Hopkins' apartment was an apartment much like ours, though far closer to Scotland Yard. I knew that Hopkins had often walked to work, an action that made perfect sense with such proximity. It lent an ironically macabre touch to the crime scene, however, as the idea that this horrible thing could happen so close to the official centre of England's law enforcement only made an already terrible event far worse.

We had walked up two flights of stairs to reach his floor where a number of other inspectors, including Jones, MacDonald and Lestrade, all waited. All eyes were on us the instant we stepped into the hall.

"Mr Holmes," Athelney Jones said, "you're just the man we want." He held out his hand, but Holmes hardly seemed to see it. Jones withdrew his hand without seeming to take any offence and covered his discomfort with a series of coughs, while Holmes drifted past him to the door of Hopkins' apartment.

I took Jones's hand, trying for a robust confidence I did not feel. "Holmes will find something," I said weakly.

Jones was shaking my hand but half-turned around to look at Holmes's back.

"Yes," Lestrade said emptily. "Yes, of course." MacDonald cleared his throat awkwardly. No one seemed to know exactly where to look.

I followed Holmes and we entered in a small, neat foyer with several pairs of boots lying tidily in the corner. Holmes briefly examined the door, but found no sign of forced entry. Gregson led the way into the rest of the apartment, his footsteps heavy, his hat in his hands.

The crime scene was shockingly easy to interpret, even for Gregson and I. So easy, in fact, that for once Holmes's presence was nigh immaterial. We all knew at once who had done this terrible thing.

Hopkins was dead at his kitchen table, his face lying in blood-spattered remains of what had been his last meal. His throat had been cut and I didn't need Holmes to tell me it had been done from left to right with a small, very sharp knife. Hopkins' face, rendered both inert and younger in death, showed only a look of bloody surprise. The poor man, a bachelor, had died by himself eating a modest meal of eggs and fried bread out of a cast-iron skillet sitting on the table. Most of the food had been tainted by the spray of blood that covered the table. Several evening papers lay by his left hand. To see the young detective, a man that had had so much promise, cut down in the middle of such a mundane and lonely task, was more than I could stand. I had to turn my face away from the sorrowful and gruesome scene.

In the kitchen, which was only a few short paces from the table where the body was, a canister of flour had been overturned and I could see, as clear as anything, the square-toed boot marks that the villain had left.

In all the years I have accompanied Holmes to the scene of innumerable crimes, never had I felt the same sense that we were unwelcome intruders. Here was a man, Inspector Stanley Hopkins, whom we had worked with for years and known casually for just as long, and now I found that we knew very little indeed. The apartment and his personal effects seemed so profoundly personal that I felt sinister to intrude upon them. I had known that Hopkins had lived alone, childless and unmarried, but had not known until I saw a picture of him as a child, alone with a bunch of other children in front of an orphanage plaque, that Stanley Hopkins had been without parents.

Hopkins had referred several interesting cases to Holmes in the past, including those involving Black Peter Carey, the Abbey Grange and the Pince-nez, and had spoken often about attempting to follow Holmes in his methods, though he had not been entirely successful. But I, at least, had never imagined the extent to which he held us in high esteem. He had a rather impressive library for such a young man, including a huge fondness for modern poetry. Among these, we also found several books of newspaper clippings detailing Holmes's cases with many notes in the margin in Hopkins' handwriting, and a volume of my stories that he had had bound all together at some expense. When I saw the photograph picturing Hopkins, Holmes and myself in a place of honour over the fireplace, where someone else might have had family or loved ones, I found my eyes uncontrollably misting over.

"What is the meaning of the spilled flour, I wonder," Jones murmured. He was still back in the foyer as he, and the rest of the force milling out in the hall, hadn't wanted to enter and contaminate the evidence.

I had rather expected Holmes to be like a bloodhound, as he had at the Ripper's previous crime scenes – who was this invisible man, Griffin, if Jekyll were to be believed – but Holmes did nothing of the sort. Instead he sat with a defeated and dejected expression on Hopkins' couch.

"The murderer spilled the flour on purpose," Holmes said with a dead voice. He spoke without looking at anybody or anything. "You can see there are a few droplets of blood underneath the nearest part of the spill, indicating that the blood fell first, then the flour. He spilled it on purpose so that there could be no mistake as to who did it. Not only did he want us to know who did it, he wanted to be sure that we understood he'd done it deliberately. He knows we're on to his identity but it does not matter. This murder is meant as a warning. He's secure in his knowledge that we cannot catch him."

"You know the Ripper's identity?"

"I know a name," Holmes said, still looking at his feet, "but it is just as likely an alias and it will not help us locate him. In fact, as this demonstration has proven, there is nothing we can do to seize him and prevent him from murdering whomever he wishes, whenever he wishes. And make no mistake, gentlemen, this…" he waved at Hopkins, "this is a demonstration, a demonstration that we cannot protect ourselves, and we cannot protect London." He put his head in his hands, the very picture of defeat. "We cannot protect anything."

Jones's face went tight and pale. The officials at Scotland Yard had been forced to suffer, over the years, many moods of Mr Sherlock Holmes. The arrogant specialist, mischievous prankster, the ebullient victor, but never had they seen the black moods that could come over him, not as I had. Jones, and the others crowded in the doorway to the hall, all looked as frightened with Holmes's air of abject defeat as I'd ever seen them.

"Holmes," I said quietly, putting a hand on his shoulder. "It cannot be without hope."

"It's all the wrong shape, Watson," he said, speaking so low that only I could hear, and even I had to strain, standing next to him as I was.

"The world is a stranger, more mystical place than I had reckoned for," he said. "I cannot get my mind around it. If I cannot do that, how can I possibly hope to succeed and bring Hopkins' murderer to justice? Even if I could bring this... invisible man... to justice, what about Van Helsing? Fleete? Holmwood? The Cult of Cthulhu is too well armed with supernatural might. Jekyll is right. Griffin is right. It is hopeless."

"I have thought that many times, in the past," I said, "and it was always you that showed me light in the darkness. Even... even after Mary... and this..." Here I tapped my fingers against my own chest, indicating my heart, the diseased blood inside me, the life of a vampire, everything. "Even after all of that, you showed me that we can still shine a light in the darkest corners. Stanley Hopkins would be the first to agree with that, as you can well see." I jabbed a finger at the picture of Hopkins, Holmes and I over the mantle. "The Whitechapel Murders, Griffin, Holmwood, Van Helsing, and this murder of Stanley Hopkins are horrific tragedies, yes, and we cannot go back and correct these things. But catching the villains that did this, that is where we come in. Griffin and Holmwood and Van Helsing need to be stopped. Our opponents may have terrifying abilities, but that just makes them puzzles we haven't solved yet." I'd been leaning over, whispering in Holmes's ear, but now I stood up and raised my voice. This wasn't just for Holmes's ears anymore. "I have never yet met a puzzle that Sherlock Holmes couldn't solve, once he had all the threads in his grip."

There was a murmur of assent from Jones and the inspectors in the hall behind him.

"Come now," Athelney Jones said. "No playing it close to the vest on this one, Mr Holmes. If you have a name that corresponds with the vile rat who did this to one of our own, you need to share it with us. Two heads are better than one, after all."

Holmes gave a small, rueful smile that I'm sure Jones did not catch. It was a smile indicating exactly what Holmes thought of Jones's little homily. Jones, while the senior inspector on the force, was a far cry from its sharpest, even in my own humble estimation.

"Very well, Inspector," Holmes said wearily. "I will make you a gift of the name I have: Griffin." He stood slowly. "I assume that to be a surname, though even there I am not certain. In addition, I cannot tell you what the man looks like, for I have not the slightest detail in that regard. Even should he fall into my lap, bloody knife in hand, I would have nothing by way of evidence that would convince a jury. I will tell you honestly that I have nothing by way of proof and I have not yet worked out any real stratagem for getting my hands on him. Even the process by which I came across the name is so convoluted, and so filled with supposition and guesswork that I could not possibly give you an account of it, even if I had the time, which I do not."

"You don't hold out much hope for a man, do you?" Jones said tartly. "You say the man cannot be caught?"

Holmes swayed a moment, a slight motion, perhaps a quarter of an inch, no more, but it seemed to me as if I could see a man shouldering one more burden among many and preparing, physically and mentally, for a long trek through dangerous weather. "I do not go as far as that, Inspector, and while I have not yet devised a strategy for finding and apprehending him, there may yet be some light at the end of the tunnel. But the path to that goal is not here, and I must go."

"You don't wish to more thoroughly examine the scene of the crime here?" Jones said, nearly apoplectic with suppressed rage. "Come now! Scotland Yard has lost one of its own here tonight. You've barely looked at anything. You really must do better than that!"

"I have seen," Holmes said carefully, "what I need to see. I can do no more here."

"That's not good enough, Mr Holmes!" Jones said. "It really isn't! I can't possibly let you leave things this way." He reached out to seize Holmes's arm.

I was mortified and a bit stunned that it should come to this, a policeman attempting to restrain Holmes. Jones's fat face was red, his eyes bulging. He looked as if he was ready to arrest Holmes on the spot.

But before Holmes could react, or I could intervene, Lestrade was there at Jones's elbow. The small, swarthy man had a friendly hand on Jones's arm, not interfering, exactly, but distracting the senior inspector. "Sir, please, Mr Holmes has always been of great assistance to us, has he not?"

Jones was a great deal stouter, but about the same height as

Lestrade, and the man had a serious grip on Jones's arm. Gregson and MacDonald, both larger men, loomed behind Lestrade, murmuring their assent.

"Holmes has his own ways," Lestrade continued smoothly, "and they are peculiar, sir…" His gaze flickered my way and I was sure, somehow, that he was thinking of Dracula's interrogation of Fleete and Lestrade's own warning to me about walking the dark path. Then he was focusing on Jones again.

"How often," Lestrade continued, "has Mr Holmes brought us a criminal that we never would have laid our hands on otherwise? How often has he steered us in the right direction when we might have put the wrong man in prison? The Lauriston Garden Mystery, the Sholto murder? Boscombe Valley, Birlstone Manor; the list goes on and on, sir."

Jones grimaced, as if conceding the point caused him physical pain. "Yes, what of it? But he hasn't brought us the Ripper, has he?"

"If anyone is likely to bring in the Ripper," Lestrade said, "we both know that Mr Holmes is the most likely to be that man. We must let him proceed his own course, sir."

"But…" Jones's officious manner dropped away and he gestured helplessly at Hopkins' body. "Something…" he cleared his throat and visibly mastered himself enough to get control of his voice. "Something must be done!"

"Yes," Lestrade said, speaking low but passionately. "Every man on the force is doing all they can. Mr Holmes must be allowed to do the same. We've seen his strange methods prove themselves again and again, have we not?"

Jones sagged in place, the stout but small man looking visibly smaller. "Very well."

I reached out and seized Jones's arm, my hand next to Lestrade's. "We will do everything we can, Inspector Jones. I promise you."

Jones nodded, still looking down at the floor. Lestrade looked up at us and jerked his head at the door, as if to suggest that we should make our exit while we still could.

I led Holmes out of the building.

Chapter 12

BEECHWOOD MANOR

The Holmwood estate was named Beechwood Manor and lay
on a good-sized piece of land on the south side of the river
in Wimbledon. Before I had seen it for the first time last week
on my turn at surveillance, I had imagined an opulent mansion
for the Lord of Godalming, and Beechwood Manor was that.
It was also, however, the darkest, grimmest, most displeasing
slab of architecture that I had seen. Even the garden, buildings
and walls around the place seemed to have been carefully
cultivated in order to present the most drab and dreary display
imaginable. Nor was there any sign of activity. No grooms, no
movement around the stables or even in the interior of the
house, as far as we could tell.

Dracula met us outside the walls and led us carefully and
stealthily to where Mina, Miss Winter and Hyde still watched
from the roof of an unused stable near the main house. The
stealth was a wise precaution, but hardly seemed necessary as

we saw neither person nor animal there. The grounds were overgrown and completely untended and the stable roof was badly in need of repair. The moon had just appeared, a sliver of pearl amid a cloudy sky, when Holmes and I finally joined the others.

"Nothing of interest," Dracula said. "Mina and I have scouted the southern perimeter, on the theory that the southern tunnel that Griffin's note referred to was aptly named. However, we have, as of yet, found nothing."

Holmes gave a brief explanation of Hopkins' murder and the rest went silent while he spoke. The stable was a large one and must have housed a great many animals when in use. The roof was well chosen and made an ideal surveillance post as it had several gables and peaks to provide shelter from any watchful eyes in the house. Dracula had the highest vantage point so that he could peer over and keep an eye on Beechwood Manor while we conferred.

"I am deeply sorry about your friend," Mina said to us. "We *will* catch them. We will catch them, and stop them."

"We must," Holmes agreed.

"Here," Miss Winter said, handing across what was clearly the last remaining vial of Jekyll's potion.

"You did not need it?" I said, looking up at Hyde, who was on the same incline as I was, only higher, with his large hand resting easily on a projection to keep his place.

Hyde laughed, softly. "No, no they didn't. They used an alternate method. I rather think the Doctor will complain your ear off when you talk to him next, and with some justification."

Holmes was intrigued. "Whatever in the world did you do?"

"Well," Mina said with a disconcertingly dark smile. "It was Kitty's idea, really, and perhaps not fool proof, but she told me that both slumber and excitement have a tendency of instigating the transformation. So I thought one of them might be worth a try and we certainly didn't have time for Jekyll to take a nap, even if he were so inclined, which he wasn't. So I decided that excitement was the method to test."

"You didn't…" I stammered. Mina was a beautiful woman, and I felt certain that she could accelerate the heartbeat of any man around her, should she so chose. But I couldn't imagine her actually doing it. Dracula wouldn't stand still for that kind of talk to another man, would he? Could it have progressed past conversation? I fought to try to keep lascivious thoughts out of my head, and failed.

"Didn't what, Dr Watson?" Mina was looking at me with a nearly undetectable smile on her face, her eyes wide and dark, her lashes very long. Dracula was still half-standing, half-sitting a few feet higher up than both Mina and I, keeping watch on Beechwood Manor and hardly seeming to pay any attention to the conversation.

"You didn't…" I repeated stupidly.

"She threatened to skin him," Dracula said without looking down. "She told a story, very compelling, about a servant that crossed us and how we proceeded to skin and bleed him for seven days and seven nights. It was very effective, as Hyde can attest and you can see."

"Jekyll was so terrified," Hyde said, "that I woke in something of a panic myself. Still, strikes me as terribly funny now. Jekyll may never come back out."

"I really hadn't meant to suggest anything quite so dramatic," Miss Winter mused. "Just… you know… thinking out loud." She shrugged. "Besides, we didn't actually lay a finger on him and he deserved a little discomfort after what he'd done."

"As to Jekyll," Holmes said, "I am still, I must confess, a bit perplexed as to one of the additives to his formula. Jekyll, of course, would not give me the details, but it is necessary that I have them and I have been attempting to analyse and extract the precise chemicals involved. I had hoped, seeing as you must be at least familiar with it, that you might be able to review a list and tell me which of these might be possibilities."

I was a little surprised to hear this, as Holmes had not shared any chemical investigations he'd had with any of us, except for his detection of the similarities between the Hyde formula and the werewolf formula. I'd had no idea that he'd been making this attempt.

Holmes wordlessly pulled a small paper, folded lengthways, out of his jacket pocket. He'd been writing in a notebook in the hansom on the way here, which seemed a haphazard way to produce a list of chemical ingredients, seemingly from memory, but then Holmes had a keen mind for details. The paper twisted in the wind that swept over the rooftops as Holmes leaned across the space between him and Hyde to hand it over.

Hyde looked perplexed and didn't bother unfolding the list. "I'm no chemist. I can't help you with this kind of work."

"Possibly not," Holmes said. "But you have spent a great deal of time in Jekyll's laboratory and may have picked up more than you realize. All I ask is that you look at the list and see if anything looks familiar."

Hyde sighed and unfolded the list. Then perused it casually, scratching his furred face while the wind played idly with his mane of black hair. "As I said," he murmured, "none of this means anything to me, but then, I hardly expected that it would. Mr Holmes, you are, I think, still working with forces you do not entirely understand. Also, I feel as if our new focus on Holmwood has led us astray from our true purpose. I want to punish the man that victimized Genie and this feels like an indirect path, at best, in that direction. I believe this is as far as I will travel with you." He stood up into a crouch, then crumpled up the paper and dropped it onto the slant of the roof, where it rolled out of sight.

"What are you saying, you scoundrel?" I said hotly.

At the same time, Miss Winter, her blue eyes wide with surprise, said, "Edward!"

"No," Hyde said, raising his voice. "I wish you the best of luck, I really do, but I wish to protect Whitechapel and its residents and here we are, very far off the beaten path. Besides, there is still a reckoning to be had concerning your dirty trick with the sherry and while I have no sympathy for Jekyll and consider it fair play that he got caught out, I cannot help but feel you have been a bit cavalier with my own person. That I cannot forgive, so I am afraid this is where we part ways."

"Edward!" Miss Winter said again.

"I am truly sorry, my dear," Hyde said, looking ruefully at her.

"I hope you can come to understand my decision in time, and forgive me." His large, clawed hand moved a bit towards her, no more than an inch, and then he seemed to think better of it. That might have been just as well considering the fire that now blazed in her eyes.

Dracula and Mina exchanged a glance, as if they had somehow expected this shocking turn of events, but did not otherwise move or speak. No one else made any move to intervene as Hyde turned, so I reached out and seized his arm.

"Do not do this, Hyde," I said. A grudging respect and admiration for this grotesque, complicated person had built up within me and I found, a little to my surprise, that I very much did not wish him to go. I held onto his arm. "You leave us just when we are most in need of your services. This is unworthy of you, a petty, callous act!"

"Do not judge me too harshly," Hyde said. Then, with a sharp glance at Holmes, he took two steps and leapt off the edge of the roof, dropping out of sight.

"Damn!" Holmes said. "We have need of him, now more than ever."

"A coward," Dracula said flatly. "One we are better off without."

"I do not think so," Holmes said.

"I wonder," Mina said, looking keenly after Hyde, and then at Holmes, but she said no more.

Holmes turned to regard Miss Winter. "You have some influence over him, do you not?"

"I…" Miss Winter's eyes were locked on the edge of the roof where Hyde had disappeared. It had all happened so quickly.

She looked back at Holmes. "I thought so, once. Now, I am not so sure."

"You must go after him," Holmes said urgently. "You must follow him and see if any of that influence will bring him back to our cause."

I thought at first that she might refuse. Her glare at Holmes was proud and angry.

"Please, Miss Winter," Holmes said. "It is of the utmost importance."

"Very well," Miss Winter said. "But I warn you, if he does not listen to reason, I shall thrash him up and down the street until he does!"

"Then let us hope," Holmes said soberly, "for his sake, that he *does* listen to reason."

Miss Winter followed the way Hyde had left, slipped over the edge, and then she, too, was gone from sight.

"Come," Holmes said. "We have already spent too much time observing as it is. But the view up here has been enlightening and I have a better idea of where to search for our south tunnel."

"How could you possibly have seen that from here?" Mina asked.

"Why is the tunnel important?" Dracula said. "There are many ways to gain entrance. What makes you sure that there is even a tunnel here at all? The tunnel referred to in Jekyll's note could be anywhere in England."

"There are still questions to be answered," Holmes said, "and it stands to reason that an examination of the house, done in secret, could yield those answers. We have seen that it is occupied, as the lights clearly declare, but no one has come or gone this entire time. Also, situated as it is, with other houses nearby, one could hardly leave using the conventional methods without being observed. We know that he *has* left during that time, unseen, from his intrusion in our home. We know from the mention of tunnels, plural, in Jekyll's note, that there are at least two, or else why be specific about which one to use? You can see from here that a great deal of the perimeter is rather well lit, but not all. It stands to reason that the dark places should be our starting points, does it not?"

"Yes," Dracula admitted. "That is very clearly thought out."

We climbed down from the stable and made our way outwards to the southeast wall of the estate, which ran a few miles, at least. However, using Holmes's method of searching the unlit areas on the outside of the wall, we very quickly found something of interest.

"Here," Holmes said, pointing to a worn patch of ragged grass several dozen yards from the perimeter of the iron fence that ran around the property. "There is a worn foot path into this drainage tunnel that begs an explanation, does it not?" Just as Holmes had said, the drainage tunnel, dug into the heavy clay underneath the street and then reinformed with field stone, a tunnel far too large and too lengthy for any realistic drainage needs, had ample room for Mina or me to walk in and stand erect. Holmes and Dracula had to stoop slightly, but only slightly. We had gone only a few paces inside when I discovered a bound iron door.

I tugged on the iron ring handle, but it was locked. Holmes was still fishing his lockpick set out of his coat pocket when

Dracula seized the iron ring in both hands and pulled. I could see, even under the dark suit and cape that he wore, his shoulder muscles tense and bunch mightily. The door gave way with a rusty groan.

Holmes, with a sigh, put his lockpick kit back into his coat pocket.

Inside, we found a rough earthen tunnel running towards the house.

"There can be no doubt," Dracula said. "Van Helsing is here, in the house. This tunnel will lead us to him."

I leaned over and whispered to Mina. "When he says things like that, is that a hunch, or does he really have some way of knowing?"

She shook her head. "I truly do not know. I'm not really certain that he does, either. Call it intuition if you will, but he's usually correct." She kept her voice pitched low, too, though Dracula could easily hear us both, I was sure.

"That sounds maddening," I said with sympathy.

"Oh yes," Mina said. "It is."

Holmes had his pocket lantern out, but let Dracula lead the way. In fact, there was no stopping him. Dracula seemed to have been a person, or a thing long inert, patiently waiting and now come to life with terrible purpose. He stalked through the tunnel as if he were on the hunt, which was no less than the truth.

We moved through the tunnel for some time, perhaps slightly less than an hour, for we had to proceed with some caution even with vampire sight. The tunnel declined in places, taking us slightly deeper into the earth. Then we heard the sound of water. In a few more minutes we came to an open chamber, more natural cavern than constructed tunnel, with a small trickle of water falling off natural rock fifty feet above us, down into a small channel that ran off to our right.

"We must be underneath the grounds," Mina said, "where there is some small pool or runoff to feed this. It does not have the scent of city water. Too fresh."

"Quite," Holmes said. "If I have not become turned around, the house is still in this direction, possibly above us." He pointed to a rough set of stairs to the left of the tiny waterfall.

"You have not," Dracula said. He moved towards the stairs.

The stairway was rough indeed, some of stone, some of packed dirt with boards sunk in at the edges to prevent the dirt stair from eroding away. We'd gone at least fifty feet up before arriving at another iron door with a heavy ring for a handle.

"A moment, Count," Holmes said, pulling his lockpick kit out again. "Unless I miss my guess, we are below the house, probably under a cellar, and it may behove us to proceed with a bit more stealth."

Dracula looked as if he wanted to object, but kept his mouth clamped shut in a grim and clearly impatient line. It took Holmes only a few minutes to pick the lock.

"The mechanism of this lock is more heavy than difficult," Holmes said, as he worked. "Next time, I'll bring a railroad spike to do the work." The lock did look oversized compared to the delicate tools Holmes was using in either hand, but finally, it opened with a ponderous click.

"Wine cellar," Dracula said as we all stepped in. Dusty bottles in racks stood all around.

"They have been negligent," Holmes said, pointing to clear traces of footsteps in the dust. "A clear trail, some of it in the last few days." He indicated several other aisles between the racks, which had no traces of disturbance. He crouched. "Indeed. Griffin and Holmwood have both recently passed through here. There can be no doubt of it."

"Can there be no other men," Mina asked, "with square-toed or pointed boots?" She seemed genuinely interested rather than looking for flaws in my friend's logic.

Holmes gave an anaemic little smile. "When I refer to the prints as square-toed, it is, of course, a simplification. Once you combine the size of the boot, or shoe, and the curvature of both toe and heel, along with the general condition of the footwear as well as the man's stride and idiosyncrasies of his gait, I assure you that each footprint becomes quite unique. Griffin's boots are quite worn, mostly on the outer edges, and his steps are a good two inches closer together than Holmwood's, for instance. Griffin also has a slight irregularity that makes me suspect an old injury to the right leg that did not heal properly. Holmwood's boots are very new, with little wear and a great deal of polish. Also, he has a much more even, precise gait." Holmes stood up and dusted off his hands.

"Square toes," he continued inexorably, "were present at the murder of Genie Babington, Lila Emmet and Stanley Hopkins, among others, while pointed toes committed the attack on Dracula on the roof while Fleete killed Luella Brown. Holmwood also killed Ben Roberts and both men were in our apartment at Baker Street the day before yesterday. If we do not stop them, it is very likely they will kill again. Come."

We quickly located a narrow, spiral, iron-grate staircase that clearly led up into the main house, which we ascended. A fair distance up, we discovered a plain wooden door and Dracula, who was in the lead, pushed it silently open.

Inside we found a rough kitchen dominated by a plain and heavy wooden table much-scarred with years of chopping and cutting. The far wall showed a clock and draped window, with edges of the moonlight seeping in underneath the heavy cloth. To our right stood an enormous cupboard filled and covered with the tools of a busy kitchen: pots and pans and rows upon rows of plates, saucers, tureens, ladles and all the like. Several stoves and an icebox stood on the opposite wall, as well as a door that almost certainly led into the dining room. The entire place had a dusty and neglected feel to it. A large hearth lay to our left, part of the same wall that the door to the cellar was in, and a fire must have burned there earlier, but it was now a sunken pile of burning embers that cast little light and little heat, but filled the empty space with the scent of it.

At the table, a man sat by himself, with his back to us, staring at the little pool of moonlight that lay underneath the window. A bottle of wine stood near the man's right hand.

"Do you know, Mr Holmes," he said, "the greatest, most merciful gift given unto man by the grace of God?"

"Van Helsing," Dracula said. It seemed that Holmes's plan

of entering surreptitiously in order to gather information was stillborn.

The man shifted in the chair, turning it partway so that he could face us. "Yes, oh yes, come, children and sit with me and I shall tell you a great many things."

He was an old man, with a fringe of iron grey around the temples and great bushy eyebrows and a stern expression. After hearing so much of such a formidable person, it shocked me a bit to see how ordinary he looked. Just an elderly man in a shabby suit. There was a keen glint of intellect in his grey eyes, but he seemed otherwise unremarkable. Even from here, I could sense that he had a quite human scent. I sniffed, almost involuntarily, trying to discern the nature of his trap, for he had clearly been expecting us. I knew he was not vampire, nor was there any of the animalistic taint I might have expected from Hyde or Fleete, or anyone else who might have partaken of a potion like Jekyll's or that which the Fleetes used.

Dracula stepped forward.

"Ah, there you are," Van Helsing said. He still had a thick accent, owing no doubt to his Dutch heritage. "Kill me now and you will never know that which I am about to tell you. And knowledge... knowledge is the key to everything. Do you not agree, Sherlock? Killing me will solve none of your problems, but will deprive you of a list of your formidable difficulties. Surely it would be better to know this?"

Mina put a hand on Dracula's arm and he paused. But his hands were openly flexing near his sides, his jaw clenched.

"Come!" Van Helsing said, pounding the table for emphasis.

"Stoker portrayed you as an unthinking beast, yes? Of the undead world? Lies, you call them, but are they? Surely you can wait half an hour for my death to disprove him, yes?"

"You interest me," Holmes said, moving forward into the room.

"Yes, yes!" Van Helsing said. "But before we start our conversation in earnest, let me pass you this, so that you might have some idea of why it is so necessary that you talk to me first." Here he took a piece of paper out of his jacket pocket. It was folded into thirds and he shook it open and handed it up to Holmes.

"This was made using your cipher," Holmes said slowly.

"Indeed," Van Helsing said. "But it is not a very good one. Come, you have claimed to be able to read ciphers as easily as the agony column and so I say, prove it! Can you make it out?"

"It is a list," Holmes said. "Of names and addresses."

"Indeed," Van Helsing said. "You had me worried for a moment there, Sherlock. A list of names and addresses. Certainly you recognize Mina's parents? Murray is a common name, but still. The names Watson, Holmes and Sherrinford will, of course, also be familiar. Your families are quite sparse and scattered, I will grant you, but they exist all the same and none of them were too terribly difficult to locate. I also took the liberty of adding the names Lestrade, Gregson, MacDonald, Bradstreet and Jones, too, in case familial sentiment has been entirely displaced by professionalism. You will note the omission of Mycroft's name, but it is not because I do not know it, but rather because I wanted to present a full and transparent threat and to make certain that you do not consider it a mere bluff, and Mycroft's self-isolation presents some few difficulties. It is not that I do not think we can reach him, but I will freely admit that he is somewhat protected and so he is not on this list. In the sense of fair play, you understand."

"I see," Holmes said.

"You note that the name of Stanley Hopkins is not there."

"No," Holmes said softly.

"Because he is already done, you see? Yes, I think you do. The list is for those that might be dead, not those that are. Also, I have no one to influence Dracula on this list, as his very few known associates are all distant, temporary, and infinitely replaceable. The only being he cares about is Mina, who is here. I shall have to rely on your influence, and Mina's, to dissuade him from dismembering me now. This is a risk, I grant you, but a small one since it is only for my personal satisfaction and comfort that serves any purpose to my existence. Your doom rolls forward and not even my death will prevent it."

"This is your plan?" Holmes said. "To use the leverage of our known associates to force us to stand down so that you and your cult can continue your plans unmolested?"

"Dear me, no," Van Helsing laughed. "This list is only my gambit for this evening, so that we may have a quiet conversation without interruption. To my larger plans, you are inconsequential. As am I. It is already drawing near and requires no further impetus from anyone.

"I also make of you a gift," Van Helsing said, "which is this: this list is a copy. The original went to my agent in the field, whom I cannot reach under normal circumstances, who cannot be detected and cannot be stopped. You know of who I speak. This is a man who enjoys killing and the restraint I have pressed upon him, slight though it is, is the only thing that keeps him from killing more frequently. In addition, there is my own vampire project, Holmwood, created through a process of my own devising; injections, you see. Inject a person with enough vampire blood, over a long enough period, and he gains all the benefits of the vampire disease without the shift in personality or the inconvenient vulnerabilities to silver or sunlight, which are products of the body's rough-and-tumble transformation. Space the transformation over a year or so and, voila, you have the super-vampire, twice as fast, twice as strong, with no weaknesses. I would have loved to have him here to demonstrate, but he is quite mad with vengeance and I fear that I could not possibly have kept him in check long enough to have this *very* pleasant conversation. Of course, there is also Madam Fleete and her monster on a leash. Who..." Here he took a watch out of his threadbare waistcoat pocket and checked it, moving without any urgency. "Yes, by now Holmwood will have liberated our monstrous tool, George Fleete, out of prison. An operation best performed while I know where all of you are and now quite complete."

He closed his pocket watch and flashed us a feral grin. "Now, Sherlock, sit down. Best if you take a chair across from me, yes, with your undead legions arrayed behind you, yes?" He swept his hand to indicate Dracula, Mina, and myself. "You will have to imagine my legions, terrifying legions, arrayed in a similar fashion behind me, yes? I know you capable of doing this, a drop of water, if you will, to infer the ocean. A logician's talent, as you say. Quite right. Sadly, I have not had time to install a black-and-white parquet floor to suggest the board, the battleground, that you and I play upon, but that is hardly necessary for two players such as ourselves, is it?" He turned to Dracula. "Or are you the player I should worry about? Certainly you beat me before, but then it was not a level playing field, then, was it?" He turned back to Holmes. "No, I think you are the real player today."

"So it would seem," Holmes said, drawing up a chair, then, as instructed, sat, and began to unpack his pipe.

"Well," Mina said, "I did not expect a warm welcome, it is true, Dr Helsing, but I hardly expected to be ignored."

"You!" Van Helsing barked, making all of us jump. "You, creature, would pretend to be Mina, when I know full well that you are the creature that murdered her and took her shape. Speak not to me!"

Mina hissed, angered beyond words, though the bestial response did not exactly put a lie to his words, in my mind. Suddenly, Lestrade's warning about travelling dark paths appeared in my mind. Was Van Helsing correct and was I just fooling myself? Had Dracula, Mina and I all passed from humanity and entered into a foul realm from which we could not escape? Had we become monsters? I could prattle on about being victims of a blood disease, but did victims run through the night, fighting on rooftops? Did victims drink blood? What had we become?

"Know this," Dracula intoned. "When we last met, you were an inconvenience, a minor obstacle between myself and Mina.

A meddlesome fool, who misunderstood my presence and therefore drew a small amount of sympathy, for you thought you were protecting your own. Now that you are truly threatening me and the ones that I love…"

"Damn your sympathy!" Van Helsing roared. "You destroyed my life! My faith, my love of God and his for me, my understanding of a world, *this* world, as a world of men and women, *for* men and women. You tore all of that away. Once I learned, from *you*, the extent to which darkness walked among us… well…" His voice grew lower. "It destroyed my *life*. I could not save Lucy, or Mina, from your clutches, and then Jonathan Harker turned to the bottle and I could not save him. By the time he was killed by drunkenly stumbling into traffic, it was hardly a tragedy because he had become a shell of a man. Seward, my best student, Morris, they both carried their own demons and it turned them bitter, turned them away from *God*. Do you understand? You murdered *all* of us when you came to England and spirited Mina away to a life of blood and death."

"I did not kill Lucy Westenra," Dracula said.

"Did you not?" Van Helsing said. "Not by your own hand, perhaps, but it was your mere *presence* in this world that damned her." He looked at Holmes. "Have you not guessed the rest, Sherlock? Hmm?"

He turned back to Dracula. "Even as you read of England and yearned to visit and made your plans, someone else in England discovered you, and made his own trip. He was already fleeing Sherlock here and it was an easy enough matter for him to seek out your home and arrange his own infection and immortality..." he turned to Holmes, "before meeting you at Reichenbach."

"Moriarty," Holmes said.

Dracula looked as stunned as I felt, as did Mina.

"Yes," Van Helsing said. "Then he went... *vrrp*... over the falls, but he did not die. Instead, he came back to England and before turning his mind to you, Sherlock, he first arranged that I should become aware of Dracula and drive him out of England. Moriarty wanted England to himself, you see."

"Ah," Holmes said. "Moriarty managed to get himself bitten, without losing his mental faculties and without becoming a thrall. One of your sisters, then?" he said, looking at Dracula. "Then, when he came back to England, it was he that was infected, and ultimately murdered Lucy Westenra."

"The Master Detective learns his lessons at last. Yes, Sherlock," Van Helsing said. "Moriarty wanted to attract my attention with Lucy's death so that I would then drive Dracula out of England. He had the willpower, you see, the willpower to survive the transformation intact and then bend Adaliene, the most tractable of Dracula's sisters, to his will. It all went marvellously for him until the two of you joined forces and ended his life."

I could feel my senses reel. I could not take it all in. I could see the others, even Holmes, similarly affected. Our answers to so many questions, all laid out before us.

"But you have not given me my answer, Mr Holmes," Van Helsing said, pouring himself more wine. "The gift, the greatest gift that God's grace has bestowed on us, do you know it?"

"Reason," Holmes said without hesitation.

"Bah!" Van Helsing said, and made a noise like flatulence with his lips. "A logician's answer. True to form, but unsatisfactory. Logic is only where wisdom starts. There is so much more than that. For logic fails to understand the unknowable. No, the true gift that God has bestowed is the *weakness* of the mind. Oh, for certain, it can be a powerful tool, as the logician has proven." He pointed to Holmes and his voice rose, as if lecturing an audience and warming to the subject. He was curiously like Holmes when galvanized by matters of interest to him.

"But while the human mind is able to write a letter or purchase groceries or solve the occasional puzzle or two, it is incapable of truly cataloguing all the information at its disposal, and this, this is a *blessing*. For we live on an island of profound ignorance, my friends, an island of ignorance surrounded by seas of infinite darkness. We are not meant to voyage on *that* ocean, I assure you. But science, oh yes, science is attempting to build vessels in order to journey on that dark sea. It is not there yet, but someday, it will peer into those depths and on *that* day, mankind will truly discover its place in the cosmos, and we will weep. Weep, and shiver in abject terror. Theology has attempted, too, to journey there, but this is an ignorant endeavour and I am truly grateful for this. For without this failure, I tell you, gentlemen, we would all go truly mad."

"You're speaking of this Cthulhu?" I said. Holmes shot me a disdainful look, chastising me for introducing an illogical element into this already illogical confrontation.

"Yes!" Van Helsing said, pounding the table again. "But

Cthulhu, while terrible, is just the tip of the iceberg, the breaching party for a marauding army. Yet still, Cthulhu is quite enough for just the sight of it, or the merest glimmer of understanding, would drive any intelligent person mad. The Ritual of Opening, you see. Such was the purpose of so many human organs, violently gathered."

"The Whitechapel Murders," I said.

"You call them murders," Van Helsing said. "I call them the forerunners of a new existence. The Ritual of Opening is an exacting ceremony in which the Cult of Cthulhu makes a crack in our reality. Cthulhu can then force open that crack as a child picks at a walnut. Cthulhu, and the rest of the Great Old Ones, will breach our reality and remake it into the primordial chaos that the Great Old Ones thrive in. Humanity is irrelevant, you see."

"Preposterous," I said, though a chill feeling settled in my stomach as I viewed Van Helsing's passionate certainty.

Van Helsing shrugged. "You shall see."

"Even if such a thing were possible," I said, "which I hardly believe, why would you do such a thing? Do you expect to rule over a shattered landscape of ruin and misery?"

"Rule?" Van Helsing said. "Heavens no. I shall surely be unmade with the rest of humanity. Such is the price for remaking the world."

"But *why*?" I said.

"Because," Van Helsing said, pointing a gnarled finger, "of *you*!" He cackled, an unsettling sound. "And you!" Here he pointed at Mina, then finally at Dracula. "And you!"

Dracula had been silent a long time, and now stood glaring down at Van Helsing with his cape wrapped around him, his expression grim and foreboding.

"Us?" I said, still uncertain if I should believe any of this madness. But I could not shake a terrible sense of foreboding.

"Vampires," Holmes said.

"Yes!" Van Helsing said. "We, men and women, are at the bottom of the food chain now that vampires are rising in greater numbers. I have already had a taste of kneeling in their thrall, watching you, Dracula, destroy those under my protection. I shall not kneel in that manner again. You once said, Sherlock, when facing your own destruction as a possible result of bringing Moriarty down, that you…" He closed his eyes, reciting from memory: "'If I were assured of the former eventuality I would, in the interests of the public, cheerfully accept the latter.'" He opened his eyes. "A noble sentiment and one I now echo for all of mankind. Humanity and the monstrous vampire shall perish together, all across the globe. There can be no other way."

"When," Holmes said, "do you plan to perform this ceremony?"

Van Helsing opened his mouth as if to reply, then a wicked gleam came into his eye. He pounded the table and roared in laughter. He laughed while Holmes glared at him from the other side of the table and the rest of us stood in confusion.

Van Helsing laughed until tears ran from his eyes and he could hardly sit upright.

"Oh, oh," he said finally, "you really do need, Sherlock, a better class of opposition. I will perform this ritual, let me see…" He pulled out an expensive-looking gold pocket watch and consulted it slowly and carefully, clearly enjoying himself. Dracula looked ready to burst a blood vessel, if such a thing could happen to a vampire. Van Helsing made a satisfied noise and closed the watch.

"It will happen approximately... oh yes, last night."

I was stunned. "W-what?" While I knew Holmes and the others gave no credence to any true mystical power such as this Cthulhu, I could not help but think of my encounter last year with the aquatic terrors associated with the Innsmouth Whaler. I remembered the chains that ran down to the very depths and evidence, slight as it was, of a monstrous beast down there. Did I believe in Cthulhu as a god, certainly not, but I could well imagine some foul beast lurking in the depths, with hordes of fish-men things at its beck and call, and the images terrified me.

"Yeah! Do you really think I would sit here and spin out my tale if there was the slightest, most remote chance of you spoiling the conclusion? Hardly. We performed the opening ritual last night, using the various trophies collected from 'the Whitechapel Murders', as you call them, and the sacrifices were accepted. Yes, there is another ritual of welcoming tomorrow, but that is a mere formality and not at all required for Cthulhu's entrance to our world. Now no force on Earth can stop it. You have..." He picked up his pocket watch, which he had set on the table, and consulted it again. "...roughly twenty hours of existence left. All the actions, entertaining as they might be, that you or me or any of the others might do, will all amount to naught."

In the end, Holmes simply got up from the table and wordlessly left the way we had come, still clutching the coded list of names that Van Helsing had given him. Even if no one else was worried about the arrival of Cthulhu but myself – and even I could not quite make myself believe it, but neither could I eradicate the kernel of atavistic fright that lingered in the back of my brain – Van Helsing's list still effectively stayed our hand.

Mina and I stood in the kitchen, confused, uncertain, but Dracula turned, wrath like a sea storm on his face, glaring at Van Helsing, who looked back with unabashed and unafraid curiosity, as if any action that Dracula could take, including Van Helsing's own murder, was of only mild consequence.

Perhaps it was.

"No!" Mina said, seizing Dracula's arm. "No! My mother, my father! It is bad enough that I can never see them again, to know that I was the cause of their destruction when I could have prevented it. Please, my love. My entire family! Killing Van Helsing does nothing for us! We need to make certain they are safe. Them and the others!"

Dracula's eyes were black, his expression empty and monstrous. He looked down at Mina and I feared he would strike her then, but then something softened in his face and he nodded.

"Very well, my love," he said. But he shot one backward glance at Van Helsing and I shivered and knew that Mina had only delayed Van Helsing's doom, perhaps just for a few days. Dracula's look said, more clearly than any long-winded declaration, that he would return and there would be a reckoning. They stood looking at each for a moment that stretched out, the almost jovial face of Abraham Van Helsing and the stern mask of remorseless revenge that Dracula's face had become.

But Dracula let Mina lead him through the door and I had no choice but to follow.

We followed Holmes silently down the stairs and out through the tunnel. At first, I beseeched him to turn back around, to plan our next moves, to do anything but trudge wearily in defeat. But Holmes would not answer.

"You cannot believe his mad tale!" I fumed. "Even if you do, you cannot think that we are defeated, that we should stop even trying! We need to protect our friends, Mina's family! We need to find out if George Fleete has been broken out of prison, and if so, track him down before there are more victims."

We emerged into the wan moonlight of the street and still Holmes kept walking and would not answer. In despair, I realized that while we were all following Holmes, he seemed to be wandering aimlessly and not heading towards any likely spot from which we could get a cab back to Baker Street.

Dracula strode forward and seized Holmes's arm. "That was a colossal waste of time. Did we go there to end the threat that Van Helsing represents to the world—"

"Exact revenge, you mean," I snapped.

Dracula waved my protest away, still focusing on Holmes. "It is the result that matters and we achieved nothing this evening. We accomplish nothing out here. We cannot allow ourselves to become paralyzed by Van Helsing's threats. Take this list, Holmes, and dispatch what agents you can to protect those named. You shall have a full day to secure their safety. Then, Mina and I shall come back tomorrow night and eliminate Van Helsing as a threat once and for all. After, we can regroup and do something about Fleete, Holmwood, Griffin." His eyes flashed, even in the half-light, and his tone grew even more acidic. "To simply wander the streets, to despair and wail and do nothing is not the act of a leader, but of an imbecile. One I will no longer follow."

"Griffin," Holmes said listlessly. "Nothing can be done while this invisible man dogs our trail." He wasn't looking at Dracula, and in fact, barely seemed to notice the Count's hand on his arm. He mumbled, as if to himself. "He would see everything and then it would become child's play for Van Helsing to thwart our every move."

My heart sank. Holmes had been under extraordinary stress with this case, working round the clock, barely eating, with minimal access to his own room or any place to get any decent sleep. Van Helsing's threats and plans and countermeasures had been the final straw and my friend's magnificent brain had clearly snapped under the pressure. If Dracula and Mina were to leave us now, after Hyde's desertion, I could imagine no way to stop Van Helsing's powerful coterie. We would all be doomed.

Dracula let Holmes's arm go with fury and disgust, clearly coming to the same conclusion as I had about Holmes's mental collapse. We had wandered into a crossroads with high stone walls on three sides and the beginnings of a dirt road in front of us and a bright pool of yellow light from two street lanterns overhead.

Dracula turned to me. "Your friend is not well. Take him home. Mina and I will go back inside and do what must be done." Mina looked uncertain as to the Count's plan and had stopped, staring back the way we had come uncertainly.

"We can do nothing," Holmes murmured. "While the invisible man dogs our trail." I stood between Holmes and Dracula, ready to protect my friend from the Count's fury, if necessary. I put my hand on Holmes's arm, as he seemed ready to wander aimlessly.

A shriek split the air from somewhere behind us and Holmes immediately stiffened and turned, all indecision dropping away from him as if by magic.

"Got him!" a voice cried out, and I recognized it as Miss Winter's. I did not completely understand what was happening, but never did I find myself so glad to hear her voice.

Miss Winter and Hyde stepped into the street a few houses away in the direction we'd come. Hyde was performing what looked like a curious pantomime, his hands clenched in front of him, dancing in a peculiar shuffling gait. It hit me like a thunderbolt!

Hyde and Miss Winter had caught the invisible man, and Hyde now had him in his powerful grip. He marched his unseen prisoner in our direction and I saw a smile split Mina's worried countenance.

"I thought I heard something," she murmured.

Dracula smiled his thin, dangerous smile. "A ruse? This was all a ruse and you did not see fit to inform us?"

"Forgive me, Count," Holmes said, not very contritely, "but there was no telling what Griffin might overhear, might see, if we could not detain him. We could, as I said, do nothing while he dogged our trail, and so it became paramount for us to apprehend him. You point out, Watson, and quite correctly, that Van Helsing's real threat was the unstoppable murder of those most dear to us. Now we have seized the tool Van Helsing would use to perform that service."

"Hyde's desertion was part of your plan, too?" I said.

"Yes," Holmes said. He raised his voice to address Hyde as he and Miss Winter drew close. "I must say, you played your role masterfully."

"You gave me every motivation," Hyde said. "I've been wanting to lay my hands on this monster from the very start. You were right, of course, he was too slippery a character, too cautious, to successfully hunt while he was on his guard. Once he thought we were out of the picture and with you providing such an interesting distraction, sneaking up on the ultimate sneak became a much easier task. It took both Kitty and I to get the job done, as you suspected, no doubt."

"You could have told me what we were up to," Miss Winter said tartly. "I near took Edward's head off before he had a chance to explain your plan."

"My apologies," Holmes said, "but it was necessary to avoid Griffin hearing or reading our plan at all costs. I rather thought that he'd feel the need to follow us inside. I confirmed this on our way out from the footprints. Van Helsing's plan was to discourage us and fill us with despair and it seemed easiest to play that part until Hyde and Miss Winter saw us exit and had a chance to follow and pick up Griffin's trail."

"You bastard!" another voice, which must have been Griffin, wailed.

"Shut up, you!" Hyde said and thumped him, none too gently, in what was probably the liver area. I heard a deep, pained gasp and Griffin kept silent. "There's more where that came from," Hyde growled. "You killed a friend of mine, remember?"

I could see that Griffin seemed to be of relatively short stature, based on the height of Hyde's right hand, which looked to be large enough to completely encircle Griffin's invisible throat.

"There is also Stanley Hopkins to answer for," Holmes said darkly.

"Here is an interesting item," Miss Winter said. "It was the devil to find, but I heard it hit the pavement when he dropped it." She handed over something I could not see. "Be careful," Miss Winter said. "Here is the handle; the other end is very sharp."

"The knife that killed Genie Babington," Holmes said, "and Stanley Hopkins. Just the dimensions I expected. And invisible, no less."

"Invisible clothes, too," Hyde said. "Coat and trousers and boots, which seems better than running starkers around London in the night. He had a hat, too, but that was lost when we grabbed him. Probably be a curious thing if someone trips over it, to be sure."

"He fought like a viper," Miss Winter said, "only Edward wouldn't let go." She looked at Hyde with shining eyes. Her fury at his departure had vanished now and her admiration was clear. Even with everything else that was going on, a jealous flood of emotion pained me. My own Mary was gone and I had little hope of another woman ever looking at me as Miss Winter did with Hyde. Then something else occurred to me.

"That list!" I said, recalling Holmes handing the paper to Hyde on the chapel roof. "You proposed your plan on paper so that you would not be overheard. It being night-time, and on the rooftop, the likelihood of it being read over Hyde's shoulder was minimal."

"Just so," Holmes agreed.

"You can fish it out of my pocket, if you like, Doctor," Hyde said. "My hands are occupied just now."

I did so. The note said:

> We must find Griffin. Our best hope is if you and Miss Winter hunt him while he follows us. It will require subterfuge, as we are likely being listened to now. You must pretend to break with our group and leave. He follows us now, but it should be easier to pick him up as we depart Beechwood. Hopefully, we can persuade Miss Winter to follow and the two of you can corral our man.

"Now then," Holmes said, wrapping up the invisible knife in a handkerchief and staring intently at the place where Hyde held our invisible fugitive. "Let us find a quiet place to talk."

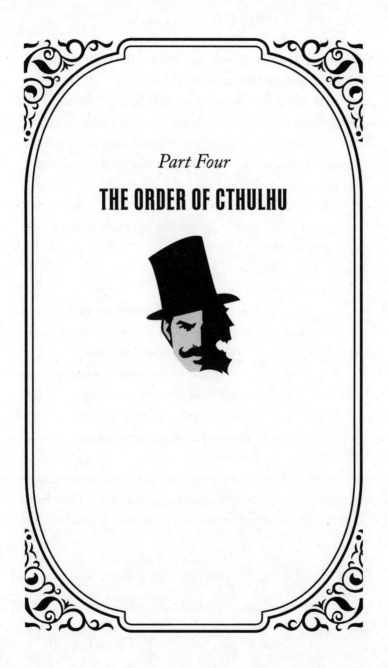

Part Four

THE ORDER OF CTHULHU

Chapter 13

THE INVISIBLE MAN

It took some planning even to get back to Baker Street, for taking Griffin, the Invisible Man, back to our home presented serious difficulties.

First, we had to make our way to a main thoroughfare, for Beechwood Manor was not on the most well-travelled of roads. This exercise alone set my nerves on edge, for the spectacle of Hyde propelling our invisible prisoner along was both comical and disconcerting. When we reached the main road, it was just busy enough that a large group such as ours drew attention and we were forced to close ranks around Hyde and Griffin in order to shield them from view.

We overcame the next obstacle with the simple ruse of having Miss Winter, Mina and I hail a four-wheeler and then pretend to have a great row in order to keep the cabbie's attention on the three of us while Holmes, Dracula and Hyde hustled Griffin inside.

"Just so you know," I heard Hyde growl under his breath just before we did so, "Holmes wants you alive, but I'm not so picky. One peep out of you and I'll be just as happy breaking your neck here and now and leaving your body in the street for pedestrians to puzzle over. One peep."

The threat must have landed in fertile soil, or perhaps Griffin did not have the disposition for a truly dangerous risk once his position was revealed, for he was silent the entire trip, which was a cramped affair with seven of us inside.

Once arriving at Baker Street, a similar diversion was necessary to get Griffin out of the four-wheeler and through our front door, but that was by no means difficult and both Mina and Miss Winter played the parts of arguing and strident divas to perfection.

On in our rooms in Baker Street, Holmes placed the invisible knife, still wrapped in his handkerchief, into a drawer in his desk, which he then locked. He then sent a telegram, though he would not reveal the contents. However, his plans and stratagems having been fully redeemed, no one demurred.

Of course, most of us were too intent on our prisoner. Both Hyde and Dracula clearly chafed to handle the interrogation, but an interrogation was hardly necessary. Griffin, in an agitated, quavering voice, claimed that he was eager to tell his tale. First, Holmes insisted on loaning Griffin clothes. The man, of course, had his own invisible garb, but the idea of addressing a *partially* visible man seemed infinitely preferable to our present situation.

Holmes occupied himself throughout the delay by rifling in quick succession through the mail.

"Ah," he said to the room at large. "Here are several urgent telegrams from Lestrade. It seems Van Helsing was telling the truth and George Fleete is quite free. At least no one was injured. It seems someone snuck in some of the potion and he burst right through the bars on his window and was gone. Back to Beechwood Manor, I expect. All our chickens in one roost."

"Snuck in a potion, you say?" I said. I glared at the spot where Hyde held Griffin. "Did you have anything to do with this?"

"Not I," Griffin said. "But you underestimate Madam Fleete, who needs no help from me. She is a witch with all manner of cunning brews and concoctions and is quite ruthless. Such a matter would be simple enough for her, though I can give you no details as she was very careful to keep her secrets. I just know she is extremely dangerous, even without her puppet son."

Holmes looked at another telegram and seemed to find that satisfactory, though he did not elaborate. He did, however, call Mrs Hudson to send for a messenger so that he could dispatch a telegram of his own.

Needless to say, none of us were foolish enough to allow Griffin to change in private, so we went through the strange pantomime of allowing him to dress in our sitting room with Hyde's hand restraining him the entire time. First, he removed his own invisible clothes, handing them over to me, where I carefully hung them on a clothes rod and then draped one of my own robes over his coat and trousers in order to make the ensemble easier to locate. His shoes and socks we treated similarly, placing them in a bag. The process of handling things that could be clearly felt, but not seen, gave a surreal quality to the entire procedure. My sense of propriety also felt injured at the idea of a man, invisible or otherwise, standing nude in our sitting room while men and women stood about, but our sitting room had already seen so much strangeness in this case, this event was only one more in a constant chain.

Finally, garbed in my trousers, shirt and socks, with a bowler hat of mine and the purple dressing gown of Holmes's, we could now see for ourselves that Griffin was a slight man, but seemed in good physical condition for his age, which Griffin claimed was nearly forty.

"Oh wait," Griffin said. "One final touch, if you please. Dr Watson, you will find in the inside jacket of my coat a pair of dark glasses wrapped in a handkerchief."

Fearing some desperate ploy, I carefully groped in his jacket pocket and found the object exactly as described. Watching my own hand disappear up to the wrist as I reached into the coat was a strange experience and one I would not care to repeat. But I withdrew the bundle, which appeared out of thin air in my newly rediscovered hand, and I handed it to Holmes, who examined them before handing them over.

"Thank you," Griffin said. "Experience has taught me that it can help enormously for others to have a representation of the eyes, the human gaze, to talk to." Griffin had a flat, oily voice now, seemingly at perfect ease. While only the general shape of his head was defined by the hat and glasses, my imagination constructed a pinched, ferrety face to go with his small frame and diabolical deeds.

"Ah," Holmes said, snatching an official-looking file of papers off the sideboard.

"Mr Ezra Griffin," Holmes said after flipping to the first page, "was born in the village of Iping with the genetic defect of albinism."

"Mr Holmes," Griffin's voice said. "You astonish me. I had no idea that you knew who I was."

I could feel the astonishment on my own face, as well, and saw it mirrored in the others around me.

"It is my business to know things," Holmes said, waving the folder. "But I was fortunate enough to find someone else who did know a great many details, once I supplied them with the proper questions. Acquiring your surname from Jekyll was helpful, but hardly necessary, which was just as well, for I had concerns that Griffin might have been an alias. I was certain that someone with your proclivities and necessary background would have committed certain deeds before the world even heard about Jack the Ripper. However, I found that when I cross-referenced such crimes with the correct schools, schools that offer serious scientific curriculums, a Griffin matched my criteria. So, somewhat to my surprise, we confirm that Griffin is your actual surname and see that you studied medicine for a brief time, but then left medicine in order to devote yourself to the study of chemistry and optics. So far this all fits."

Holmes shuffled the papers and went on. "You then managed, partly by accident, to invent a chemical compound capable of rendering flesh invisible. You had left Iping before, leaving behind no friends and family since your father was unknown and your mother passed in due course, but you returned to Iping after your discovery and had several altercations there while trying to find a way to reverse your process. You were unsuccessful. You eventually were discovered and forced to flee, but not before you assaulted several of the townsfolk, even shooting one Colonel Adye, the Port Burdock Chief of Police. One man," Holmes consulted his letter, "Benjamin Rice, died of wounds you inflicted with an iron crowbar. It was thought you perished in Iping, as well, torn apart by an outraged mob. But it seemed this body wasn't as completely invisible as I knew you to be. It is both the opinion of the government agent suppling this information, and my own, that this is more likely a tramp you enlisted by the name of Thomas Marvel. You had either an imperfect or insufficient amount of your invisibility agent left for the process?"

"Yes," Griffin said nervously. "My lab was destroyed and I wasn't able to make any more for quite some time, and then even only at great expense. What's this about the government?"

"Their assistance was necessary," Holmes said cryptically. I thought of Mycroft Holmes's position in the government and his astonishing ability to correlate seemingly unrelated parcels of information and felt that I had a pretty good idea who the government agent Holmes referred to was.

"Yes," Griffin said. "I was unable to reverse it, but did have enough of the chemicals required to change Marvel against his will. They caught him, instead of me. Of course, I drugged him to facilitate that. They thought it was me and I escaped." He seemed very proud of his actions, paying no attention to the clear revulsion that everyone around him showed.

"They lost track of you," Holmes went on, "for a long time

after that and were not aware that you had come to London and begun an association with the Fleetes and the Cult of Cthulhu until I informed them. Later, you initiated the first Whitechapel Murders, did you not?"

"Well," Griffin said. "You seem to know so much that it seems I might as well fill in the few remaining gaps. Yes. Yes, I did."

"Why?"

Griffin laughed, a nasal chilling, sound. "Why not? I was bored. Frustrated, angry. I had expected the Cult's library to assist me in refining my discovery, but it was mostly esoteric nonsense and mystical drivel. Oh, there were a few useful volumes, I suppose, but only a few. Also, Fleete and a few of the others, most of them are elderly or dead now, performed that foolish opening ritual every year and needed human organs to make it seem serious, I guess, to their gods. So I had their blessing and financial assistance. They were willing to pay a pretty penny for a liver or a spleen and who was I to turn away their money?"

"Why women?" Holmes asked. "Why Whitechapel?"

"Easy targets," Griffin said. "Poor, neglected by society, easier to manhandle. I didn't want to take too many risks wrestling with some beefy farmer. Especially in the nude."

Miss Winter made a low noise, something between a moan and a growl. Meanwhile, Mina was holding Holmes's jack knife and transfixing Griffin with a narrowed gaze. I nearly expected one of either of them to have done with it and dispatch our prisoner despite Holmes's wishes. In fact, I could hardly blame them. I myself felt a severe loathing for the man, more intense than I can remember ever having with the many other murderers and cutpurses Holmes and I had dealt with in the past. Dracula looked impassive, but I could see that Hyde felt much the same. Ironic, a small hindmost portion of my brain noted, since I'd once felt a similar loathing for him, but this had been merely on account of his primitive manners. With Griffin, however, I felt certain it was fully deserved.

"Then the murders stopped," Holmes said. "Why?"

"Nearly got caught," Griffin said. "This was before I'd managed to create invisible clothing or a weapon and a Jewish butcher nearly disembowelled me when he saw a floating knife and struck out in panic. After that, I restrained myself."

"Later," Holmes went on, "Dr Jekyll became a member of that same organization, for much the same reasons."

"That ponce," Griffin said. "Never was there a man less deserving of scientific progress."

"You did not get along, then?"

"No."

"Then Van Helsing and Holmwood came into the fold after that and a great many things changed."

"Oh yes," Griffin said, and now his voice oozed with enthusiasm. "He showed me that my methods of experimentation had been relying as much upon haphazard luck as scientific method. With his refinements, I was able to expand on my discovery and make the clothes and the weapon, as you see. Well…" he chuckled, amused at his own puerile joke.

"Then you resumed the Whitechapel Murders," Holmes said.

"Yes," Griffin agreed. "I was much better equipped. Fleete, and now Van Helsing, wanted to perform the opening rituals again, convinced that somehow the stars or dimensions or chicken entrails were all better aligned."

"Then you do not believe in Cthulhu or the Great Old Ones?" I asked.

"Lord, no!" Griffin said with a laugh. "But I don't need to. Van Helsing, Holmwood and the Fleetes are bad enough. They think the end of the world is a grand plan. Destroy the entire world before it's run over with vampires and humanity has to kneel to them. You have to understand that Van Helsing was driven mad by his encounter with you, Count." His bowler hat tipped in Dracula's direction. "His failure to contain you, I mean. But him being mad makes him more dangerous, not less. He and the Cult continue to amass scientific and mystical power while working to cause the end of the world in order to bring the vampire low with all the rest. The latter may never happen, but there's no stopping them on the former. Not even with the extraordinary persons you have here."

"That's curious," Holmes said with a twinkle in his eye. "Van Helsing said that we would never be able to stop you, but here we are. Now, why the cipher? Van Helsing implied that you created it."

I couldn't quite remember Van Helsing saying that, but then remembered what he *did* say, which was that it wasn't a very good cipher and understood Holmes's reasoning.

"Yes," Griffin said. "I didn't trust most of the busybodies in the cult and wasn't sure that I trusted Van Helsing, if I'm honest. This gave me an excuse to take their money, but also get out from under their control. I moved my quarters and lab to a secret location and kept in contact with Van Helsing and the rest of the cult through coded message."

"Quite," Holmes said. "What of this Holmwood?" He looked at Dracula.

Dracula gave the mildest of shrugs. "I know little more than you know. He seemed much like any other man when I first met him. Dull, rich, ineffectual. We have discussed what happened to Lucy Westenra and it was, I understand, Holmwood that drove in the final stake, so he must have discovered his mettle. I cannot say any more about him."

"Oh, he's a mad hatter and no mistake," Griffin said. "But Van Helsing infected him gradually, so that he did not go through the same transformation that vampires normally go through; he was never a feral beast like the rest of you."

I felt a rush of shame as Griffin's words, completely true, struck me, and saw a similar flash of shame in Miss Winter's eyes. Dracula and Mina, however, showed none of this feeling.

"But he's mad all the same," Griffin continued. "With power. He's completely unstoppable and he knows it. Kills for fun. I stay well clear of him and you'll do the same if you know what's best for you."

"Well," Holmes said. "I think that is clear enough. It is about time anyway."

"Time for what?" Hyde and Griffin asked in unison. Griffin's voice had a quavering note to it.

Heavy, ponderous footsteps came up the stairs and the door to our sitting room opened to admit the corpulent figure of Mycroft

Holmes. Undoubtedly, the recipient of Holmes's telegram was now clear and there seemed to be little need for explanation between the two brothers.

The elder Holmes surveyed the room with a pair of watery grey eyes filled with introspection, which he mopped briefly with a sapphire handkerchief. While he did so, two beefy men in identical suits and bowler hats appeared in the hall behind him. From the scuffling and sounds on the steps, I thought it might be more like four, all together, but the other two stood out in the hall.

"Well, Sherlock," Mycroft said in his whispery voice, which always struck me as a little higher pitched than one might expect out of so large and stout a figure. "This is quite the little coterie you have gathered around yourself." He nodded. "Count Dracula and Countess Dracula, I presume. I am Mycroft Holmes." He held out a hand like a well-manicured flipper, which the Count and then Mina took with automatic cordiality and a little surprise and confusion.

"Just Mina," Mina said. "I insist. Affairs of Christian wedlock and sovereign titles get a little muddled in Castle Dracula."

"Just so," Mycroft said. "Since I am here as a representative of the crown, I must confess and beg your indulgence that the crown cannot recognize either of your titles officially, but you have our heartfelt thanks nonetheless."

He turned next to the curious picture of Edward Hyde holding the only partially visible Ezra Griffin.

"Edward Hyde," Mycroft said. "Which means that Dr Jekyll will be absent."

"You seem awfully well-informed," Hyde said with a glare at Holmes the younger.

"Sherlock has kept me apprised of affairs," Mycroft admitted.

"You'll forgive me if I do not shake, but I've got my hands full at the moment."

"Just so," Mycroft Holmes said. "Which is the very reason that I'm here."

"What?" Griffin said. "Why?"

"Yes, why?" Hyde said.

"Come now," Holmes said. "Surely it has occurred to you the predicament that Mr Griffin presents. There can be no question of sending him to regular prison and I can hardly countenance murdering him on the spot. What is required then is a portion of the British government capable of dealing with such a unique situation. Mycroft here represents that division and is an agent that I trust."

Mycroft signalled to the two men behind him, one of whom produced a syringe.

"Wait!" Griffin shrieked. "You can't!" He struggled in Hyde's grip, but to no avail.

When the two men came for Griffin, Hyde looked as if he might still object.

"I promise you," Mycroft said, seeing his reluctance. "We are quite able to look after this kind of problem. Whitechapel has seen the last of this menace. He will never have a chance to inflict the terrible fate that he inflicted on Miss Eugenie Babington, Lila Emmet, and Stanley Hopkins on anyone else."

Hyde nodded and the two agents with Mycroft each took a

hold of the squirming Griffin. The easy, near blasé demeanour with which they handled him made it seem as if this task was a frequent occurrence. The syringe had administered a powerful sedative and the figure of Griffin slumped to the floor. The two men from the hall came in bearing a rolled-up carpet. In a few short minutes, Griffin was rolled up into the carpet and the men hoisted it, and him, and left the room.

"You'll be given a knighthood for this, Sherlock," Mycroft said with ebullience.

"Please no!" Holmes said with a deprecatory laugh. "I have no time for such tedium. Give it to Watson."

"I had meant to offer one to you both," Mycroft said. He looked a little offended. "At least you will not spur the gratitude of the crown?"

"I'd better not," I said. "Too many questions would come of it, I think. But please, send my thanks to... you know." Referring to our clandestine activities in such a direct way seemed somehow inappropriate and the rest of the government, I suspected, was unlikely to know the details of our 'service'. At least, I could only imagine such to be the case.

"What would serve much better," Holmes said, "is if you could attend to this list. These people need protection in case Van Helsing has other tools to turn against them besides Griffin." Holmes had clearly deciphered the list, for Mycroft took one look and shot him a look of surprise.

"The address for the Sherrinfords should not, at the very least, have been accessible to him." Mycroft eyed his younger brother with what looked like a very personal outrage and it came to me in a flash that Sherrinford must refer to a part of the Holmes family that I wasn't yet familiar with.

"Precisely," Holmes said. "I have every reason to believe that the other addresses are equally accurate. You should pull the Scotland Yarders on here out of rotation first. Being public figures makes them the easiest to move against. Also, I need your assurance – and when I say 'you', I of course mean the government – that we have caught the perpetrator of the Whitechapel Murders. I have already sent telegrams to Lestrade, Gregson and MacDonald, but Bradstreet and certainly Jones will require more official pressure before they stand down from their investigation in order to accept protection. Then, I would move to protect those in the country. The Murrays being the closest of these to London, they should be first."

Mina gave Holmes a look of heartfelt thanks. Even Dracula nodded slightly at this.

"Very well," Mycroft said. "It shall be done, and swiftly. Sherlock, be careful if you plan to go up against Van Helsing and the rest of the Cult. Griffin has likely told you, they are every bit as dangerous as Griffin here. In fact, you *could* consider this case closed. Certainly the Whitechapel Murders and Jack the Ripper have been dealt with. No one could ask more of you."

"I am inclined to disagree," Holmes said. "What say you, Watson?"

"The incarceration of the Ripper might remove one danger," I said promptly, "but the Cult of Cthulhu represents a very serious threat to all of England. I couldn't imagine just standing by and doing nothing."

"Well said!" Holmes agreed. "What say the rest of you?"

"Van Helsing has just as much to answer for as Griffin does," Hyde said at once.

"Besides," Miss Winter said, "you're going to need every good hand you have, going against that lot. I'll not shirk my duty now."

"Indeed," Dracula said. "Hyde has the right of it. Van Helsing must answer for his crimes." Somehow he made it sound like a much more personal crime he referred to, rather than crimes against the public, but no one corrected him. Mina nodded, clearly saddened by the necessity, but also clearly determined to see it through.

"I believe you have our collective answer, Mycroft," Holmes said.

"As you will," Mycroft said. "I never could dissuade you once you made your mind up on something, not even as children. I will send what assistance I can, but all I have at my disposal are ordinary men. Competent, but not up to the task that you set yourselves."

"Best if you keep them out of the way, then," Holmes said. "But you had mentioned a certain piece of equipment."

"Yes, yes," Mycroft said. He looked at one of the agents with him, who went out into the hall and brought back a large, leather-covered suitcase.

"I warn you," Mycroft said, "it has never been used for the purpose you intend. It may not work."

Holmes nodded his understanding.

"Be careful," Mycroft said, holding out his hand. Holmes took it and they shook solemnly.

"Well then," Mycroft said. "I have an unexplainable phenomenon to incarcerate. Good hunting."

He left.

Mycroft had hardly cleared the room before Hyde picked up the oversized briefcase and said, "What do we have here?"

He moved to open it, but Holmes put his hand on the top of it, preventing him.

"Peculiar that you should ask," Holmes said, "because I have need of your services if this toy Mycroft brought is to be any use to us at all. Or rather, Dr Jekyll's services."

Chapter 14

THE CULT REVEALED

We dispersed in the morning, since Holmes declared there was no further need for enforced sequestering. In addition, he wanted to work on the mysterious plan that required Jekyll's presence. Thus Holmes and Hyde went to Jekyll's residence, taking Mycroft's suitcase with them.

Miss Winter, grateful for the chance to return to her own quarters, left right after them. Dracula and Mina did the same and I suddenly had my room and quarters returned to me.

That evening, we gathered again, we arrived all together at Beechwood Manor. This time, there was no attempt at subterfuge.

"Are you certain this is the best approach, Mr Holmes?" Mina said as we all alighted from a four-wheeler in front of the Beechwood Manor gate. The moon, newly risen, hung fragmented and wreathed in mist. A beaten silver disc, partly occluded, but no less bright. The night was silent. Almost... *waiting*.

"There is hardly time for anything else," Holmes said. "After this farce of a ritual tonight, they may well scatter to the four winds. Our last attempt at subterfuge and clandestine entry was necessary in order to let Van Helsing think he had the upper hand…"

"Still not so sure he doesn't," Miss Winter mumbled, looking up at the massive and mostly dark manor.

"As I said," Holmes said tartly, "it was necessary to have Van Helsing think he held all the cards, lest he caution Griffin and prevent our laying our hands on him. Eliminating Griffin was a critical first step. Not only does it leave us free of surveillance, but it eliminates his threats against our friends and family. In addition, I believe Van Helsing has shown his hand a trifle too soon. He truly believes that he will bring about the end of the world with this final ceremony, so what need has he of intricate plans and protections after tonight? He spoke nothing less than the truth when he claimed that his list was only meant to restrain us for a very short time. I find it hard to credit Van Helsing's opinion as to our certain doom, but it is a certainty that this cult represents a grave threat to the citizens of Britain even with Griffin indisposed. No, I think it is time for the direct approach." He gestured at Dracula and then the sturdy lock on the front gate.

"Sounds like pure balderdash to me," Hyde said cheerfully. "But delightful balderdash. I'd just assume the direct approach. Tactical considerations be damned, especially with the end of the world coming." He laughed as he said the last few words, but I thought I heard a thin strain in his voice. Holmes had scoffed at such an idea earlier, but I couldn't feel his confidence on the matter. I'd seen too many things these past two years to discount the impossible anymore. Perhaps I wasn't the only one, either, if the twitch in Hyde's furred cheek were any judge.

"I accused you once of foolishness," Dracula said. "I used the word 'imbecile', as I recall. I see now that your judgment and perception has never faltered and is the superior of Van Helsing's and my own. You have kept your plans closely guarded, Mr Holmes, but what commander in war can be faulted for that? If you feel it is the time for brash action, then I will agree. You, sir, are a leader I would gladly follow into battle."

Mina had looked startled during Dracula's speech and now, on its completion, looked positively stunned, then suddenly proud.

Dracula, seeming not to notice how everyone was looking at him, stepped to the gate and wrenched the lock free in one easy motion. While we hadn't necessarily needed *him* to deal with that lock, the symbolism of the act gave me a swell of hope in my heart and I felt profoundly more secure with Dracula and Mina on our side. Still, it had taken all of us working in concert to bring down the werewolf Fleete. Meanwhile, Holmwood, of whom we had heard only superlatives and absolutes, had already brought Dracula down with ease once, and there had been little we could do to prevent it. Even if Van Helsing didn't have any more horrors waiting for us in Holmwood's house, and I was not at all certain that he didn't, confronting them was a terrifying proposition. Still, I wasn't ready to back out now. While Van Helsing was clearly mad, the idea of him completing any more unnatural and unsavoury rituals with the stolen organs from murdered London citizens made my stomach turn. He had to be stopped.

"Well, Mr Holmes," Hyde said, "do we get to see what Holmes the elder has given you now?" He jabbed a heavily knuckled and hairy forefinger at the leather suitcase that Holmes still carried.

In answer, Holmes set the case on the ground and opened it in the moonlight.

"What in the world?" Hyde mused.

Holmes drew out a heavy chrome contraption unlike any I had ever seen before, shaped somewhat like a 'T'. He then drew out a folding lever with a forked end and using that, fitted it onto the first contraption so that it could draw back a cable stretched across the top, which was when I realized that he was holding a modern and heavily modified crossbow.

"Highly specialized," Holmes said. "Not… too… difficult to load using the goat's foot lever." He suited action to word, pulling the cable back. It gave a heavy click. These two pieces had come out of fitted cavities in the bottom of the suitcase, while five arrows lay in similar cavities on the top portion. One of these was marked with a black 'X', the other four with silver ones. Holmes pulled the arrow marked with black, a ponderous ungainly missile to my eye, and fitted it into the crossbow.

Then, with the weapon loaded, he handed it to me. "Watson, if you would be so good as to bear the burden of this ungainly device for a time? Mycroft assures me it is fairly accurate as far as forty yards, but no more, on account of the payload delivery system. Your target, should he present himself, is the inestimable Mr Fleete, as this may do a great deal to suppress his transformation. I will carry the rest of the ammunition, though I tell you plainly that I do not hold much hope that these will be terribly effective, but it is our only option. You are now armed with the most powerful arrow, as I only had enough of Jekyll's werewolf antidote for one attempt. The other four are large quantities of silver, which may slow him down, but are not likely to end the battle themselves."

"What is our objective?" Dracula asked. "Do you plan on arresting them, Mr Holmes?"

Holmes shook his head, his mouth tight. "I do not see that as an option, unfortunately."

"Then your brother has a government labour camp prepared, perhaps? One for each of them?"

"I do not think that there will be any quarter asked in this confrontation, and none given," Holmes said, though it clearly pained him to admit it. "If we can capture them, so much the better, but with Holmwood and Fleete, at the very least, it seems a highly unlikely possibility. They must be stopped, at all costs."

"We are to be judge, jury and executioner, then?" Mina said softly. She did not sound as if she questioned Holmes's judgment on the matter, but only regretted the necessity.

"Yes," Holmes said. "It seems so."

Wordlessly, I took the crossbow. One shot, and one shot only. Of course, both Holmes and I had silver bullets in our guns, as well, but Fleete had absorbed enough damage from those last time to bury seven vampires and had kept on fighting.

Thus armed, we went in.

Any house of that size required a sizable staff to maintain it, but we saw no sign of any such people as we made our way boldly up the gravel drive, between moon-drenched poplar trees and to the front grand porch. The front doors opened to our touch to reveal a recessed foyer. It was not just as if Holmwood had dismissed his people for the evening, but as if they had been permanently dismissed months ago. No lights were lit and Holmes led the way with his lantern raised.

So surreal did our invasion of Beechwood Manor feel to me that I find that my memories of the place are fragmentary, at best. Opulence neglected under a layer of dust and no sign of person or light or activity. A general impression of massive rooms with vaulted ceilings and grand archways, darkness lying heavy all around while Holmes and his lantern were a single star moving through a thickly textured night sky, with the rest of us in tow.

"Holmes," I murmured, "do you smell that? Smoke, I believe."

Many of the others around me nodded while Holmes lifted his nose in the air. "Excellent, Watson. I do believe you are correct. We would do well to follow, I think."

While Miss Winter, Hyde, Dracula, Mina and myself all had excellent night vision, it was still Holmes's keen eyesight that spotted marks on the floor that led him to discover a hidden door behind a large collection of miniature ships in the billiards room. The entire nautical display rolled smoothly out of the way and we beheld an iron staircase descending down into open darkness. It was an intricate and clever apparatus involving a counterweight that slowly drew the case back into position once left unattended.

"The smoke comes from this direction," Dracula said, "it being the only activity on the property. Our enemies clearly lie this way."

"Do they expect us, do you think?" Miss Winter asked.

"They may not," Hyde said, "seeing as how we have eliminated their method of keeping tabs on us. Of course, if Van Helsing tells the truth, and my gut says he does, he cares little about what happens anymore. He had his revenge, so he feels, and the rest is but a foregone conclusion. Think he'll be put out when this Cthulhu doesn't show?"

I shuddered at the thought, not ready to be so cavalier about any reference to Van Helsing's pagan god and not at all as certain as they were that the haunting and misshapen entity would not somehow put in an appearance.

We descended, Holmes again leading the way and the cramped space quickly opened up on our left. The iron-gridwork stairs clung to some kind of rock face on our right as we twined deeper and deeper around a vast open cavern. Even to our augmented night vision, the pitch outside of the lantern's light spill was complete and the air all around us was redolent of smoke and of fish washed up onto a deserted beach and left in the warm sun. When Holmes once knocked a pebble off the ironwork, it was a long, silent drop until the small splash came back to our ears. Gradually, as we went several storeys down, the smell of smoke grew stronger and I could hear voices raised in unison.

Holmes turned back to me and cupped his hand so that he might whisper into my ear. "There is light coming from a doorway off to the side about a storey down. We shall proceed carefully and without light to betray our presence. Make no move until I have indicated to. Let the others know."

I turned to Dracula, immediately behind me, and repeated Holmes's message, so that he might do the same. Finally, we were all prepared and ready. I hefted the awkward mechanical crossbow, trying to get a feel for the thing.

Vampire or no, nominal creature of the night, my heart quailed when Holmes snuffed the lantern and darkness enveloped us. We inched forward carefully, faces and hands pressed against the cold rough stone wall on our right, with both the scent of fire and the chanting voices gradually becoming clearer. As it did, a strange phenomenon occurred wherein the harsh and inhuman-sounding words started to work some kind of insidious charm in my brain, chill fingers in my thoughts that brought fear and the sudden need to take flight. I do not know about the others, but I was in desperate need of all my nerve as we drew closer to the chanting. Every fibre of my being wanted to run and my hands, holding the strange crossbow, began to shake such that I could imagine no possible way to take any kind of shot, no matter how close, and still expect to be on target.

If Holmes felt any similar urge, I could not tell. But, looking back, I could see that Mina, Miss Winter and Hyde all had a peculiar tightness to their expression that led me to believe the chanting was working its will on their minds, too. Only Dracula looked unaffected, but his countenance was less than relaxed in the best of conditions.

Light flared suddenly from the doorway as we approached,

a red, lurid spill across the iron staircase that brought to mind pitchforks and torment rather than light and warmth. It wasn't a comforting sort of light, but I felt grateful for a break in the darkness.

Finally, we arrived at the doorway in question and Holmes set down the extinguished lantern and peered round the corner. He looked back at us once, nodded, and went on. I followed, manoeuvring the crossbow into a firing position as I did. But there was nothing yet to shoot at.

We were in a tunnel, sloping gently down. Only a few feet in, a long, oval opening in the side of the tunnel let in both the chanting and the light from a bonfire, while the tunnel itself continued down, curving slightly to the left, presumably leading to the large open space I could see through the aperture. Holmes peered briefly through the opening before prostrating himself on the tunnel floor and sliding onward. There was a small lip on the oval opening so that this performance screened him quite adequately from any of the persons who might be below.

When he was past the opening and I followed his lead and performed the same manoeuvre, my quick glance showed me that there were, indeed, persons below.

Van Helsing was there, his grey hair and wrinkled features painted by the rusty light as he stood on top of a low dais before a large, ornate mirror and led the others in the alien chanting. The mirror seemed a strange business, taller than Van Helsing and octagonal with a heavy iron framework holding it in place. The intricate ironwork around the edges held, I could not doubt, unsettling images as all the artifacts associated with this cult seemed to, and I felt a sense of relief that I could not decipher them from here.

A man stood next to him, tall and solidly built, in a wiry sort of way, with short, dark curly hair and an insouciant smile. Almost certainly Arthur Holmwood. He had an ordinary, average face with the exception of a pair of vibrant dark eyes that hinted at something untamed and violent beneath them. Both George Fleete and Madam Fleete were there, as well as a dozen other persons, some with their hoods up, but most down. I did not recognize any of the others. They all wore long, ornate robes of black and purple, possibly ermine, with pale characters stitched into the lapels and around the hoods. I did not recognize the characters as part of any human language that I knew and they had a way of shifting, almost *crawling*, as I looked at them.

In the centre of the ring of worshippers lay a huge burning firepit, flickering to throw wild shadows all around. Van Helsing had stated that the trophies from the Whitechapel killings, the various internal organs, had all been used in the opening ritual, but I began to wonder if this might have been a subterfuge, for the unsavoury reek of burning meat defiled my senses.

"Watson," Holmes whispered, though it hardly seemed necessary to whisper over the din the chanters were making. "Your target is Fleete. But not until he is transformed. You must wait here for this, watch for the transformation and only when *that is complete*, shoot him. If that fails, use the remaining silver arrows on either Fleete or Holmwood as you see fit. After that, it will fall to your revolver."

I nodded, not entirely comfortable with this strange weapon, but recognizing that the others were likely better hand-to-hand combatants and so were needed there. I pondered, briefly, the fact that Kitty Winter had been a vampire only slightly longer than me, but would be such a fierce and terrifying force, once roused. I concluded, as always, that she seemed to be far more at ease with the feral aspect of her nature, an aspect that I shunned. That seemed such a trivial difference in the abstract, but it made all the difference. I also wasn't comfortable with the military nature of this mission. We weren't here to solve a crime or bring a culprit to British justice, but to attack and destroy. It was necessary, in the extreme, and I had no doubt of that, but a dire mission nonetheless.

Holmes looked at Dracula and Mina. "Can you engage Holmwood? It will be exceedingly dangerous."

"I would have it no other way," Dracula said ominously. "I still owe him for the cowardly attack on the roof."

"As do I," echoed Mina. That statement, along with her intent expression, brought a look of surprise to Dracula's face, but then he reluctantly nodded. I wondered if, being a solitary and fierce predator for so long, the Count now underestimated his lady's own ferocity. Having seen her violence first-hand myself, I certainly did not.

"That will leave Fleete to you," Holmes said to Hyde and Miss Winter, "until or unless Watson is able to neutralize him. After that, it may very well take all of us to bring down Holmwood, if his abilities have not been exaggerated."

Both Miss Winter and Hyde nodded, clearly determined, but not quite as eager as either Dracula or Mina were.

"It's been a pleasure working with you, Mr Holmes," Hyde said gravely. Holmes nodded.

"What about you?" I asked Holmes.

"Van Helsing is not likely to be a terrible combatant," he said. "But he has the potential to be very dangerous nonetheless and I shall keep my eye on him as well as the others and see what develops." He shrugged, indicating the impossibility of predicting the chaos and violence that we were about to initiate.

"Very well," Dracula said, standing up. "There is no point in delay." Mina stood, as well. Hyde and Miss Winter looked at each other, clasped hands briefly – his massive furred hand entirely encompassing her small dainty one. When Dracula and Mina strode down the ramp and into the cavern with the firepit, Holmes, Hyde and Miss Winter were right behind.

I took up my position in the opening overlooking the cavern, trying to keep out of sight. It mattered not at all; no one was even looking in our direction until Dracula reached the bottom of the incline, and then they all looked at him and the others.

"Van Helsing," Dracula boomed. "Holmwood! A time has come for a reckoning!"

Van Helsing looked up, the chant trailing off with a look of severe irritation. The other chanters trailed off too and I couldn't help but feel an enormous sense of relief. Van Helsing had claimed that this ritual was of little importance, that the Great Old One already had its entrance to our world, from whatever shadowy and unreal dimension it might hail from, and that his arrival was but a matter of time. He had called this ritual a mere formality, but I was relieved at a primal, atavistic level to hear it stop. A trick of the flickering firelight made it seem as if something cloudy moved in the mirror independent of any of the persons in front of it. I had to tear my eyes away from that insidious movement so that I did not get distracted from my duties.

Several of the hooded figures quailed and stepped away, breaking the circle. I discounted them at once as having any involvement in the upcoming battle. Wealthy socialites joining the Cult of Cthulhu out of boredom, perhaps? Purses to fund their activities, I guessed. Madam Fleete and her son were among them, she behind her larger son with her hand on his shoulder. I wondered about Holmes's instructions that I wait until the change before shooting. Perhaps it would have been just as well to put a bullet, silver or otherwise, into George before he had time for such a change. Still, I was glad for Holmes's instructions being as they were, for I suspected I did not have the heart to shoot an unarmed man, regardless of what cold logic would suggest, and regardless of how dangerous he would soon become.

"Fools!" Van Helsing spat out. "Fools, to come here! Can't you see you are far too late?"

Holmwood, however, allowed a great smile to split his face, practically beaming at us. "What an unmitigated delight. I knew you would come, no matter how Van Helsing tried to keep you away."

Miss Winter, followed by Hyde, was slowly edging her way around Holmwood and towards the crowd of milling and terrified cultists, of which Madam and George Fleete were a part. I saw

Madam Fleete cast a look at Holmwood, a look containing so many conflicting emotions that I could not identify them properly. I thought affection had a place there, and regret, though both expressions flashed by so very quickly that I could not be certain.

Holmwood paid her no attention. He stood, that beaming smile unbroken while he held Dracula's gaze, took a long time drawing his silver sword, enjoying the dramatic moment, the noise a whispering susurrus that commanded more attention than a gunshot.

"This is meaningless…" Van Helsing started.

But he never finished as Holmwood, gaze still locked on Dracula, in one easy movement, switched his blade to his left hand and whipped it around and behind him so that the tip passed neatly, with surgical precision, through Van Helsing's throat.

Van Helsing's eyes bulged and he clapped his hands to his throat, for all the good they did staunching the blood that spurted through his fingers and ran down his waistcoat. Outrage flashed through his eyes, then anger, and pain, and finally, understanding. He collapsed to his knees, gurgled, twice more, then fell stiffly to the cavern floor where he twitched a few times more before laying still. The blood looked very black in the lurid firelight.

"Now that *that* foolishness is dispensed with…" Holmwood said, and his smile twisted into something dreadful while a madness danced in his green eyes. The sword stroke had been so quick, and had come back to bear on Dracula with such speed, that it seemed I might have almost imagined it if not for the dying professor at his feet.

"But," one of the hooded cultists wailed, "Van Helsing? Who will lead the ritual? What have you done?"

"The ritual!" Holmwood spat and he finally took his gaze from Dracula long enough to sweep it over the cultists with pure disdain. "And this, from a man of science." He stepped down off the dais and looked back at Dracula again before saying, "It's your fault, really. Both of you." He swept his hand to include Mina, too, in his condemnation. "His encounter and failure with the two of you broke something in his mind. Thereafter, he strove with science, and made the greatest discovery of our age, but was too blind to see it. No, he was always striving for something *beyond* science, which he thought he needed to combat you. He, along with that Stoker drivel, thought that you had a bargain with Satan, you see, to explain your power, but I know better. There is no God, no Great Old Ones, there is only *us* and *we* are the gods!" He tapped his chest while walking closer. He was less than half a dozen paces from Dracula and Mina now. "Oh, the gall of it! Having to listen to that old man's drivel, all the while biding my time."

"Biding your time for what, Arthur?" Mina asked.

Holmwood's smile became, somehow, a fraction wilder. "For this, of course." He gestured at Dracula and Mina with his left hand while the right kept his sword in line. "Our grand reunion. Don't you see? We should not be fighting. We should be in union! A force so magnificent that none can stand against us. Why destroy the world, if you believe Van Helsing's fanciful tales, when we can *rule* it?"

"You would join forces with us?" Dracula said, bemused.

"Well," Holmwood said, "not exactly." He stopped, the tip of his sword a mere six feet from Dracula's heart. "I would rather, *rule* you."

"Really?" Dracula laughed, this last statement finally breaking Dracula's impassive mask. "You *are* ambitious."

"Granted," Holmwood said, "I hardly expect you to submit to me without an ample demonstration of my power." With a movement so blindingly fast that I barely saw it happen, he stepped forward and struck. Dracula hissed and fell back, clutching his face, from which a black wetness now emerged. I'd seen both Dracula, Mina and Miss Winter all move with astonishing speed. I supposed, too, that as the disease progressed in me I was also, contrary to the progression of any other disease, a great deal stronger and faster than I was. During the fight with Fleete in Whitechapel, Dracula in particular had moved with a dangerous speed and grace that was positively inhuman.

But Holmwood, astonishingly, was even faster.

His actions didn't have the same fluid grace that Dracula's movements had, only the sudden impression that something had *just happened*, but happened faster than the eye could view or the brain could comprehend. Again, Holmwood moved and again I could not even begin to follow the motion, but now Mina staggered and fell back, a nearly identical line of blood across *her* cheek. The silvered blade Holmwood carried clearly did its work, for the wounds on Mina's and Dracula's faces bubbled and smoked.

With a feral snarl, Dracula launched himself at Holmwood, sweeping the air with a clawed hand.

And hitting only empty air.

With casual ease, Holmwood, his dark eyes flashing and his grin wide, avoided the blow. The man moved with alarming speed, his every step a blur. Dracula raked at Holmwood with a brutally quick backhand, then an angled sweep of his other hand. Holmwood avoided each blow by fractions of an inch. But these were not narrow escapes, he simply needed only the narrowest of margins and moved just the smallest degree necessary to evade contact. Fast as he was, each motion was so neatly performed that it seemed almost lazy, requiring no effort whatsoever.

"You know," Holmwood laughed, "it's a relief, really, now that you're here and I can see how sad this all really is." He whipped his sword to one side, stepped closer so that he could seize Dracula by the back of the neck, like one would seize a naughty kitten, and flung the other man negligently out of his way.

Dracula flipped end over end, out of control, and just barely landed on his feet. He staggered and braced himself against the cavern wall, narrowly avoiding smashing face first into it.

Mina had jumped into the fray, slashing repeatedly at Holmwood while he danced easily out of reach.

"A fearsome pair," he said, and laughed again. "Oh, I *am* sorry. I really meant to comport myself with the seriousness and solemnity that this night deserves. But, you see, Van Helsing has been making such a *business* of you that it quite went to my head. Count Dracula! The Wallachian Warlord, the King of all Vampires, the Scourge of Mankind… he was always raging about it and I was starting to believe it myself, in the end, remembering how fearsome you were and thinking, deep inside, that I was *nothing*."

Holmes had taken up a position on the lowest part of the incline, braced against the cavern wall near the tunnel, tracking Holmwood with his revolver as best he could. He now waited, as I did, for a clear shot, though we concentrated on different targets, Holmes focused entirely on Holmwood, while I focused, as instructed, on Fleete, who stood with his mother, merely gawking at the battle in front of him.

"But now, now it is different and history is of little importance. Science! It is science that matters now and Van Helsing, for all his foolishness, transcended God in this area. I am faster, stronger, nigh invulnerable."

Mina swung again and Holmwood evaded again easily, smacking her clawed hand aside with smooth confidence, then driving his shoulder into hers. Mina, unbalanced by his quickness, stumbled for several paces before turning with a feral hiss. Her hair was wild, her eyes black.

Dracula was much the same, clearly letting a brutal, savage part of his personality surface as he always seemed to during battle. The two of them gathered their composure and began to circle Holmwood like cautious predators.

Holmwood, by contrast, showed none of the anger or savagery that his opponents displayed, merely a supreme control. He had the sword tucked behind his back now in his left hand, as if it was a tool he hardly needed for the likes of these two, held in abeyance.

Suddenly, I had no attention for Holmwood, Dracula, Mina,

or even Holmes, for George Fleete had seen Hyde and Miss Winter, who had been edging closer to him.

Madam Fleete turned to her son and whispered something with intensity. George's face went slack and his eyes glazed over. When she handed him a vial, he moved it automatically to his lips, presumably now under her powerful hypnotic control, though I'd never seen such manipulation effected so skilfully or completely.

George Fleete drank and the result was instantaneous.

He collapsed to his hands and knees, the muscles in his obese back rippling through the fabric of his robe. The cloth tore open, revealed a dark, furred back unlike any man walking on two feet. His flesh swelled, filled with turmoil like a stormy sea.

My finger tensed on the trigger. *Not yet.* Only when the transformation was complete, Holmes had said.

Hyde, thinking perhaps to end this battle before it had properly begun, sprang at Fleete, his huge fist pulled back to deliver a terrific blow, but Fleete, still caught in the throes of transformation as he was, reared and backhanded Hyde with the force of a battering ram. Hyde flew across the room, impacting the wall near me hard enough to send vibrations through the wall and stone floor, and crumpled to the cavern floor. He did not move. Fleete towered over the others around him now, his huge mass redistributed into the furred killing machine we'd faced in Whitechapel.

Miss Winter jumped at Fleete next, but then jerked herself back as Fleete took a swing at her. He missed. He swung again, and missed, and I realized that Miss Winter knew just what she was doing. Fleete was a slavering beast now, enraged and furred all over. The transformation was almost complete. His face twisted and elongated itself, forming a muzzle wide open, roaring and dripping saliva.

And he stepped fully into the light, away from his mother and the milling and screaming cultists.

It was time for me to take my shot.

Bless you, Miss Winter, I thought. She'd given me the perfect chance.

I pulled the trigger.

My heart leapt for joy when I saw the bulky crossbow bolt fly true and lodge itself in Fleete's barrel chest.

Fleete howled and grappled with the arrow, but there was not much of it left unburied and he only scrabbled ineffectually at the thing. He sucked in a breath, and there was a brief moment of relative quiet in which I heard a hydraulic noise come from the missile lodged in Fleete's chest. He snarled, then gave a sudden whimper, and collapsed yet again. This time, he did not move.

Just as quickly as the man had changed to beast, I could see him shrink and shift back again. He was completely human when he went very still, knocked completely catatonic by the mechanical quarrel.

"You foul animal!" Madam Fleete cried. "You killed him! My only son. Well, it will be the last act you ever do." She opened her hand and another vial fell and broke on the floor with a tinkling sound.

She started her own transformation and it took only seconds

for me to realize that we would, in seconds, have another werewolf to contend with and I had just used the only crossbow bolt capable of stopping her. We hadn't come prepared for *two* shape-changers. There were other custom bolts, yes, but these, Holmes had said, contained not the antidote to the werewolf potion, but silver. We'd seen in Whitechapel that silver could damage the werewolf, but it had taken many wounds inflicted with silver and finally, a fall from the top of a building to put a stop to Fleete before.

A soft groan came from the floor underneath my sniper's vantage point and I realized that Hyde was still alive and coming to. I felt relief and fear in equal measure, trying to imagine, against impossible odds, how this battle could possibly come out in our favour. I peered down to see him stumbling to his feet.

In the meantime, Miss Winter was on her own against the werewolf that was Madam Fleete. She, in a fit of misplaced violence, seized one of the cultists that had been taking shelter in the far side of the cavern with her, and tore the man messily in half.

Hyde, a little unsteady on his feet, and Miss Winter, moved to fight. Madam Fleete, her lupine face howling with rage, levelled a blow at Miss Winter that would have felled trees, but Miss Winter narrowly ducked under it.

I scrambled as best I could with the next crossbow bolt, but I would not sit in my relative safety and play the sniper while Miss Winter alone faced down the fearsome beast. I stuffed another of the bolts into my jacket pocket, patted the other pocket to made sure that the service revolver was still there, and slid through the opening in the wall, letting myself fall – crossbow still clutched in my hand – the twenty-five feet or so down to the cavern floor.

I landed neatly and fired. The bolt hit Madam Fleete in the shoulder just as she was about to spring on Hyde. At first, nothing happened, but then I could hear the bolt discharging and the enormous muscle in her right shoulder seemed to burst asunder from within, bubbling and boiling silver splattering and leaking from the wound as if it had been a bomb.

She screamed and, ignoring Hyde and Miss Winter, charged the twenty feet or so to where I stood. I tried to duck, but something hit me with the force of a locomotive and I pinwheeled end over end as I went the length of the cavern.

I hit something that gave with a crash, I wasn't sure what, and fell to the ground.

I was conscious, but just barely. Also, I miraculously still held onto the crossbow. My blood pounded in my ears as I struggled to get my bearings. I peered uncomprehendingly at a shard of glass on the floor between my hands, noting the murky shape that coalesced there. I saw, very briefly, an enormous eye, bulbous and huge, huge as worlds, with a black horizontal slit. Then the image cleared and I was staring at a broken piece of glass. I realized that I'd been thrown into the mirror, shattering it. I kicked the fragment of glass away with an involuntary cry of disgust.

I didn't have time to ponder that malignant eye. Instead, I struggled to make my legs work. Standing was no easy proposition, however, and just getting to my feet took a full minute and then some. While I was engaged in this struggle, I could see, through blurred eyes, that Madam Fleete had turned back to Miss Winter and Hyde, while Dracula and Mina, now much closer to me than the others, still fought their one-sided, hopeless battle with Holmwood.

"Now then," Holmwood said, "you see now that your position is an impossible one, do you not? How can you not?" I'd missed part of their engagement while focusing on the Fleetes, and both Dracula and Mina sported new wounds. Dracula bled from a large gash on his shoulder while Mina held one hand to her side, but both of them circled him again, like hounds around a wounded stag. Only they were the ones wounded and I could not, for the life of me, see so much as a mark on Holmwood.

"Please," Holmwood said with utmost sincerity. "I have no wish to kill you, either of you. I would much rather have your allegiance than your death. But I will have one or the other. Please, see the reason of submission. For either of you to die the real death here would be a pointless waste."

Dracula's face was a mask of fury, Mina's the same, and Holmwood's smile broke for the first time.

"Don't make me kill you, Mina," he pleaded. "After being forced to end dear Lucy, I really don't think I could bear to be the death of you, too."

"You won't," Dracula said, springing at Holmwood.

Holmwood sighed, then neatly stepped out of the way of first Dracula's rush, and then Mina's. They had timed it wonderfully, so that they had launched in what should have been a dizzying flurry of strikes from several directions. But all of that was nullified by Holmwood's unbelievable speed. He simply wasn't there any time they attacked and I could see the frustration building in Dracula and Mina both.

"You will not yield, then?" Holmwood said. He still had his silver blade tucked neatly behind him, not having any real need for it thus far.

"Never," Dracula spat.

"Pity," Holmwood said, and seemed to actually mean it. "Perhaps," he said, brightening, "perhaps Mina will be more tractable once you are gone."

When Dracula next lunged, Holmwood did not dodge, but snapped the blade out and pierced Dracula as tidily as if he were a butterfly collected for the specimen jar.

"No!" Mina wailed as the silver sword sliced into Dracula's torso then out through his back. Dracula groaned and stiffened, the sword still in him as the silver reaction started bubbling around the horrible and unmistakably mortal wound.

"A pity," Holmwood said. "I really didn't want it to come to this. Alas." He leaned back to pull his weapon free, already turning to face Mina.

Only his sword didn't move.

Holmwood turned back to Count Dracula, then, his saddened expression turning to one of surprise as he saw that Dracula's hand was now clamped onto his own.

Dracula flexed, strengthening his grip and then, instead of pushing, *pulled* himself further onto the silver blade then seized Holmwood's neck.

"Never," Dracula said, as his hand squeezed Holmwood's throat.

An expression of pure, unadulterated fear crossed Holmwood's face as he suddenly realized the danger that he was in. He struggled, but to no avail. Van Helsing had boasted of Holmwood's unassailable speed, and also his strength, and I was terrified that even Dracula's grip, fuelled as it was by the Count's inexorable will, would not be enough. I lifted the crossbow then realized that not only was the bolt missing, but the cable that would propel it was dangling, severed in half. It was hopelessly ruined. I dropped the useless thing.

Then two shots rang out.

Holmes! Biding his time, waiting patiently, watching with the keen eye of his for the right moment to strike. He'd fired two bullets and I could see the blood spurt, twice, from Holmwood's left eye. With Van Helsing's claims, and the display of power that we'd seen so far, there was a moment of doubt that even that would be enough and I turned, fumbling my revolver out of my pocket, to deliver yet another coup de grace, when Mina acted.

She slipped in behind Holmwood, embracing him from behind almost as a lover might and seized the hilt of Holmwood's sword. Dracula, seeing his wife's hand on his, released his unbreakable hold, and Mina slid the sword from Dracula's body and, in one fluid motion spun around so that she brought it down in a deadly arc, parting Holmwood's head from his shoulders.

Dracula, freed from the deadly sword, sighed, gave his wife the barest of smiles, and fell to the ground.

But Madam Fleete was far from done. Although I noticed

now that for all her power, she had not started with the sheer bulk of her son, and so had not transformed into a werewolf of quite the same size. This was all to the good, as it had taken a supreme effort to bring the larger Fleete down. Still, Madam Fleete did not look at all ready to surrender.

She howled fit to shake dust from the cavern ceiling and sprang at Miss Winter.

Miss Winter dodged, then crouched low and rolled as Madam Fleete bounded over the place she'd just vacated. Hyde was recovered somewhat, too, and sprang onto Madam Fleete's back, clasping her around the neck in a desperate wrestler's hold.

Surprisingly, it held. Madam Fleete clawed at Hyde's hands and arms, drawing profuse amounts of blood, but Hyde would not let go. While the grip did nothing to quite nullify Madam Fleete's powerful strength, he was clearly a serious encumbrance to movement. While half the height of the werewolf, he was at least as heavy, and the weight of him threatened to topple her with every step. She clawed again, snarling in rage, but still he would not let go.

I was on my feet, finally, with my revolver in my hand and staggering in their direction. I could see Holmes doing the same. But with Hyde on her back and her twisting around in fury, there could be no clean shot. We'd be just as likely to hit and injure Hyde as Madam Fleete.

Then Miss Winter was there, and I realized that while she had rolled away from Madam Fleete's savage attack, she had also managed to retrieve something.

The silver bolt that I'd lost.

She stepped towards Madam Fleete and drove the bolt into the werewolf's heart.

Another ear-splitting howl tore through the cavern. Hyde and Miss Winter both jumped away as Madam Fleete fell, screaming. Then she was on her feet again and stumbling, that howl unabated, towards the cavern's exit.

I fired then, as did Holmes, each of us putting at least two silver bullets into the creature's chest, but she kept on running.

She rushed past Mina, who now held Dracula, and sprang up into the opening, scrabbling through it onto the slope. I could see the horrific wound that the silver was still inflicting on her chest, the silver burning a hole large enough to put both your fists in. It was a wonder, werewolf or no, that she still lived. Still, Holmes and I rushed up the slope to give pursuit.

But such was not to be.

Madam Fleete, with a bestial roar, burst out of the doorway that we'd come in, tripped over the iron staircase that we'd descended so carefully earlier, and fell over the edge.

Holmes and I rushed to the staircase, hearing the baleful howl as she fell, and fell, and fell. We heard the relatively soft thud that indicated that she'd finally reached the bottom.

Holmes and I exchanged a glance, then retraced our steps to see about the others.

Dracula still lived, and I wondered again at the man's unbelievable resilience.

Mina hovered over me as I checked the wound, a horrid hole in the upper part of the stomach and another, equally grisly exit wound partway up the back. It had not pierced the heart or done any damage to the spine. Still, it looked ghastly, but not *quite* as ghastly as I expected. Then I realized the answer as I noticed one of the cultists lying a few feet away like a discarded toy and knew at once that Mina had offered up the cultist's blood to save her husband. That action should have outraged my stolid British morality, but I found I just hadn't any outrage left. Besides, I could see that the cultist still lived. Mina had allowed her husband to feed, but not enough to kill the man, who had, in turn, planned to end existence for the entire world. Some blood seemed a small enough price to pay for his crimes. Now Dracula rested easily and I had no doubt he would recover. Still, I thought it best not to move him for the moment as any motion would likely be excruciating for him and we had nothing like a stretcher. Had Holmwood pierced the heart, it would have been a different matter entirely.

The rest of us were relatively unscathed, for which I thanked my lucky stars. Several of the cultists had fled back up the staircase, but several of the others had sat, stunned on the dais, one of them holding a piece of the mirror with a hangdog expression. I noticed several faces known to the public including one famous artist, a wealthy matron known for philanthropy, and a peer of the realm. Holmes, I knew, would take note of them all and while I could not imagine them being charged with a normal crime, I could well imagine Holmes, or Mycroft, taking measures to prevent them causing any more mischief after this. I only hoped, for their sake, that Mycroft did not see fit to put them in a cell next to Griffin for the rest of their lives. Of course, considering the horrific damage they had tried to perpetuate on London and the rest of the world, as well as being complicit in the Whitechapel Murders, I did not hope as hard as I might have.

It was another hour after that before we heard voices and footsteps coming down the stairs. By then Dracula had regained consciousness and was sitting up and looking better, if not himself. Holmes had drawn out his notebook and taken surreptitious records of the cultists there and then had Miss Winter usher them out and up the staircase into the house. Holmes then examined and carefully covered the corpses of Arthur Holmwood and Abraham Van Helsing. Hyde moved the catatonic, but still-living, body of George Fleete out of harm's way.

It was a short time later that we heard multiple footsteps coming down.

"Ah," Holmes said, turning toward the sound. "This is likely Miss Winter returning with Mycroft's men, as he promised to send what support he could."

"Good," Hyde said. "We can send them for a stretcher and get the Count out of here."

"Are we comrades, now," Dracula inquired, seemingly amused, "that you would bear me out yourself?"

"What else, Count?" Hyde said, standing up so that he could make an extravagant bow. "I would happily bear you and count it my honour. I've never seen a man do something as brave as what you just did."

The Count gave a brief, wan smile, an automatic and dismissive response to Hyde's flamboyant way of speaking, but I thought I saw a flash of true pleasure in his eyes. Mina's smile left no doubt as to her own feelings.

But Holmes's prediction of Mycroft's men was a hopeful and incorrect one, as a loud and brash voice suddenly proved.

"Well, Mr Holmes," Athelney Peter Jones called out, "this is a fine and pretty mess, if I do say so myself."

The portly senior inspector was followed by MacDonald and the smaller Lestrade, as well as half a dozen other constables, two of which had Miss Winter by either elbow. The two constables holding Miss Winter were polite, but also clearly under orders not to let her go.

I could see Hyde's face when he saw Miss Winter's escort. He hastily stood to his feet, his hands flexing in a manner that I recognized as presaging a physical altercation. For that matter, Miss Winter looked ready to throw off the constables herself. Mina and Dracula looked equally grim, but I saw Mina raise her hand to stop Hyde, who, amazingly enough, obeyed.

"What is the meaning of this?" I said, my hackles on the rise.

The portly Jones, his fringe of red hair all askew, advanced on us, the tall, bony figure of MacDonald following diffidently in his wake.

"There had been enough esoteric methods and fanciful theories in this case, Mr Holmes!" Jones railed. "I know you are a man of unusual methods, but our allowance for that kind of thing went out the window with our prisoner. When I say 'out the window', Mr Holmes, I assure you that I am not exaggerating.

We have the torn-up cell masonry to prove it! Tore the bars right out, I tell you! What's more, I think you know more than you let on about this case and I'm tired of being kept in the dark! Now the Ripper is on the loose again as well as the person who broke him out and my superiors are frothing at the mouth! There will be a public outcry! Charges of incompetency to my department! The press will rake us over the coals for years over this! My constables are already collecting statements from various persons and what we're hearing is somewhat difficult to credit, Mr Holmes!"

Holmes and I had risen to greet the inspector. I found myself quite taken aback as to this sudden attack on Holmes's virtue and yet I could not help but acknowledge that Inspector Jones had a fair point, for we had certainly not shared all that we knew. But then, how could we?

"Don't think that your brother can save you, either, Mr Holmes!" Jones went on. The man was practically apoplectic with rage. "Whatever branch of the government he works for, it has no jurisdiction here. No, this is strictly a police matter! I'm holding him and his men upstairs now, for they arrived on our heels, but I'll not have this crime scene tampered with before Scotland Yard has done a full investigation! We'll be going over every inch of this pretty mess, believe you me! Everyone here will be detained for questioning until I have a full account of what happened here!"

I could see that Lestrade had already gone over to where Holmwood's body was covered with the sheet. Holmwood's *headless* body, that is. Laying not too far away was the unconscious form of George Fleete. I shuddered to think of Madam Fleete's body at the bottom of the cavern, too, and wondered if Jones's determination would cause him to send men down there where they might recover it. Of course, they hardly needed to recover Madam Fleete to find plenty of questions we couldn't answer. Two dead, well-respected member of London's elite, one of the them decapitated. The silver sword and crossbow bolts along with the spent silver bullets.

"How have you come to be here at all?" Holmes asked, looking as nonplussed as I'd ever seen him.

"Oho!" Jones crowed. "Didn't think any of us were sharp enough to have your place watched, did you? We took note of the four wheeler you ordered and were able to put our hands on the cabbie after he delivered you here."

"We?" Holmes said, his gaze sliding over to MacDonald, who had the grace to flinch.

"Sorry, Mr Holmes," MacDonald said with his Aberdeen lilt. "Orders, after all."

"Inspector!" Lestrade's voice called out. "Holmes had found him! Fleete's master, Jack the Ripper, fallen during what appears to be a pitched battle."

"What's this now?" Jones said.

Lestrade whistled low and bent down to pick something up. "Here you have it, Inspector. If this is not the murder weapon itself I'll eat my hat!"

Here, the ferret-faced inspector walked over and presented his superior with a thin, curved, extremely sharp-looking knife very much in the nature of an instrument for fish-boning. It was a nasty-looking thing and had streaks of what I could only assume were dried blood on it.

It was also completely unfamiliar. In fact, I was certain I'd never seen this knife before.

"You're looking for two weapons, I believe, Inspector," Lestrade went on. "I'll bet my pension that the sword lying over there is your second one, but this—" He'd wrapped a handkerchief around the handle and handed it over in this fashion.

"Yes!" Jones said, taking it eagerly.

"You see, Mr Holmes," Lestrade said, "it was Inspector Jones here who figured it out, about there being two killers and how Fleete over there was a subordinate to a much more diabolical murderer. It was the inspector's opinion that Fleete couldn't possibly be the mastermind. He knew that the mastermind was still at large and reasoned that it had been him that had arranged for Fleete's prison break. Carefully engineered, that was, or how else do you describe a man that brazenly uses block, tackle and a team of disciplined men to tear free the bars of Fleete's prison window?"

"That's right!" Jones beamed.

"What in the world…" Holmes started, but Lestrade, uncharacteristically, cut him off.

"There's no help for it, Mr Holmes," Lestrade said. "Inspector Jones has reasoned it all out and he would have turned over every stone to get to the bottom of things. Jones will have both murderers and the murder weapons to prove to our superiors and the press that we have apprehended the Ripper once and for all." He gave me a significant look and the briefest and smallest of winks. In fact, the wink had come and gone so quickly that I was hardly sure I'd seen it.

"Otherwise," Lestrade went on, "the interviews and investigation will continue."

Lestrade had clearly planted this wicked-looking knife as evidence, but I was hard-pressed to understand how he could have known that we would need it. Griffin's actual knife still lay safely in Holmes's desk drawer. It being invisible, it would have been a convincing, if inconvenient piece of evidence. Certainly no newspaper photograph was going to do it justice. I was curious about Lestrade's theory of the crime, too, which had the virtue of being close to the truth without any inconvenient mention of invisible men, vampires or werewolves. In fact, it was as close to the truth as we dared reveal to the public.

Even so, I could see Holmes visibly struggle with this facsimile of the truth that Lestrade had offered. But what could we do? It would certainly do no good to have Jones and the rest of Scotland Yard dig too deeply into what had happened here tonight. Van Helsing, Holmwood, and Madam Fleete had already paid the ultimate penalty for their crimes and George Fleete was as destined for a cell as any man I'd ever seen.

Still, Holmes looked very much like he'd swallowed a starling when he said, "I really must congratulate you, Inspector Jones. A very well-reasoned out theory. One that has paid dividends as you now have all the details and culprits at your disposal."

"Closed case," Lestrade said helpfully.

"Yes," Jones said. "Well, Mr Holmes, now that you see it is no use hiding things from the official force we can be friends again and it is very true that we have you to thank for leading us here. But next time, you could be a little more open about your plans and save us all a great deal of trouble! We'll see it all eventually!"

"Yes," Holmes said in a hoarse voice. "I'm sure."

"That's settled, then," Jones said and strode purposefully away to give orders to the constables, including the release of Miss Winter. She and Hyde embraced, causing a few curious looks from some of the surrounding constables.

"Now that he has what he deems necessary in order to keep his job and appease the press," Lestrade said, "I believe he will lose interest in the smaller details of this case. I can control the interviews and we'll have no need to detain either you lot or Mr Holmes the senior. We'll have a freer hand now."

"How on earth did you know..." I started, addressing Lestrade.

"Mycroft," Holmes answered for him.

"Indeed, Mr Holmes," Lestrade agreed. "He even passed me the knife while no one else was watching. A most insightful man. It seems the Holmes family is doubly blessed."

"Thank you, Lestrade," Holmes said, his grey eyes thoughtful.

"The doctor entrusted me with a great deal of information," Lestrade answered, "and I hope you see now that I can be a man of great discretion."

"No doubt about it," I said.

"Then I am happy to assist," Lestrade said. He reached out and shook both Holmes's hand and my own. "It seems England owes the two of you, and your friends, another great debt, even if not everyone at Scotland Yard knows the full extent of it. For my part, I thank you, gentlemen. Now, let me see about Mycroft and a stretcher for your injured companion." With another wink, he turned and left.

"What a remarkable man," I said.

"So it would seem," Holmes agreed. He shrugged. "Come, Doctor, let us gather our flock and beat a hasty retreat while Inspector Athelney Peter Jones is feeling well-satisfied. I should hate to see another turn of events that led to us all getting arrested."

Chapter 15

AFTERMATH

Three weeks later, I returned from my billiards club to find Holmes standing at the sitting room window, sawing out a plaintive and melancholy tune on his violin. He did not look in my direction.

"Afternoon, Holmes," I tried.

He made no acknowledgement of my greeting but continued to play while I poured out some sustenance from the red-ribboned teapot and considered whether the verb 'play' was entirely appropriate to the desultory and barely coherent noises.

"Really, Holmes," I said finally, sipping at my cup. "We've solved and stopped the Whitechapel Murders and Jack the Ripper as well as the nonsense cult who perpetrated it. Griffin is in your brother's keeping and Van Helsing, Holmwood and the Fleetes are all dead or in jail. You are known as the man who captured Jack the Ripper and the respect for your methods from those at Scotland Yard has reached new heights. Other than

Mycroft threatening both of us with knighthoods on a weekly basis, I really don't see what you have to be despondent about. Don't tell me you're bored already?"

"Whitechapel Murders solved! Ha!" he burst out. He picked up a folded newspaper and tossed it negligently in my direction. It fluttered and landed on the floor, but he didn't seem to notice that, either. He put the bow back on the strings and gave it a savage pull, making the instrument squawk like a kicked chicken.

I crouched and picked up the paper, still holding the teacup in my other hand. I looked at the front page and sighed. It was paper from almost three weeks ago, shortly after our battle with the cult, and Holmes had been complaining about it since.

The headline read: JACK THE RIPPER DEAD. ACCOMPLICE FOUND GUILTY! and showed George Fleete's simple and surly face and another next to it with Holmwood's visage. A smaller photograph showed Holmes's face and another caption underneath said: 'Sherlock Holmes critical to solving the case'. A further caption revealed Lestrade's curved boning knife.

"Fleete," I said.

"Fleete!" he exploded. "Not Griffin! Not Jack the Ripper! Not the correct murderer at all and the imbeciles are buying it. What are they using for brains down there? Sawdust? Entrails? Soggy, used tea pot dregs?"

I sighed and set the paper down. "You would rather see Griffin's face in this photo?"

"If that was an attempt at humour, Doctor, it was a rather poor job of it."

"Lestrade is right," I said. "Both Scotland Yard and the public need a face to put to the Ripper murders and George Fleete did kill Luella Brown. It's not as if he's innocent."

"He's completely innocent of Eugenie Babington's murder, and Stanley Hopkins', and most of the others," Holmes shot back. "I'll not be party to this…" He was near shaking with rage. "To this… host of lies!"

"George Fleete is guilty of murder and he will be convicted of the same," I said, trying to keep my tone reasonable. "What about the Shannons?"

"Yes," Holmes admitted. "He is certainly responsible for their demise."

"Griffin, for obvious reasons, cannot be tried for the other murders. No fair trial could be had for someone that cannot be seen and just his appearance at a trial would raise questions that we cannot answer. People feel safe again, and they are safe. Public opinion of the police, and also of you, by the way, are higher than ever. Where is the problem?"

"It's all built on a lie, Watson!" Holmes fumed. "I cannot, in good conscience, allow this bloating of my reputation built on such… such falsehood. Better my name were kept out of it entirely."

"Holmes," I said. "Be reasonable. The press knew very well that you were on the case. Mycroft's fiction is the story that we can tell that is closest to the truth. What else would you have done?"

He dropped both violin and bow with a discordant thump and twang that made me flinch and collapsed into his chair. While Holmes had purchased his Stradivarius for a mere fifty-five shillings on Tottenham Court Road, I well knew that it could be valued at five hundred guineas or more and cringed that it should be treated so cavalierly. Holmes fumed, staring out the window with his back to me.

"Ah, Watson," Holmes said finally, his shoulders slumping. "I suppose you are correct, but it galls me to have the truth dealt with in such a slipshod manner."

"It is the best we could do under the circumstances," I said.

"I suppose…" he repeated. Then he turned back in my direction and waved his hand as if he could clear the air of all falsehoods and dismiss all of life's unsatisfactory compromises. "That is not even the most distressing part of the case."

"Oh?"

"Van Helsing," Holmes said. "I find his mind distressing."

"Well," I said, confused. "That is hardly likely to be a problem anymore."

"That is precisely what bothers me, Watson, the colossal waste of a mind of the first order."

"You regret his death?"

"Perhaps," Holmes said. "But I refer to the encounter with vampires that diverted such a brilliant career into a channel replete with pagan gods and superstition. Take this fragment, for instance." He lifted a small piece of broken glass from the table near him and I saw with an absolute wave of horror that he held a portion of the mirror that had been in the subterranean chamber of Holmwood's house.

"Holmes! You brought a piece of that foul thing home? Where have you been keeping it?" I could see, in my mind's eye, that huge aquatic eye I'd seen in the mirror before and broken or not, the idea of any piece of that mirror residing in the house gave me a feeling of dread.

Holmes gave me a derisive look. "Surely you do not give credence to the fairy tales surrounding Van Helsing's claims that a monster god would come and end all of humanity. Not even his own people believed him at the end. Holmwood's deranged ambition, Griffin's murderous desires. As damaged as their psyches both were, none of them believed in Van Helsing's delusion. That is what pains me, the thought of those inferior minds laughing all those many years at a brilliant mind's decay. It is a depressing thought. But for the grace of God, Watson."

"Certainly you don't think there's any danger of that happening to you, Holmes?" I said, shocked out of my dark contemplation by this absurd concern.

"If the Sherlock Holmes of today," he said, "could converse with the Sherlock Holmes of a few years ago and regale him with tales of vampires, werewolves, Jekyll and Hyde, and invisible assassins, well... I should think myself absolutely without reason."

"Would not the you of years past bow before the evidence of such strange persons and phenomena when it was placed before him, just as you have?"

"I suppose," Holmes said.

I walked over to the small end table where he had laid the mirror fragment and looked down at it with some trepidation. "Holmes, must we keep this vile thing in our home?"

"Really, Watson," Holmes said. "You'll be believing in ghosts and goblins next. Very well; if the idea of it disturbs your peace, I shall send it to Mycroft in the morning. Will that suit?"

"I shall sleep better knowing it is gone," I admitted.

"Well," Holmes said, "it is just as well that you do not usually go to bed until the morning, then, isn't it? By the way, how did your visit to Jekyll's household go?"

"Miss Winter has settled in nicely," I said. "It certainly is a more central location for her duties on the Midnight Watch and with Hyde to help her, I think it is a great improvement for both of them. I was a bit worried that their relationship was a fragile one, built on the necessity of living together in close quarters and forged in the extreme danger we all faced, but I am happy to report that I was mistaken on that score. They seem better suited than ever for one another."

"At least it will give Hyde some money of his own," Holmes said. "He will no longer have to rely on Jekyll for his sole source of income. What of Miss Winter and Dr Jekyll?"

"She will never like the man," I admitted, "or enjoy his company, but I think they have all come to understand and appreciate the qualities of the others. Certainly they are all very reliant on the others. Jekyll's standing in the community is something the other two sorely need, as well as his chemical expertise so that the potion continues to be made. In fact, he has been working on some small refinements to the potion that he seems excited about. Hyde provides him, through your payments to him as one of the Midnight Watch, with a small income and Jekyll recognizes that Hyde is performing an invaluable service, assisting Miss Winter as he does with monitoring the graveyards and morgues and making certain that any new vampire outbreaks are dealt with. Miss Winter, in addition to her relationship with

Hyde, is quite capable herself and has already started acting as a sort of bridge of communication between the two men. Everyone seems very content with the arrangement."

"Very good," Holmes said.

"What of Dracula?" I asked.

Holmes indicated a letter on the sideboard. "Mina writes that they have arrived safely in the Carpathian mountains and all is well, and will likely stay there the rest of the season and return to England in the summer."

"Just in time for a London summer," I said.

"Yes," Holmes said.

"Have you anything pressing this moment?" I asked, looking at his disorderly pile of correspondence.

"I have two blackmail cases, one murder, and a half-dozen thefts on hand at the moment, which is to say, nothing much of interest at all. I tell you, Watson, it will take a pretty case indeed to present as many features of interest as we have seen in this one."

"You have neglected yourself during this case, Holmes," I insisted. "What you need is a holiday."

"Well," Holmes said slyly, "I have been pondering a trip to Scotland for a while now. There are a couple of people there that I should like to see."

"Excellent," I said. "We shall make arrangements and leave as soon as feasible. I have nothing urgent at the moment. What is it you wish to see?"

"Who, Watson, who. There is a doctor in Edinburgh that tells me that he has some new information on that American brigantine, the *Mary Celeste*. Also, someone else has reported a new sighting of Alexander MacDonald's salamander near Inverness."

I could feel a groan rising up from inside me.

"Now where did I put my hat?" Holmes said.

NOTES ON THE TEXT TO THE ASTUTE READER

Astute readers will notice several discrepancies between this text, my previous stories, and the works of other authors using similar characters.

As to the inconsistencies in my own text, I have been forced to change many dates and names in order to preserve the privacy and dignity of several of Holmes's original clients, muddling both the timeline in this tale as well as in my original stories. Again, I can only beg the reader's indulgence, but these small trivialities are necessary to preserve the secrecy under which Holmes and I have been sworn on many of Holmes's most delicate cases.

ACKNOWLEDGEMENTS

Tremendous thanks to Sarah Zettel, Steven Piziks, Cindy Spencer Pape, David Erik Nelson, Diana Rivis, Mary Beth Johnson, Christine Pellar-Kosbar, Jonathan Jarrard, Erica Shippers, and Ted Reynolds of the Untitled Writer's Group who suffered innumerable versions of this story with grace and aplomb and many coloured pens. Also to Janine Beaulieu, Heath Lowrance, Ron Warren and Carole Ward for helping nurture several stories that led into these.

Also to my agent Lucienne Diver and editors Sophie Robinson, Fenton Coulthurst and Hayley Shepherd at Titan, who provided extraordinary levels of encouragement and understanding in order to keep me on the straight and narrow while navigating the pitfalls of so many iconic characters.

To my parents, Craig and Pam Klaver, and my mother Suzanne Klaver, who encouraged me in this endeavour for far longer than I care to admit.

As always, thanks to my daughter Kathryn, who continues to inspire and encourage me on so many levels.

Lastly, and most importantly, to my wife, Kimberly, for constant encouragement and endless tolerance for a husband constantly sequestered.

ALSO AVAILABLE FROM TITAN BOOKS

The Cthulhu Casebooks:

SHERLOCK HOLMES AND THE SHADWELL SHADOWS

By James Lovegrove

It is the autumn of 1880, and Dr John Watson has just returned from Afghanistan. Badly injured and desperate to forget a nightmarish expedition that left him doubting his sanity, Watson is close to destitution when he meets the extraordinary Sherlock Holmes, who is investigating a series of deaths in the Shadwell district of London. Several bodies have been found, the victims appearing to have starved to death over several weeks, and yet they were reported alive and well mere days before. Moreover, there are disturbing reports of creeping shadows that inspire dread in any who stray too close.

Holmes deduces a connection between the deaths and a sinister drug lord who is seeking to expand his criminal empire. Yet both he and Watson are soon forced to accept that there are forces at work far more powerful than they could ever have imagined. Forces that can be summoned, if one is brave—or mad—enough to dare... Holmes deduces a connection between the deaths and a sinister drug lord who is seeking to expand his criminal empire. Yet both he and Watson are soon forced to accept that there are forces at work far more powerful than they could ever have imagined. Forces that can be summoned, if one is brave – or mad – enough to dare...

⌒

"The pastiche is pitch-perfect; Lovegrove tells a thrilling tale and vividly renders the atmosphere of Victorian London."
The Guardian

"[A] crossover tale for the ages that's bound to please fans of both literary canons."
Starburst Magazine

TITANBOOKS.COM

The Cthulhu Casebooks:

SHERLOCK HOLMES AND THE MISKATONIC MONSTROSITY

By James Lovegrove

It is the spring of 1895, and more than a decade of combating eldritch entities has cost Dr John Watson his beloved wife Mary, and nearly broken the health of Sherlock Holmes. Yet the companions do not hesitate when they are called to the infamous Bedlam lunatic asylum, where they find an inmate speaking in R'lyehian, the language of the Old Ones. Moreover, the man is horribly scarred and has no memory of who he is.

The detectives discover that the inmate was once a scientist, a student of Miskatonic University, and one of two survivors of a doomed voyage down the Miskatonic River to capture the semi-mythical shoggoth. Yet how has he ended up in London, without his wits? And when the man is taken from Bedlam by forces beyond normal mortal comprehension, it becomes clear that there is far more to the case than one disturbed Bostonian. It is only by learning what truly happened on that fateful New England voyage that Holmes and Watson will uncover the truth, and learn who is behind the Miskatonic monstrosity…

$\backsim$

"Will delight fans of Doyle and Lovecraft alike."
The Guardian

"A fascinating and gripping read, deftly uniting the worlds of Holmes and Lovecraft."
The Crime Review

"First rate entertainment."
Crime Fiction Lover

TITANBOOKS.COM

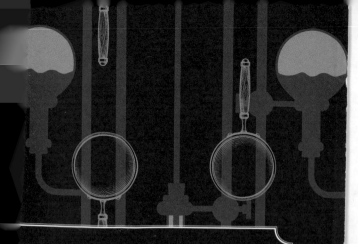

IAN KLAVER has been writing for over [..]ears, for a number of magazine publications, [..] *Escape Pod*, *Dark Wisdom* anthology, and [..]*ter*. He's the author of *Shadows Over London*, [..]twalker series and has written over a dozen [..] both fantasy and sci-fi. He's worked as a [..]r, bartender and a martial arts instructor [..]tling into a career in internet security. He lives [..]de Detroit, Michigan, with his wife, daughter [..]up of animals he refers to as The Menagerie.

CHRIST

twenty y

including

Anti-Ma

the Nigl

novels i

booksell

before se

just outs

and a gr